DARK SPACE

ADVENA ABDUCTIONS
BOOK THREE

HOLLIE HARTWRIGHT

PINDIKA PRESS

CANBERRA

Dark Space (Advena Abductions Book Three)
Published by Pindika Press
Canberra, Australia

All characters in this novel are over the age of 18.

Paperback ISBN: 978-0-6456731-2-8

For Nanny and Robyn.

Author's Note

DARK SPACE IS THE third book in the high-heat *Advena Abduction* science-fiction series, which began with the short novel *Count Down* and continued with *Into Orbit*. Please be aware that this third story is darker and more harrowing for the heroine than the preceding two novels; it also has a slower burn. Though each book features a different human heroine and a resolved why-choose romance with a HEA, the *Advena Abduction* series is intended to be read in order and has an interconnected series arc.

Dark Space is a super spicy, medium-to-slow burn, insta-connection alien romance where the lucky human heroine will not be choosing at the end. It contains M/M/, M/F, and group scenes, along with alien *bits,* some low-gravity fun, and some swearing. It is suitable for adult audiences only.

Content warnings include kidnap and attempted kidnap; incarceration; the victim falling for her captors; personal violence and injury; space violence; allusions to r*pe, forced breeding, and trafficking; homophobia and toxic masculinity (not perpetrated by any POV character); death (including the off-page death of a grandparent and the on-page death of a mentor); references to dementia and its symptoms; allusions to theft and criminality. If you think I've missed anything from this list, please, *please* contact me and I will update it; I am committed to keeping my readers safe.

This series is written by an Australian author, using Australian English. Formal Australian English is largely based on the spelling and conventions of UK English, though sometimes US spellings will slip through for certain words, depending on which TV channels our parents let us watch when we were younger.

Terms & Definitions

Pod: A SMALL, TWO-BEING craft used by the Tirian peace-keeping force. There are two kinds: those used for short-distance transport, and those flown into battle as part of a larger fleet.

Claiming: the Roth equivalent of marriage.

Dread Order: the Roth's priesthood, dedicated to worship of the dread gods.

Scytha: the Roth's home planet. Much of it in uninhabited; the majority of the Roth population reside underground in the capital, Scytha City.

The Spire: the Roth King's palace in Scytha City.

ANNA

If I don't come back, call the police love ya xx

THE MESSAGE FLASHED UP on my screen, then disappeared. *I must have read that wrong,* I thought, laying my knife to one side and wiping my hands. I grabbed my phone and read it again.

The words didn't change.

'Is Maeve still at the bar?' I called to Ellis, trying to keep the tremor from my voice.

The sous chef craned his neck, looking through the service window. 'Can't see her. Her chips are still there, though.'

'What about Claire?'

He shifted, searching. 'Nope. She might be back in the office.'

I chewed on my lip. 'Can you take over? Maeve just sent me a weird message.'

Ellis glanced at the pile of order receipts and visibly repressed a sigh. 'No problem, Anna.'

I untied my apron and hung it up before washing my hands properly. Bracing myself for the noise, I headed out to the bar.

Belle was there with two new staff, and they looked happy enough, despite the crowd. I stood on my toes and searched through the crush of patrons, but I couldn't see Maeve anywhere.

'You were *right here*, Maeve,' I muttered to myself. The bowl of chips I'd shoved at her was still mostly full, but her cranberry juice was finished; at least she'd gotten some vitamins in before sending anxiety-inducing text messages. I thought she would have known better; after Tessa's disappearance, we were all raw, all on edge, and a message like *that* had my stomach churning.

I unlocked my phone to call her, but before I could, another number popped up. I answered it immediately.

'Viv? Is everything okay?'

'Anna, honey?' I put a hand to my ear, trying to block out the noise of the club so I could hear Vivien's soft voice. 'Anna, can you go somewhere quieter?'

'One second, Viv.'

I steeled myself and pushed through the crowd.

I loved working at Advena, I really did, but I preferred to experience it from behind the safety of the kitchen wall. Though I liked people as a general rule, Advena was full of so *many* of them, and they were drunk and loud and confident. I was small and quiet and shy, and I didn't have Tessa's self-assurance, or Maeve's brazen confidence, or Claire's sense of mysterious calm. Instead, I had a tongue that got tied up with nerves, and the general air of a frightened deer about to bolt towards a set of moving headlights.

You need to find your courage, girl, my grandmother had always said. Sometimes she'd say it emphatically, and sometimes sadly.

I never had a response, either way. It was easy for people to think that what you showed on the outside was all there was. I knew that the way I looked didn't help matters: too pale, too delicate, too *breakable*. A doll just waiting for someone else to move her arms and legs into position, to tilt her head, to choose which dress she wore.

Never mind that I ran my own kitchen. Never mind that I could lift industrial bags of flour and handle a knife with my eyes closed. The outside of me always seemed to eclipse anything I worked for, anything I *earned*.

Dolls just sat there, after all, waiting for someone else to play with them.

Claire was at the club's doors, chatting with the bouncers. She must have dyed her hair earlier that day; the tips of her dark brown tresses were a bright, vibrant pink. There was a long line of patrons standing down the street, waiting to get in; I didn't like their chances.

Did you see where Maeve went? I mouthed at Claire.

She pointed towards the line. 'She went that way. She was with someone, though,' she answered quietly. 'She might have gone home.'

I shot her a smile of thanks and walked outside, shivering as the cool night air hit my skin. 'Viv? Can you hear me now?'

'I can hear you now. Anna, honey, I've got some bad news.'

Vivian was my grandmother's part-time carer; she visited for a few hours while I was at work so my grandmother was never alone for too long. 'What is it?' I said, my throat going tight.

'Honey, she's gone.'

I blinked. 'Gone? What do you mean?'

'Gone, honey. Passed. The paramedics confirmed it a few minutes ago. She had a stroke.'

I staggered. A boy in the line wolf whistled at me as his friends guffawed and pushed each other.

'Anna?'

I made it past the end of the line and leaned on a shopfront wall. 'Gone?' I managed.

'Gone, Anna,' Vivian said gently. 'Can you come home?'

'I ...' I swallowed, pulling on the end of my braid, realising I was still wearing my beanie. I pulled it off and let it fall to the ground. 'Yep. Yes, I can come home.'

There was a short silence. 'Honey, my babysitter –'

I checked the time on my phone; Vivian had stayed far past the end of her shift. 'Go home, Viv. Of course, go home.'

'I'll email you some resources, okay? And a doctor will be around in the morning to sign the death certificate.' There was another short silence. 'Anna, is there someone who could come with you? Will you be okay?'

Would I be okay?

My grandmother was my single remaining relative. She'd been a constant in my life for the last five years, and my house-mate for four. I'd looked after her myself until I realised we needed extra help, then I'd hired Vivian. I'd started researching care homes in the last few months, because I wanted to be prepared for when it got too much for us to handle.

My grandmother had been a geologist and had worked all over the world. It was one of the things she still always remembered. She couldn't work the microwave, got confused about money, and she sometimes needed help getting dressed in the mornings, but she could talk about different types of soil for hours on end.

She'd said *goodbye* to me that afternoon. She'd called me Arabella – my mother's name – but she'd looked happy, sitting on our tiny balcony with a cup of tea. I'd put some of her collection of ammonites on the table, along with a couple of reference books, and she'd been looking through them, a blanket around her shoulders, the sun on her silver hair.

Would I be okay?

Her life had ceased to be in her full control; she'd forgotten some of her family members and friends. My past grandmother – the one before dementia – would have hated it, hated the lack of control over her mind and emotions. Death meant that she was past the frustration and confusion, past the continual loss, past the agitation at her own helplessness and the anger at the increasing unreliability of her body.

But for five years, she'd been my universe, and now she was *gone*.

I had absolutely no idea what to feel.

'I, ah. Yes, I'll be okay, Viv.'

'I know this is a shock, honey. There are some community grief counsellors we recommend – I'll send you their numbers. And I'll call you tomorrow, yeah? I can help with the funeral director.'

'Yeah,' I said. 'Thanks, Viv.' I hung up the phone.

I stared at the wall, my eyes following the path of the shadowed mortar. I felt sick, though I wasn't sure why – was it grief?

Shock? My body reminding me that I'd skipped my break and hadn't eaten for six hours?

I opened my phone and pulled up a browser tab. I typed in: *What do you do when someone dies*, then closed the window before I could read the answers.

I need to talk to someone.

Claire. I need to talk to Claire.

I turned around and took two steps back towards Claire before I remembered why I was out here in the first place.

Maeve.

I peered down the street. It was empty of people and full of shadows, unnervingly quiet given the noise of the line and Advena behind me.

It's just a street, I told myself. My hands were trembling. *You're allowed to be here. You're safe.*

I walked further away from Advena, crossing my arms over my chest. A movement across the road caught my eye; I jumped before I realised what it was.

'Cat,' I muttered. I ventured further. 'Maeve?' I called.

One of the streetlamps was out; the absence of light cast a pool of blackness across an intersection. The shops here were all closed, their windows dark. 'Maeve?'

The back of my neck prickled, and I realised that this wasn't a good idea. I pulled up her number.

The call went straight to voicemail, as if she'd turned her phone off.

Maeve *never* turned her phone off. I flicked her text open.

If I don't come back, call the police love ya xx

I bit my lip. Surely it was too early to panic.

I called her number again; this time, I left a voice message.

'Maeve? Can you call me, please? I'm worried. And, um. I have to talk to you.'

I hung up and shook my head. Four years studying literature at university and I could barely put together a coherent voice message.

Medical expenses were starting to eat into my grandmother's savings by the end of my degree. I'd wanted to go into teaching, but that would have been another two years living on study assistance and the little extra I made from weekend shifts at a bookshop, and that barely covered rent and food; I couldn't help my grandmother with that. I'd always loved cooking, so when I'd seen an advertisement for an apprentice chef offering above-award rates at a new club opening close to my apartment, I'd taken a gamble and applied. Jessa had still been cheffing then, balancing owning the club and running the kitchen. She'd taken me on, and, when I'd learned enough, she'd ceded the kitchen to me and bought another club; she now had her own mini empire of bars scattered up the east coast.

'Heck.' I stopped still and closed my eyes, leaning on an obliging wall as another thought struck me. 'The apartment. Her stuff. Her will. Her ... *her*.' I opened my eyes. *Would she still be there?* Or would the paramedics have taken her somewhere else?

I could deal with a lot, but I wasn't sure I could deal with my grandmother's *body*.

I unlocked my phone and called Maeve again with shaking fingers. 'Maeve? Please, I –' My voice shook; I swallowed. 'I'm worried. I need to talk to you. Please.'

There was a scuffling sound up ahead; I shivered again, unnerved. Deciding I'd go back to Claire to wait for Maeve's response – and work out when I called the police – I turned my back on it.

And caught the sound of a soft footfall.

I spun back around. 'Maeve?' I called, trying to keep my voice strong, my fingers hovering over the emergency call button on the keypad.

A shadow moved.

Not Maeve, I realised. The shadow was too big, too broad. Too ... *male*. Pale skin turned pearlescent in the moonlight. Black hair, eyes like pools, beautifully-shaped lips, and –

'What the *heck*?' I blurted out.

An odd growling sound ripped through the night air.

You didn't imagine it, I told myself. *Horns*. Two horns, black as jet, curving elegantly back from above his temples.

'It's not Halloween,' I said stupidly.

His black eyes blinked. I stared into them, mesmerised, the churning in my stomach turning into something hot and hungry. I stepped forward without thinking, an odd pressure blooming beneath my ribs, drawing me closer. My fingertips were tingling; my hand twitched with the need to touch, the need to trace over the square line of his jaw, the curve of a horn. Heat flared between my legs and I took a shuddering breath, my lips parting as I moved to take another step, to close the distance between us.

What are you doing, Anna?

Somewhere deep inside, instinct shouted a warning, and I froze as he took a step towards me.

Too late, the heat in my core turned to fear and crawled up my spine. Too late, I turned, then shifted my weight to run.

Too quickly, a hand took hold of my waist; my skin twitched as something hot pricked my neck. Every muscle in my body tensed; pain rolled through me, buoyed on the crest of an excruciating wave.

Too quickly, I was slung over a massive shoulder.

Too easily, my boneless fingers dropped my phone; I heard the screen shatter as it hit the pavement.

Too easily, my eyes rolled back, and the street disappeared.

CALLAN

WHAT ARE YOU DOING, Callan?

The female was limp over my shoulder. Her hair escaped its plait in pale wisps as she hung upside down, her sharp chin bumping my back with every step.

What are you doing, Callan?

The scuttler hatch lifted silently as I drew close. I'd stunned the female in a kind of mindless reflex, panicking when her expression flickered into fear and she'd turned to run.

There's still time to put her down.

I did put her down – in the scuttler's co-pilot chair. I positioned her gently, trying to support her head; I winced when I saw the bruise from the stunner on her slender neck. I strapped her in carefully, then slid into the pilot's seat.

What are you doing, Callan?

It was never my voice I heard – it was Alcide, always Alcide. *Callan, you're better than this*, whenever I turned up with eyes bruised blue after a fight. *Callan, you can do this*, when I'd failed the theoretical component of my pilot's exam and needed to re-sit the test. *Callan, this isn't you. Go home*, when I'd drunk too much spiced wine and the other trainee pilots were trying to drag me towards the long line for the public brothel.

Callan, I need you to see what they're doing, when we'd tailed a Tirian peacekeeping ship to an unknown planet in an ass-end of the universe Sector. We'd been telling Alcide's father that the Tirians were on *our* tail, and not the other way around; Alcide thought knowing what they wanted with this small blue planet might help us keep up the ruse. *Callan, you can look, but don't touch. Be careful. Don't be seen.*

'So much for that,' I muttered, glancing at the female as I flicked on the scuttler's start sequence.

The female moaned.

'You're all right,' I murmured to her. 'You're safe.'

You've stunned her and you're in the process of abducting her from her home. While she's unconscious. I doubt she'd agree.

'Shut it, Alcide,' I growled.

I strapped myself in and tapped the control screen to launch the engines.

Last chance to let her go, Cal.

I looked across at the female. Her head lolled to one side. Her skin was dewy, her hair a blend of honey and wheat. She was small – *so* small – and her frame was slight; she was made of angles, her body planes of light and shadow.

My heart constricted, just as it had the moment I'd first seen her, glowing in the starlight. Despite that, despite how beautiful she was, despite how much my heart thumped and my body tightened, I could have walked away in that moment. I could have stayed in the darkness, could have let the shadows hide me from view. I could have stayed quiet, and let her slip away. Instead, I'd stepped forward, stepped into the light, into her line of sight, and I'd *let* her see my pearlescent skin and my curving horns – the things that screamed *not like you* – all because I'd caught her scent on the cool night breeze.

Spring.

I'd never known a spring – our home planet, Scytha, was too far along in its own death to have any season other than endless drought – but somehow, somewhere deep down, I still knew what it should feel like. What it should *smell* like. All freshness and hope, all life and blossoming, all determination and rebirth. The female's scent was all that and more, and once I caught it, I knew I couldn't let her go.

I *needed* her.

Even if I never saw a spring, I'd have her scent, have the life and the hope and the blossoming it promised. Have *her*.

'I'm so sorry,' I told her quietly. 'But I'm taking you with me.'

It felt wrong and right all at once. Sometimes, I couldn't tell the difference.

That was what I had Alcide for.

'What the *fuck*, Callan?' Alcide said, his black eyes wide with horror. 'What is *that*?'

I lowered the female onto his bed. 'A human.'

'A human,' Alcide repeated. 'Right.' He closed his eyes. '*Take it back, Callan. Take it back right now.*'

'Her,' I corrected. 'And no.'

'I – *what*?'

'No. I'm not taking her back.'

He opened his eyes and fixed them on me. 'I think I misheard you.'

'I'm not taking her back, *Prince*.'

'Callan, you can't *keep* her.'

'I need to keep her,' I said, as calmly as I could manage.

'You *need* to keep her? A human female you found –' Alcide checked his wrist screen '– less than *one turn ago*?'

'I can't explain it,' I said. 'I need to keep her.'

Alcide's nostrils flared. 'I assume you've spoken to *her* about this?'

I didn't answer.

'Callan. You *abducted an unwilling female*?' He ran his hands through his unruly red hair. 'What were you *thinking*?'

I wasn't, of course; that was the problem. I was *feeling*, instead.

'Callan, if Dainn hears about this, he'll either take her for himself, or he'll put her in with the crew. You *know* what they'll do to her!'

I winced. I *did* know. Just thinking about it made my stomach churn and bile creep up my throat.

I wouldn't let them touch her. And fortunately, I'd had an entire turn to think about how to ensure they didn't.

'There's a way we can keep her safe.'

Alcide frowned down at her. 'Enlighten me.'

'You claim her.'

He whipped around to face me. I didn't think his expression could be *more* horrified, but he somehow managed it. '*I beg your fucking pardon*?'

'You claim her,' I continued. 'Your father would have forced you to claim a stranger in any case. At least you'll be *choosing* this one. And if you claim her, then Dainn and the crew can't touch her.'

Alcide pulled on both horns, a sure sign I'd driven him from *concerned* to *I'm going to kill you, Callan.* 'So I claim a complete stranger from an alien species, declare her my princess, and work every day to keep her safe from Dainn and the other males on the ship – *so that you can keep a female you kidnapped*?'

'Cide,' I said softly. '*Look at her.*'

He turned reluctantly to the unconscious female.

Roth males were monsters. I was one, so I could say that and know that it was true. Our home planet was dying, drained dry after a millennium of unbridled consumption. The seas were too hot to sustain life, the ground leeched of anything natural and good by irresponsible farming. The Roth had been a subterranean species for centuries now, existing – if you could call it that – on artificial foods and ice harvested from space.

It wasn't just Scytha that was dying. Our species was, too. There hadn't been a Roth female born for fifty years, and it was twenty since the last male bairnling.

The King's – Alcide's father's – solution was expansion. He ruled over a collection of six planets in Sector Nine, using Scytha as his centre. All it did was spread the problem; the other planets couldn't sustain us, either, so his empire was one of thirst, starvation, violence, and death.

Long live the King.

He'd sent Alcide on a mission to reap *suitable alien females* to give to his generals. We'd been on the orb ship for months now; Alcide had managed to not reap anything, using the Tirians as an excuse.

And now I'd fucked that up.

Alcide inhaled, then gave a rumbling growl, the sound springing from somewhere deep in his chest.

Roth males had always been protective. In the past, our females hadn't needed it, but we'd done it anyway. Generations of socialisation had corrupted us into something different: our protective instincts became possessive. Our inclination to defend became a tendency towards aggression. Our bodies, built for strength, built to be a barrier between our females and danger, became vehicles for violence. Over time, our females went from being partners, to glorified servants, to possessions, and when they stopped being born, they became commodities, something only available to the rich and powerful.

I'd seen one Roth female in the flesh my entire life: Alcide's grandmother. I'd been seven summers old the first time I'd seen her, and I still remembered the way my body had straightened, my shoulders rolled back, and every muscle had tensed with the *need* to protect her, to serve her. I hadn't been able to use a weapon then, but I'd reached for the ceremonial knife at my side anyway, ready to lay down my body in her defence.

I felt the same need for the human female.

I knew that Alcide would feel it, too. I was relying on it, relying on his instincts overriding his logic – and his conscience. I'd kidnapped her, after all, the very thing Alcide had spent months trying not to do. I studied his profile, watching his instincts – the core of him, what made him Roth – war with his morals – the things that made him *Alcide* – through his flickering expressions. Her unconscious state would be wreaking havoc with his hormones: he'd feel anxious, restless. His stomach would churn with the pressure to protect, to eliminate any potential threats. And when he caught her scent ...

His hand went to his sword as his eyes turned to me.

I held up my hands. 'Calm, Prince,' I said softly. 'It's me. It's Callan.'

'Callan,' he repeated, my name rolling off his tongue, igniting a flare of desire that licked up my spine. I tried to ignore it. Alcide was handsome, with a strong jaw, high cheekbones, and a nose that would have been straight had it not been for his father's fists. He was tall and muscled and graceful, but it was more than that; he was *Alcide*, the male I'd known since before we could speak. He was as much part of myself as my own hands, as my own *soul* – not that I'd ever tell him.

I'd be killed on sight if the King ever found out, and even if it was only ever one-sided, I couldn't bear to think about what the King might do to Alcide.

My Prince took another deep breath, inhaling the female's scent, then rubbed his eyes with long, strong fingers. 'You're going to be the death of me, Callan.'

Never, I vowed. 'So ...?'

His black eyes swept over her small form; his expression was at once possessive and full of regret. 'Where will we put her?'

I pushed away a thrill of triumph, and the stab of guilt that immediately followed it. 'She can't go to the cells.' The cells should have been full of the females we were sent to collect; instead, they were locked and empty. 'And she can't go anywhere near the crew.'

'No. It won't be safe.' He paused. '*Nowhere* on this ship is safe, Cal.'

'She'll be safe in here with you.'

'I can't keep her in my room,' he snapped. 'What would she think?'

'Or,' I said tentatively, steeling myself, 'you could keep her *here* but *not here*.'

Alcide rubbed his temples. 'Callan –'

I gestured to the door at the far end of Alcide's quarters, the door that only Alcide could open. It hid a short corridor with a single window, and, at the end of the corridor, a cell.

He frowned at me. 'You *can't* be serious.'

'Think about it. Only you have access. No one will be able to get to her. No one will know she's there.'

'*No one* except the being *already chained in there*, Callan.'

'He's neutralised,' I argued. 'He can't do anything with that dark matter chain wrapped around his ankle, Cide. He can't even *move*. He won't be able to touch her.' I paused. 'When it comes down to it, will she be safer with *him*, or with your crew?'

Alcide stared at the human, then leaned down and covered her in the blanket from his bed, careful not to touch her. 'Fine,' he said softly. 'I'll adjust the security overrides to give you access.' He looked up, pinning me with his gaze. 'She is your responsibility, Callan.'

I saluted him. 'Yes, Prince. You won't regret this.'

I gathered the female in my arms and carried her to the door as Alcide tapped on the screen next to his bed. I wasn't far away enough to miss what he said.

'I think I already do.'

VESPER

A BURNING PAIN SHOT through my finger as I tore another nail.

I stared at the hand – *my* hand, I reminded myself. 'What good are you?' I asked it. 'What is the *purpose* of fingernails?'

It didn't answer.

I couldn't decide whether I was disappointed or relieved at its lack of response. On the one hand – *ha* – I was entirely, exceedingly, mind-numbingly bored. On the other, I was slightly concerned that I was dancing on the edge of madness, and surely talking body parts would signal that I had slid over the precipice and fallen straight into that abyss.

I wasn't made to be alone. And I *especially* wasn't made to be alone and trapped in a form as dull and soft as this one.

'Stupid fleshbag,' I muttered.

I blamed this ridiculous humanoid brain for my current predicament. Surely it was the useless mass of wrinkled grey matter within this thick skull that tempted me to raid the Prince's on-board treasury for a third time, rather than walk away with the considerable fortune I'd already amassed during the first and second visits.

And surely it was this form's dull instincts that hadn't warned me of the fact that the Prince was capturing every moment of that third raid on his security feeds, recording my plundering visit in the kind of detail that would have me thrown straight in a Council cell for a millennium.

And *surely* it was the same weak instincts and the slow response of this meatsuit that gave the irritatingly pretty Prince and his black-haired companion time to clamp the dark matter chain around my ankle, a chain that blocked me from drawing new light.

Surely.

I scowled at my fingers. *Who travelled with their treasury, anyway?*

Perhaps it was all the Prince's fault. He was basically *asking* to be robbed.

Now, I was not only trapped in some kind of secret, high-security cell, I was trapped in this odd, distasteful body, a form I'd based on my twin sibling, who wore it to please his cyborg and cephalopod partners.

I did *not* see the appeal. Bits of it were hard and bits of it were soft. For something that so closely resembled pillars, the legs and feet were oddly clumsy. The muscles were held together with some kind of fragile flesh-straps, which seemed like a critical design flaw. The hair didn't seem to serve much purpose, other than falling into the eyes and obstructing vision. The skin organ needed a surprising amount of upkeep, and surely needed to be thicker to serve its purpose.

And toenails. *Why?*

I hadn't spoken to him since my capture, but the Prince came to glower at me every week or so. At least, I thought it was that often; I had no idea where we were, or what the time was, and therefore no idea how much of it might be passing. I suspected he was checking that I was still alive, which I assured him in the affirmative by greeting him with a wide, taunting grin. I might be bored out of this tiny mind, but I wasn't going to tell *him* that. I also wasn't going to let him know that I *was* getting weaker by the day. The dark matter cuff stopped me changing back to my trueform – or into any other form, for that matter – and although I could still control the light residing inside me, I couldn't gather any more to consume, or to use, and therefore to escape. I'd been already drained when they caught me, and the light I had was all there was – until the Prince let me go, or I starved.

Despite the threat of slow death, I enjoyed his visits. I liked his shimmering skin and his black eyes, liked his waving auburn hair, and enjoyed the way his horns curved back from his face in a graceful arch, bracketing his serious expression. The Roth forms were humanoid, too, but were built with considerably more muscle than the one I was wearing. Their skin grew a layer of impenetrable scales when they were threatened, and their black fingernails turned hard as claws.

I looked at the hands attached to my arms. 'I bet *his* nails wouldn't break,' I told them, and I started working on the dark matter chain again.

The cuff around my ankle didn't seem to have a weak point, though logically I knew it must. The technology to fuse dark matter with a malleable metal found on the moons of Ellin in Sector Twelve was ancient, and the knowledge to reforge more of it lost, but dark matter chains still existed here and there. Some were with the Tirians, and some in a locked facility controlled by the Intergalactic Council. Clearly, the Roth had gotten their hands on a pair, which the Prince had used to great effect.

My broken nail tore; blood welled as pain flared through my hand.

'Useless,' I told it, and scraped the next available unbroken nail over the cuff.

I knew it was a long shot, but I couldn't sit here and do *nothing*. I'd rather do *something*, no matter how hopeless that task was, than sit here and slowly waste away until I starved to death, or the Roth Prince decided to give me to his King, or drag me before the Tirians and the Intergalactic Council.

My nail wore down to the quick. I paused, considering my toes. Could I make them bend that way?

Light flickered at the edge of my awareness.

Even stuck in this ungainly body, I retained some of my true nature. My eyes had not changed with the shift, so they could still detect light in any form. Sometimes I'd watch the comings and goings of the ship, seeking out the light and heat signatures of the Roth Prince and his crew as they went about their business. They were an odd lot, going through the motions each day, with the ship plotting an erratic course across the stars; if there was a logic to our travels, I couldn't determine it. For a ship carrying the crown Prince of a species obsessed with conflict, this orb seemed remarkably reluctant to seek it out.

It didn't make much sense, but I also didn't care. I'd been stealing from species that had died out long before the Roth decided to slither out of the sea. The Prince could do as he pleased, as long as I eventually found a way to escape.

The light flickered again.

I frowned. It was a heat signal – a *new* one. Too small to be Roth, too bright to be dead.

'What are *you*?' I said to it.

It didn't answer, which was fair enough. It was an odd little thing, its light layered like a star, with a core so bright that even other species could have almost seen it. The Prince and a second Roth – the black-haired one – were clearly interested in it, standing close and watching the little light as it stretched out prone on the Prince's royal bed. The Roth were having a conversation – they gestured and shifted their stance and nodded – but the light didn't react.

Eventually, the Prince wrapped something around the light; I grew bored, turning my attention back to the cuff.

I examined the chain's anchor for what felt like the thousandth time. It was attached to the cell's smooth floor by a thick ring of metal, and no matter how closely I looked, I could never find the joint.

'Right,' I said to my toenails. 'Time to see if you serve a purpose.'

Light flared outside my cell.

I looked up, surprised.

One wall of the cell was glass, opaque on the inside – to any species but a starling, anyway – but transparent to those watching from the outside. The glass slid back, revealing the black-haired Roth, and the thing – the new, many-layered light – in his arms.

The light was small and unconscious, with soft-looking, fair hair falling from a loose braid, some kind of organic life form. They were wrapped in a blanket that had clearly come from the Prince's own bed.

The Roth stepped inside the cell.

'You couldn't have called ahead?' I said politely. 'I might have had something important on.'

He ignored me, and lowered the light – the *being* – onto the cell's single cot.

I examined them. They were slight of build and pale all over, with full, lush lips. Their face was finely boned and delicate, fragile-looking, as if they'd break if I touched them.

But the light at their core was strong and warm; my fingers stretched out towards it. It was the kind of light that would burn for a lifetime, the kind of light that might flicker, but would never dim.

'What are they?' I said, unable to look away.

'Human,' the Roth grunted.

'Human?' I wrinkled my nose. 'Oh, that little blue planet.' I broke into a smile. 'That little Category-3 blue planet that is decidedly *not* a signatory of the Universal Pact.'

The Roth's lips twisted. I liked his face; his expression was even darker than the Prince's. He wasn't as handsome, but he was striking, with straight black brows and beautifully curved lips balancing a wide jaw and cheekbones. There was a pin of rank attached to his black uniform, but I didn't know what it meant.

Had I been in a different situation, it was the kind of face I'd try to seduce – not for a purpose, not because he'd be part of a play, but just because I wanted to spend more time looking at it – looking at *him* – from closer up.

I grinned at him. 'You've stolen something you shouldn't have. How *interesting*.' I cocked my head. 'Where does kidnap from a Category-3 planet lie on the list of intergalactic crimes, do you think? Is it higher or lower than theft?'

The Roth stepped towards me, his chest rumbling with a low, dangerous growl.

'Now, now,' I said chidingly, intrigued by the sound and the resulting shiver up my organic spine. 'You know I'm helpless, currently. But it's something to keep in mind, isn't it? My kind take a *very* long time to kill, and if you give me to the Tirians, I might just have a little song to sing. But perhaps we could come to an agreement. I could keep my metaphorical mouth shut about *your* crime if the Prince decided to forgive *mine*.'

The Roth's eyes narrowed. 'This is all you are, isn't it? A petty criminal looking to turn every situation to your own advantage.'

I put a bleeding hand to my chest. 'Petty? Oh, handsome, I'm not *petty*. And I've never kidnapped a being before, so don't go shooting a lasergun in a glass starcraft and all that.'

He snorted and turned to leave.

'Ah, meatsuit,' I called after him, 'I'm no expert, but won't they *need* something? Sustenance? Moisture? What do humans need to grow?'

He turned towards the little light, his cheeks flushed with blue shadows, his forehead creased in worry.

I laughed again, delighted. 'You don't know, do you? How are you supposed to look after a human if you don't know what they *eat*?'

He spun to face me. 'You want the Prince to consider forgetting your crime? Then *you* find out. When she wakes up, ask her what she needs, and we will find it.' He gave the human one more sweeping glance, then pinned me with his black stare. 'Touch her and I'll end you.' He turned and marched from the cell without another glance back.

The glass slid closed, and I was left alone with the little light.

I frowned at her small body. I liked company, but that company fell into three main categories: marks, associates who would eventually become marks when I inevitably betrayed them, and temporary sources of pleasure. The Roth Prince and his black-haired friend had formed a surprise new category – captors I would eventually get the better of and maybe wouldn't mind fucking if the opportunity arose – but I wasn't sure where this alien female fit.

'This is fine,' I told myself. 'It will be fine. She'll wake up, I'll find out what she needs to grow, and that will be that. The Roth will come back and get her, and it will be … fine.'

The human stirred; her light flared.

I pressed myself against the wall, unnerved, then looked up into the shadows, where I knew several small recorders were installed in the corners of the cell.

'Come back and get her soon,' I said.

ALCIDE

'I KNOW WHAT OUR orders are, Dainn,' I said, as calmly as I could manage. 'But we've yet to find a suitable planet. And the Tirians are too close for us to do anything, even if we *did* find one.'

The ship's medic tapped his fingers on the table. 'You know what the King will say, Alcide.'

I knew it all too well. *Failure, disappointment, weak. Wretched, clumsy, stupid.* I knew all my father's favourite adjectives by heart, down to the order he'd use them in, and which ones he'd say louder to emphasise. And to top it off, his finale: *If only I'd had another son.*

He hadn't, though, so he was stuck with me. Unfortunately, I looked so much like him that there was no way he could reasonably deny parentage; whoever my mother had been, she'd given the King himself in miniature.

Not in spirit, I vowed. *I will never be like him.*

If all the Roth histories did was compare me unfavourably to my father, then I'd consider my life well-lived.

Over time, we Roth had become a violent species, with strict hierarchies, rigid rules, and an unshakable belief that we should be governing the universe and imparting those rules on other species, as if it would somehow improve *their* lives. What we really wanted was power. We were hungry for it, ravenous, even, because we knew that we were dying, and we were making one last, desperate grab for life through universal expansion.

And until the dread gods claimed my father's soul, I couldn't do a thing about it.

Well, that wasn't strictly true. I could do very little about it, but I could still do *something*, keeping in mind all the lessons my grandmother had given me about the history of our species and about *right* and *wrong*. When my father gave me an order to collect alien females, for instance, I could deliberately direct my orb ship towards a galaxy where databases suggested there were very few females to find, and I could ask the orb's co-pilot, Callan, to discreetly hack our course to mirror that of a nearby Tirian ship so that if any of the crew questioned me, I could pretend that *we* were being shadowed by the universal peace-keepers, rather than the other way around, and protest that if we sent out a reaping party the Tirians would realise and take action.

I didn't think the Tirians even knew we were there, which was why I'd risked Callan's unsanctioned trip to Earth, succumbing to my curiosity about why the peacekeepers would send a single tiny Pod to a Category-3 planet.

Unfortunately, I was reasonably certain that Dainn, one of the few males my father called *friend* and my advisor since I grew horns, knew what I was doing, and I was equally certain that he'd tell my father if I didn't start following the King's orders soon.

Dainn gestured to the map on the screen. 'Here. Sector Thirteen. The notes say there are three planets with complex life forms that may be compatible with ours. Or we can turn around and go back to Earth. As a Category-3 planet, we could probably do whatever we liked there.'

I thought of how the human had looked lying on my bed, her eyes closed, her hair spilling from her braid and shining on my blanket, thought of how her fresh scent had invaded my senses and tied my stomach in knots. 'No,' I said, trying to ignore the sudden heat at the base of my spine, the heat that had come the moment I'd noticed the sweep of her eyelashes against her cheek and wouldn't seem to release me from its grip. 'We're not going back to Earth. Let us look forward. We'll plot a course for Sector Thirteen.'

Dainn patted my shoulder. 'Good. I'll get back to the lab.'

When the door slid closed behind him, I allowed myself to slump. I pressed the screen on my wrist. 'Callan,' I growled into it. 'The nav room. Now.'

My pilot arrived barely a minute later. Our orb ships were always piloted by two officers: one who served the military, and one who served the highest-ranked dignitary on board. That way, if anything went wrong, the dignitary could escape one way with their pilot, while the rest of the crew went the other. Callan was different to other pilots; an orphan given to the military at birth, he'd been raised with me as half a companion, half a bodyguard, before my father decided to appoint him as my personal pilot. My father meant it as an insult, inferring that Callan was nothing more than a chauffeur with a shiny pin, but

Callan had smiled and thanked him and said that nothing could be a greater honour.

I pretended not to admire him as he stepped through the door, pretended not to see the pattern his muscles made beneath his uniform, pretended that my fingers didn't itch to run through his jet-black hair, pretended that my lips weren't burning to be pressed against his.

I pretended a lot of things, when it came to Callan.

'What do you need, Prince?' he said quietly.

I shook my head. 'How are we going to do this? There's no way we can keep her a secret.'

'Alcide, you're the *Prince*. You don't have to justify your choices to *anyone*.'

'But Dainn –'

Callan growled. 'I know you grew up with him, Cide, but Dainn is nothing but your father's echo. He doesn't have your best interests at heart. He's a pawn in your father's game, a piece the King uses to stop all your moves across the board. Forget Dainn.'

'Who does have my best interests at heart, then?' I said quietly.

'You know the answer to that.'

I met his steady black gaze. *You*. 'One being in the entire fucking *universe*.' I sighed and rubbed my temples.

'I know it's hard,' he murmured. 'But remember your grandmother's lessons. Remember what you dreamed together. Bringing Scytha into the light. Saving our kind through peace, not violence. Replanting the forests. Cleansing the water. Ending the corruption, the consumption. Building a world where our species lives with *balance*, where *elya* can flourish once more. Where the Roth are *happy*. Where *you're* happy.'

'Sometimes I think it will never be anything but a dream,' I said glumly.

Callan took a step closer. 'Cide. If I'd taken that human female to your father, what would he have done?'

I swallowed, feeling sick. 'I don't want to think about it.'

'Exactly. What will you do if she refuses to let you claim her?'

I frowned, thinking of the way her hair had fallen across her cheek, of the way her scent made my muscles tight and loose all at once, the way it made everything seem *right*. 'I suppose we'll take her back to Earth.'

'Do you think your father would do the same?'

'No,' I sighed. 'No. He wouldn't.'

'Then, Alcide, *think*,' Callan said, touching my shoulder. 'It's *already* more than a dream.'

I looked away, trying not to flush. 'Has she woken?'

Callan stepped back. 'No.' He paused. 'I wish that starling wasn't so much ... himself.'

'I wish that starling *wasn't*, end of story,' I growled. 'I wish Dainn had never seen that footage. I could have just pretended not to know we'd been robbed, and we wouldn't have the Intergalactic Council's most wanted chained in our cell. I don't want to deal with that, Cal.'

'So toss him out the airlock. He's a starling. He won't even notice.'

I snorted. '*Dainn* would notice, and then he'd tell my father how much was stolen from the treasury, and I'd have the skin stripped from my back. Again.'

'So *Dainn* is the problem. Got it.'

'Callan,' I said carefully, 'do *not* go after Dainn. My father would have you pulled to pieces in his throne room.'

Callan grinned. 'Fine. But I'm not going to stop imagining how satisfying it would be to stick my knife into that old bastard's kidney.'

I waved my hand. 'Imagine away. But keep your knife sheathed.'

'Only for you, Alcide.' He paused. 'The starling said something about the human. What do humans eat?'

I stared at him. 'Oh, *fuck.*' I pinched the bridge of my nose. 'I have no idea. I don't suppose you know how to hack the human satellite systems?'

'I'm a pilot, Prince, not a systems engineer.'

'Then get Bryn to look at it. Bryn *only*, Cal. Tell him it's a direct order from me, and that he is to use encrypted systems and share the knowledge with *no one else*. Him, you, and me. That's it.'

'Yes, Prince.' Callan turned to leave.

'And Cal?'

'Mmm?'

'Let me know as soon as the human wakes up.'

Callan was silent for a moment too long. 'Yes, Prince.'

I stared at the closed door once he'd left.

So many problems, so little time.

ANNA

My head hurt.

I groaned, my temples throbbing. I rolled on my side, which made the pain worse. It felt as though I'd been struck on the side of the throat; my fingers quested over my skin, finding it unbroken but sore to touch. Something soft was around my shoulders, so I snuggled down into it, trying to breathe through the sharp stabs of my headache.

My stomach roiled, threatening to push its contents up my throat. 'Gonna be sick,' I croaked, and sat up so fast my head spun.

'Could you not?' said an unfamiliar voice.

I swallowed down the bile, then opened my eyes.

I was in a strange, dark room. I blinked a few times, hoping that my sight would adjust to the darkness, but everything was shadows.

'Where are you?' I rasped.

Two glowing golden orbs flared to life a few metres away.

I shrieked and scrambled back, my shoulders hitting the smooth, cold wall behind me.

'Well, that's rather rude,' the voice observed. The orbs blinked, and I realised they were *eyes*. 'You look odd to me, too, but you don't see me commenting on it.'

'You literally just did,' I said wildly. 'Where am I? Who are you?'

'The first question is rather easier to answer than the second,' the voice said cheerfully. 'You're in a cell. The highest security cell the Roth could manage, which would be a joke if it weren't for this stupid dark matter cuff.'

I stared at the orbs. 'I ... I don't know what *any* of that means.'

'Oh. I forgot. *Human*. Hmm. Category-3 planet. Let's see.' The voice paused. 'Well, you know that when you look up, you can see a sky? And when that sky goes dark, you can see more sparkly things than you can count? Well, those are *stars*, and –'

'I know what space is,' I said tersely.

'Of course you do,' the voice said condescendingly. 'Well, each of those stars is part of a galaxy, and each of those galaxies has planets, and some of them are quite similar to Earth, I imagine, in that they have breathable air and drinkable water and they can sustain complex life. Now, over time –'

'You're not going to explain evolution to me, are you?' I said, rubbing my throbbing temples.

'Oh, you know that one? Good, that will save some time. So, the more complex species obviously developed and mastered space travel, and they came together to form the Intergalactic Council, and from that Council came the Intergalactic Pact, and the Council decreed that to be part of the pact, species had to meet a certain level of development. Anyway, Earth isn't quite there yet, but there's this species called Roth who *are* at the level of development but who *aren't* part of the Pact, and they have an unhealthy obsession with expansion and for reasons unknown to me their Prince has flown his orb into the gutter of the galaxy. Anyway, the Prince's friend, or minion – I have no idea what his job is, actually, but he has an overabundance of muscle and quite nice horns – went on an illegal sojourn to Earth and seems to have picked you up along the way. So now you're here, in this cell, with me.'

I pulled the blanket – at least, I *hoped* it was a blanket – tighter around my shoulders. 'The … *person* with the horns and the black eyes? He took me?'

'All Roth have horns and black eyes, so definitely, yes, but he is absolutely *not* a person.'

'And who are *you*?' I asked again, trying to tamp down my panic.

There was a moment of silence. 'My name is Vesper,' the voice said eventually. 'I'm a starling. I got trapped in a humanoid form when the Prince captured me, so I don't look like I'm supposed to. But I can turn the light up a bit, if that would make you more comfortable.'

'Please.'

The orbs – *eyes* – glowed brighter, and a warm light spilled outwards, illuminating the room.

It was bare, with featureless black walls and a matching floor. There was a smaller wall opposite me, which seemed to be a kind of screen for whatever lay beyond it; carefully craning my sore neck, I could see a kind of bench and some fixtures that seemed like taps. It might have been a bathroom – but there was no door.

Eww.

I was sitting on a narrow, cot-like bed. It looked like a bench, but it was surprisingly comfortable; the mattress seemed to be made of something like firm memory foam, and I was wrapped like a burrito in the softest blanket I'd ever felt, dyed a lovely forest-green.

I let my eyes focus on the owner of the voice.

He was sitting on the floor, one long leg stretched out before him, the other bent, his bare foot pressed into his thigh. His shape was entirely human – not a horn in sight – and if I'd seen him on the street, I would have stared. He was beautiful, with black curling hair and skin that seemed golden in the warm light. He had a straight nose and curving lips that were made to give devastating smiles.

But his eyes were still glowing, so ... not *entirely* human.

'Um,' I said, because honestly, what else *could* I say?

He cocked his head. 'Do you have a name? I don't know much about humans. Do they use them?'

'Y-yes,' I stammered. 'We use names. Anna.'

'An-na? *That's* your name?'

'Anna, yes.'

'That just sounds like ... sounds. It's one sound, forwards and then backwards. What kind of a name is that?'

'*Any* name is just sounds,' I said crossly. 'What kind of a name is *Vesper*? You sound like a vehicle.'

'At least vehicles go places,' he said. 'Where does an *An-na* go?'

'Further than you,' I snapped, gesturing at his chain.

To my surprise, he gave a wide, charming grin that made my heart try to jump out of my chest. 'You're fun, An-na.'

Great. Stuck in a cell with a handsome, shit-stirring alien with glowing eyes.

I swayed on the bed.

'An-na?' he said, alarmed.

'All good,' I managed. 'Just, you know, processing the whole *cell* thing.'

'Don't forget the whole *Roth* thing,' he said. 'They really are the worst species you could hope to be abducted by. They don't think very much of females, you see. Although the fact that you're here – somewhere relatively safe, actually – and not in the breeding rooms at the mercy of the crew is probably good.'

'*Probably*?' I squeaked. 'What are *breeding rooms*?'

'Exactly what they sound like,' Vesper said with a careless wave of his hand. 'There are very few Roth females left, so they have a habit of stealing females from other species and sharing them. And the females are most decidedly *not* willing. From the outside, one might observe this practice and consider the very low birth rate and conclude that the species' fertility issues lie not with the females, who were blamed for producing only male younglings – and not very many of those – but with the males, who seem to father very few young, and only those of one sex.' He shrugged. 'But no one asks *me*.'

'Will they take me to those rooms?' I whispered.

I wasn't being dramatic when I thought I'd rather die.

Vesper frowned. 'That's what I can't work out. I am sorry, little An-na, but I have no idea what they'll do with you.'

I sniffed. 'Why are you here, then?' I said. 'Unless … Can they breed you, too?'

'They'd better not try, if they value their breeding apparatus,' he answered airily. 'I may be chained, but I can still burn the hand – or any other appendage – that touches me. No, I'm here because I tried to liberate some of the Prince's possessions, and he unfortunately caught me at it.'

I blinked. 'Liberate? Do you mean you were *stealing* from him?'

'Oh, little An-na. Your tone is rather too disappointed to be appropriate for such a short acquaintance. You sound like my sibling, and you don't know me well enough to judge me like they do.'

'Why were you stealing?'

He frowned. 'What?'

'*Why* were you stealing? Were you hungry? Were you suffering? Did you need what you took? Were you taking it for someone else who *did* need it?'

He sniffed disdainfully. 'My sibling says that there's no issue with beauty for beauty's sake. What's wrong with crime for crime's sake?'

I didn't really have a sensible answer for that. I took a deep breath. I was feeling so many different things that it was all but impossible to tease out a single emotion to process; my entire body felt alight with it, as if every instinctual warning was simmering inside my blood and turning my skin to flame. 'To sum up: my grandmother died today, I've been kidnapped and taken from Earth and from everything and everyone I know by an alien species bent on intergalactic expansion but with serious fertility issues, and I'm currently being held in a cell with a thief.'

'A *charming* thief,' he corrected.

'I think that makes it worse,' I said, and burst into tears.

I don't know how long I cried. There was no way to tell time in the cell; the light didn't change, and no one came to disturb us, but I kept sobbing until my eyes were aching, my temples were throbbing, my throat was dry, and my voice cracked. It was as if I'd broken open, letting all the grief and the shock pour out. *Nothing wrong with having a good cry,* my grandmother would have said, and I let myself sink into how much I already missed her, how much it hurt to think of her as *gone,* and I wrapped myself in the fact that my entire world had changed in a matter of hours, in a number of different ways. My face was a puffy, tight mess, and my chest hurt. Vesper had stayed quiet all the while, watching me curiously, but offering neither comfort nor censure.

'That was quite a lot of liquid,' he observed, once I stopped hiccupping.

'*Tears.* They're called *tears.* Humans cry them when they're sad.' I paused. 'Or angry. Or happy. Or overwhelmed. We cry for a lot of reasons, actually.'

'Yes, I know what *tears* are,' he said impatiently. 'I am familiar with the concept. We cry ultraviolet light. What I meant is that there are rather a lot of them *outside* your body, when before they were kept *inside* it. Do you not have to replace them?'

'I am thirsty, yes.'

Vesper turned a sudden, fierce glare up at the corner over my bed. 'Hear that, fleshbags? The human needs liquids. Have you managed to figure out what she absorbs yet?'

'*Drinks,*' I muttered. 'We *drink* liquid.'

'You put it in your *mouth*?' Vesper said. '*Why?* That's disgusting.'

'Well, where do *you* put it?' I sniped.

'We don't need liquid. We're a higher life form,' he said archly.

'Not from where I'm sitting,' I muttered.

He chuckled and looked up at the corner again. 'I think you should have stolen a different human. This one is very mouthy.'

'Who are you talking to?'

He pointed. 'There are several recording devices in the corners. I don't think they're hooked up to the ship's main security systems, because only two Roth have ever visited. If this cell was part of a proper incarceration block, there'd be a rotation of security personnel.'

'Know a lot about jails, do you?'

'Well, yes, it is one of my professional interests,' he said modestly. 'I make a point of knowing as much as I can about them, in order to never, ever see one up close.'

'And how did that work out for you?'

Light flickered in the corner of my eye; I turned towards it, then screamed.

Where a wall of the cell had been, there was now glass, and behind it stood the horned male – the *Roth* – I'd seen on Earth.

'You're not very good at greetings, are you, Anna?' Vesper said.

The Roth scowled, and held something out – a large bowl, filled with clear liquid. He gestured, and made a series of growling, snarling noises that made the hairs on the back of my neck rise.

'He says they figured out you drink water,' Vesper said. 'He's going to bring it in; he said try not to scream again, or he could spill it, and it took them an hour to get this much.' He frowned at the Roth. 'He says they're going to harvest some ice for you. Well, that's nice.'

A panel in the glass wall slid aside, and the Roth stepped in.

He was huge, at least six-foot-six, and his shoulders were almost as wide as the doorway. He was clad in an odd, sleeveless suit that looked to be a uniform, black in colour and tight to his pearlescent skin, highlighting his defined abs. Like his skin, the uniform shimmered as he moved, as if it were made from tiny scales, and there was a round pin on the right side of his chest.

Stop staring at his abs, stop staring at his abs, I chanted to myself, lifting my eyes to his shoulders.

Oh, that doesn't help.

Something beneath my ribs pulled towards him, just as it had in the shadows when I'd first seen him. But I hadn't seen his body properly then, and now it seemed I couldn't *stop* seeing it.

'Are all aliens cut?' I blurted out.

Vesper wrinkled his nose. 'What is *cut*?'

'Never mind,' I muttered, and forced my eyes up further.

His eyes were still the darkest black beneath straight, thick brows. His mouth was still lovely, even twisted. His silky-looking black hair was braided back from his face.

Exposing his horns.

They were as black as his eyes, but not smooth; when the dim light caught them, I could see that their surface was scale-like, too. My eyes caught on the side of his strong throat, and I realised that the pearlescence of his body was coming from *beneath* his skin, where more scales in shades of blues and purples and pearl-white waited.

I took a deep breath, panic threatening to overwhelm me once more. If I could somehow ignore the scales and horns, he could simply be a very tall, very well-muscled human who possibly needed a little more sun in their life.

And I *definitely* didn't think he was attractive.

'Nope, Anna, absolutely not,' I said to myself.

Vesper frowned at me. 'Anna, are you going to leak again?'

The Roth offered me the bowl of water and I took it, ignoring Vesper. 'Thank you,' I told the looming wall of muscle.

He made a snarling noise in response.

'He says that they are trying to generate you some human food now,' Vesper offered. 'He said that the first meal they tried smelled so vile they threw it straight out the airlock. *Fish*?' He shook his head. 'Disgusting. They're trying *chicken* now.'

I stared at him. 'They're making me chicken?'

'Technically, he said *trying to make*. But yes.'

'Oh.' I cleared my throat. 'Thank you?'

'Yes, it's all very nice,' Vesper said, 'but don't forget that if it wasn't for this horned bastard, you'd still be on Earth, making your own chicken. Whatever that means.'

The Roth growled.

'Oh. He's asking if your mate – your partner – would make you the chicken on Earth.' Vesper scoffed. 'Very subtle.'

I flushed. 'I don't have a partner. And no, they wouldn't. I'm a chef. I don't trust anyone else to make my chicken.'

Vesper turned to the Roth. 'She doesn't have a mate,' he repeated, and I realised that the Roth couldn't understand me any better than I could him. 'And you should let her make her own chicken.'

The Roth snarled.

Vesper sighed. 'He said you can't leave the cell just yet; it's too dangerous. But he asked if you need anything.' He twisted his lips. 'Pillows,' he continued, without waiting for me. 'Humanoid species need neck support, do they not? Tell the Prince to give her pillows.'

'Freedom would be nice,' I said. 'But if not that, then yes, pillows.' I looked around. 'Is there a shower in there?'

Vesper repeated my question; the Roth made a hissing sound. 'Yes,' Vesper confirmed. 'A light shower, and a waste disposal system.'

My cheeks flushed hot. 'You mean a toilet?'

Vesper scrunched his face up. 'I don't know. Like I said, higher being. I don't *need* to know.'

The Roth snarled.

'He says do you need a different type of shower?'

'Water,' I said, relieved. I decided to push my luck. 'Humans need a *lot* of showers.'

The Roth gave a sharp nod when Vesper repeated the information, then turned and left the cell, leaving me with the bowl of water. It looked clear and clean; I picked it up and sniffed it, though I wasn't sure what I was looking for. It smelled fine.

I lifted it to my lips and took a tiny sip, then set the bowl aside carefully. If I got sick, I'd know not to drink more.

'Smart,' Vesper said approvingly. 'Although if they wanted to harm you, there are several more straightforward ways than that.'

'Why can I understand you? And you can understand me? But the Roth didn't know what I was saying?'

'I can understand any species,' Vesper said breezily. 'And I can make it so they understand me, regardless of the language I'm actually speaking. So I can speak with both of you, but you can't speak with each other.'

'Oh.' I drew my knees up and hugged them. 'Do you know his name?'

Vesper looked surprised. 'I didn't think to ask. To be fair, I don't think he knows mine, either.'

'And the Prince?'

'Alcide,' Vesper said, making it sound like a caress. 'The Prince's name is Alcide.'

CALLAN

Humans were harder to care for than I'd anticipated.

Firstly, the information Bryn had accessed suggested that their bodies were about sixty percent water, and that two of their major organs had an even higher percentage of the liquid. My kind needed water, too, but we could survive for months without it. Bryn and Alcide had been able to create some in the lab, but it had taken hours and it wasn't a sustainable method, so Bryn had agreed to harvest some ice for us to use instead.

Secondly, their food was *awful*. Roth ate meat, but we ate it lightly seared, if not entirely raw. We didn't add *spices* to change the taste. And we *certainly* didn't have it with a side of green things grown in dirt.

'This is disgusting,' Bryn said.

Alcide poked at one of the vegetables, steaming hot from the food generator. 'Are you entirely sure this is right?'

Bryn shrugged. 'This is what their internet said, Prince.'

Bryn was a burly engineer I'd met during the military component of my pilot's training. When Alcide's orb ship needed a head engineer, I'd recommended Bryn due to his ability to think on his feet, and for the fact he'd been kind to me when others hadn't. I didn't trust him completely – I didn't trust *anyone* but Alcide – but we couldn't have found the information without him. We didn't confirm we had a human on board, but Bryn was smart enough to know that we needed the information for a reason. Luckily, he was also smart enough not to comment.

'Pillows, chicken, and water,' Alcide said dubiously, when Bryn left to find an ice net. 'This seems very odd.'

'She'll let us know if it's not what she needs. She wasn't shy with the starling.'

'The starling is also chained to the floor and can't touch her,' Alcide pointed out. 'She might be more wary with two strangers twice her size who are under no such restrictions.'

'Well, if you want to claim her, you'll have to get her to trust you.'

Alcide flicked me a glare. 'I will remind you whose idea claiming was.'

'Yes, Prince,' I said, ignoring the twinge of jealousy in my stomach. I wasn't entirely sure what I was jealous of – whether it was jealousy that *she* would be claimed by Alcide, or jealousy that *he* would claim her.

Alcide tried – unsuccessfully – to smooth down his unruly hair, his expression tight. I bit my tongue; I hadn't seen him this nervous – well, *ever*.

I understood; simple foot soldiers could go to the public brothel after too much spiced wine and come away knowing what a female felt like, even if they didn't remember much about it afterwards. Princes couldn't. I assumed he wasn't a virgin, but couldn't be entirely sure; he was fairly tight-lipped about the various educational experiences his father subjected him to in the name of his *training*. It was entirely possible, I supposed, that Alcide had never touched a female. Given the current state of our home planet, it wouldn't have been unlikely.

I hadn't.

Other planets and Sectors had pleasure houses, I knew, where the beings within them were paid and worked under fair conditions, like any other job. The public brothel in Scytha City wasn't like that. The females were captives; there was no payment, and no escape. The first time my brothers-in-arms had stumbled towards it and dragged me with them, I'd taken one look at the females – some terrified, some resigned, some simply *empty* – and had vomited straight onto the red mud cobbles.

I became something of a joke after that – the trainee pilot who couldn't handle his wine and had to be put to bed before the evening even started. No one recognised the coincidence of my excess drinking and their visits to the brothel – no one but Bryn, who, every time the other soldiers planned that particular outing, suddenly had *too much work to do*. The others would go without us, laughing.

I didn't know how they *could* laugh. Somewhere along the line, they'd misplaced the knowledge that those females were sentient beings, and what they did was abhorrent. I could make sure *my* actions were in line with my values, but I didn't have the courage – or the charisma – to speak up, to try to change the actions of others.

Alcide did. It was part of why I believed in him so fiercely. His grandmother had taught him that princes worked to make their world a better place, and that's what he'd always done.

He'd spoken publicly about the Scytha City brothel already. Short, to-the-point speeches to his father's Court about the history of our kind, and the sort of power females had held in the past. Reflections on when it had changed, and why, and persuasive arguments on why the females in the brothel should be freed and returned to their planet of origin with a hefty reparation. *It would not erase the crime*, he would say, *and nor will it give us a fresh start, but it is a step in the right direction, and a step we must take.*

His father thought it was amusing, and when the King laughed, his Court laughed with him. Alcide tried to let their mocking slide off him like rain, but it took its toll.

He squared his shoulders and kept doing it anyway.

As long as you believe in me, Cal, I can do this, he'd said, and I would *never* stop believing in him.

And so no matter how I felt about the little human – no matter how much I kept thinking about her delicate features, her shining hair, her enticing springtime scent, the way she made my chest coil tight – if she wanted Alcide, that was that. He deserved something beautiful in his life. She'd be close by, even if she was never mine.

We'll just hope she forgives the whole kidnap thing, or at least knows who to blame. And I'd try not to break under the weight of my guilt in the meantime.

And if she refused Alcide, and he took her back to Earth –

I didn't let myself think about it.

'Come on, Cide,' I said, aiming for lightness and failing. 'Let's take the female what she needs.'

I took up her food, and Alcide carried the extra water that he'd managed to extract in the lab. Remembering Vesper's instructions, I grabbed some of the pillows from Alcide's bed as he entered the code to unlock the cell door.

When we'd walked down the tiny corridor, he studied the cell through the glass. It would be opaque from inside. I was aware it didn't mean a thing to the starling, but the female wouldn't be able to see us.

My Prince frowned at the small wash station and the narrow cot. The female was sitting on it, apparently examining her hands. 'I don't like this,' he muttered.

'Do you have any better ideas?'

He sighed. 'No. May the dread gods keep us.'

I touched between my horns for luck, then pressed the control screen on the wall.

The glass went transparent.

The female jumped at the change; I imagined it would be a surprise to see two horned figures suddenly appear, watching you, and I resolved to be less unnerving. Exactly *how* I was going to manage that, I wasn't sure.

'What an honour,' the starling drawled, as we walked inside.

'Hullo, Vesper,' Alcide answered levelly. 'How's the ankle?'

The starling reached down to touch his leg. 'A bit uncomfortable, actually. Do you happen to have the key? A short walk would do me a galaxy of good.'

'I don't have it on me, no,' Alcide answered, straight-faced. 'Perhaps next time.'

'Perhaps,' Vesper echoed. He gestured at the female. 'Well, go on then. She's curious as to what you plan to do with her. I let her know about the breeding rooms and the generalities of the Roth. She's understandably interested about where she might fit in.'

'I'm sure you were extremely helpful,' I said.

The starling grinned; his eyes danced. 'I *live* to be helpful. Now, I'm sure you can speak to her yourself, so I'll just pretend I'm not here.' He closed his eyes; the room dimmed.

I gave a wordless snarl, then immediately regretted it as the female trembled. Our translators didn't include human languages, which the starling likely knew.

'We would be most grateful for your assistance, Vesper,' Alcide said politely. 'Unless you have something better to do.'

The starling opened his eyes; the human female blinked against the sudden light. 'Are you sure you trust me, Prince?'

'Of course I don't trust you,' Alcide said. 'You already know I'm not stupid.'

Vesper snorted. 'What you are, Prince, is *lucky*.' He glanced at the female. 'But I don't have anything better to do, actually, so I might as well.'

I offered the female the covered food, keeping my body well back.

She sniffed the air and took it a few moments later, clearly cautious, and careful not to touch my fingers. She lifted the lid; her eyes widened.

She looked to Vesper and made a series of noises.

The starling laughed. 'Oh, that's too good. *What the heck is this*, she said.'

'Chicken?' Alcide said, confused.

Vesper apparently relayed this; she looked horrified.

'She doesn't like it?' Alcide worried.

'She said it's like someone heard of chicken second-hand and then tried to make it themselves.'

Alcide flushed. 'Roth food is different,' he said defensively. 'We didn't think she'd like it. We tried to make Earth food with the generator.'

Vesper shook his head. 'Bring her Roth food next time, Prince. She's not as fragile as she looks.'

She poked at the vegetables, and lifted one long tube of green, nibbling tentatively on the end. Her face brightened; she spoke excitedly to Vesper.

I watched her mouth, entranced. I would have given a lot in that moment to know what she was saying.

'This is better, apparently,' Vesper said, wrinkling his nose. 'She can eat this. Not forever, I imagine, but it's a start.'

All three of us waited, watching her eat. She realised after a few moments and blushed a lovely, deep pink.

Alcide's claimed. She will be Alcide's claimed, I told myself.

'She said *why are you staring*?'

'Can you tell her we have a question to ask her?' Alcide said.

Vesper repeated it; her eyes widened. She looked at us expectantly.

Alcide swallowed. 'Will you ask if I may claim her?'

VESPER

I stared at Alcide. 'I think I misheard you,' I said carefully.

'I don't think you did, starling. Ask her if she'll let me claim her.'

'You *do* know what that means in other languages, don't you? *Marry, wed, bond*?'

'Yes, Vesper, I know what it means,' Alcide said, with exaggerated patience.

'Just so I have this clear: the Roth Prince is asking a stray alien he's known for approximately half a milliclick to let him claim her. As in, binding, lifelong, formal claiming, where she will become the princess consort of a species she hadn't even *heard* of yesterday.'

'Yes, you've pretty much got it.'

'I see.' I paused. '*Why*?'

Alcide sighed and rubbed his temples. 'Starling, do you really care?'

I considered the question. *Caring* was something outside my general experience, even when it came to those it theoretically should have applied to; I wasn't sure what it was supposed to look like. I didn't miss my parents, and didn't really mind that my sibling was halfway across the universe. I deliberately went out of my way to avoid attachments, and had associates rather than friends, chased pleasure rather than affection.

But the stomach currently belonging to me was roiling with something I didn't recognise, and, if I didn't know what it *was*, then I couldn't confidently say what it *was not*.

'I don't know,' I said at last. 'But I might.'

Alcide stared at me. 'Are all starlings like you?'

I waved a hand. 'Don't flatter me, Prince. Why do you want the little human for your claimed?'

He exchanged a glance with his companion. 'We want her to stay safe,' he said at last. 'And on this ship, at this time, we think this is the best way. The *only* way. We won't be able to hide her down here forever.'

'So take her back to her home planet,' I said, unimpressed.

'No,' the other Roth growled.

I snorted. 'Ah. I see. There is only one option, because you're only *offering* one.' I turned to Anna. 'The Prince wants to bond you.'

Her reaction was better than I could have imagined; she blanched and dropped her food back on the plate. 'He wants to *what*?'

There are many times when the meaning of language may be difficult to grasp, but the tone of delivery is decidedly not. Alcide flinched, stepping back. The black-haired Roth's lips twisted; he stepped closer to the Prince, as if ready to catch him if he fell.

'The Prince wants to claim you, marry you,' I repeated calmly. 'You're in danger on this ship, and they think this is the only way to ensure your safety.'

'The only way,' Anna repeated flatly.

'That's what he said.'

Anna turned her stare to the Prince. 'But *why*? He knows I'm not some Earth princess, right? I'm a *chef*, for cake's sake. I have a degree in English Literature that I have never used, no family as of my abduction day, approximately three friends, zero savings, and my worldly possessions can be packed into a humiliatingly small suitcase.' She crossed her arms. 'Or is this some kind of space harem situation, and he collects wives of different species?'

'Space harem?' I said, amused. 'Is that a thing humans really think happens?' I remembered my sibling's two partners and almost took it back, but Anna had flushed a glorious pink colour and so I snapped my mouth closed, unwilling to do anything that might make it go away. I stared at her blush, fascinated; I'd never known a species to blush *pink*.

'How would I know what you do in space?' she retorted, throwing her hands up. 'I don't know where I am! I don't know why they took me! I don't know what this ship looks like! And I don't even know their names!'

'Ask them,' I said.

She put a hand to her chest. '*Anna*,' she said clearly. '*Anna*.' She pointed at the black-haired Roth. 'Name?'

'What?' the Roth growled. He looked at me. 'What does she need?'

I decided I wasn't feeling helpful. 'Ask her,' I said flippantly.

'What do you need?' he repeated; to Anna, it would have sounded like a long, deep snarl.

I laughed when she flinched. 'This is too good.'

'Enjoy it while it lasts, starling,' Alcide said calmly. 'When we figure out our next step, you'll be alone again. You think she'll want to come back and visit?'

'Given I'm the only one who can talk to her, Prince, I can almost guarantee it,' I shot back.

Alcide sighed. 'Fine, Vesper. Play your games. I know that's all you're good for. Did you know the Intergalactic Council has several files on you? And do you know what's in them?' He leaned forward; the position made him loom over me. His unruly auburn hair framed his face in gentle waves; he looked suddenly like a creature of fire and darkness, and all the more handsome for it. 'A selfish asshole who leaves crews scattered behind him, ruined at best. Someone who uses other beings and discards them when they're no longer needed. Someone with a pretty smile who's dead inside, who sets up his allies to take the fall once he's gone. Someone who does all that – *but doesn't even* need *what he takes*.' He stepped back. 'You're utter trash, starling. The bored child of wealthy parents who thinks the universe exists to fulfil your every whim. My species might be monsters, but it's taken us generations to get here. You managed it all on your own.'

'Again, Prince, flattery,' I said airily, but something unfamiliar twisted in my chest.

Between what had happened in my stomach and what was happening in my chest, I had experienced quite enough of an organic body for one day.

'We'll leave you,' Alcide said, inclining his head to Anna. He looked oddly majestic doing it, his horns dipping gracefully as he moved. 'The offer stands. I ask you to be my claimed. I will wait for your answer.'

With that, they left, the black-haired Roth favouring me with one last scowl, and giving Anna a lingering look that made my nostrils flare.

'Please, Vesper,' she said softly, once they were gone and the glass wall had gone dark again. 'I don't understand.'

I didn't meet her eyes. 'I don't have much more information than you, but I suspect that you're in danger here,' I said bluntly. 'If *any* of the Prince's crew work out there's a female on board, you'll be fair game. They don't want to keep you in this cell indefinitely, but at the moment, they can't let you out. If you let the Prince claim you, you'll be untouchable.'

'He wants to marry me to *protect* me? Why?'

'I suspect because you're eminently protectable,' I snapped, tired of the conversation. 'You're delicate and beautiful and small. I don't know what humans are like, but for many of the known species in the universe, that's something irresistibly desirable. And you're on a ship filled with one of those species.'

'So they think I'm weak,' she said angrily. 'They want to protect me because I couldn't *possibly* protect myself.'

I laughed harshly. 'Little lodestar, when it comes to the Roth, I imagine that even *the Prince* needs to watch his back. From what I've heard, his crew wouldn't just hurt you. They'd *eat you alive.*' I crossed my arms. *The* arms. I felt sick, snappish. I tried to quash the feeling, to push it down, but it wouldn't obey. *Stupid animated carcass*, I snarled internally. *Stupid bag of meat and instinct.*

Anna was quiet for a long time. 'What would you do?' she said at last.

'I'd save my own skin.' I closed my eyes, throwing us into darkness. 'That's what I always do.'

ANNA

The Prince wants to claim you.

I tossed and turned for hours, thinking about what the Prince had said. About what he'd *asked*.

It can't be real, I thought. He had nothing to gain, and I had everything to lose.

Claiming sounded rather more possessive than *marriage*, but Vesper had used the terms interchangeably, and I gathered it was all the same for the Roth.

I'd never imagined getting married *at all*, let alone getting married to an alien prince because my life was in danger. If I read it in a book, I'd scoff. But being locked in a cell indefinitely – or, alternately, facing a crew full of aliens twice my size who might do things I didn't want to think about – weren't options, either.

Marriage looked like a fairly reasonable choice in the context, actually.

And despite having horns, the Prince had kind eyes, and a face that would make anyone's heart race.

And he had an incredibly ripped friend. *Tall, Dark, and Looming*, I decided I'd call him, in lieu of anything better. *His* eyes weren't kind; his eyes were *hungry*, and they made my heart race, as if my body would be more than happy to be his feast.

I shook my head. I was imagining things, projecting my own desires onto males I couldn't even *speak* with. *Head in the clouds*, my grandmother would have muttered, sometimes affectionately, and sometimes in censure. *Don't worry about us mortals down here*.

Plus, I couldn't have both of them.

Why choose? Tessa would have said, but I was pretty sure that *choosing* was the point of marriage.

'Vesper?' I said tentatively, but he didn't answer. For some reason, his silence made me irrationally angry; it wasn't as if *he'd* put me in this situation, but my temper didn't care.

'Fine,' I snapped crossly, an ache forming in the pit of my stomach. 'Be like that. This isn't my fault, you know.'

Since I couldn't sleep *or* talk to Vesper, I decided to work out the shower situation. Evidently, Vesper had been right about the whole *harvesting ice* thing, because when I pressed the button, water sprayed out of the wall instead of light – and it was *hot*. I took the opportunity to use the toilet while the water was running, my face burning the entire time, but I relaxed once I was standing under the shower, the heat pounding on the tense muscles of my back.

The Prince wants to claim you.

I thought of Vesper's shocked expression.

You're eminently protectable. You're delicate and beautiful and small.

The butterflies in my stomach fluttered their wings at the notion that Vesper thought I was beautiful.

I ignored them.

'If I can't have two, then three is even less likely,' I told myself, washing my hair with the sweet-smelling liquid left in a pouch by the sink. I had no idea what it was, but it did the trick. 'And they seem to hate each other, anyway.'

I dried my hair as best I could and dressed in my dirty clothes, resolving to ask if there was anything else I could wear, or at least a way to clean what I had. Despite the hot shower, putting my clean skin back into the clothes I'd cooked – and then been abducted – in made me even more cross, so I got back into bed and pulled the blanket over my head, ignoring Vesper, who had opened his eyes and was watching me from across the cell.

I slipped so gently into sleep that when I dreamed, it seemed as if I were still awake, every detail of the cell vivid, from the stark black walls to the softness of the blankets on my bed. I stretched languidly, enjoying the feeling of the blankets on my skin – skin that was suddenly bare.

It didn't seem strange when the wall opaqued and Tall, Dark, and Looming was there, waiting, watching. In my dream, I wasn't scared of the hunger in his eyes, so I arched, letting the blanket fall away and his gaze brand my heated skin from throat to hip. My nipples were hard and aching, so as he watched, I cupped my breasts, rubbing my thumbs across the stiff peaks, at once a pleasure for me and a show for him.

It didn't seem strange when the wall slid open and he walked inside the cell, nor when I realised that Vesper was freed from his chain, sitting within arm's length, watching, his eyes glowing gold in the dim light. The black-haired Roth pulled the blanket from my bed so I was naked before them both, bare and waiting.

The Roth fell gracefully to his knees next to Vesper, so I spread my own and let them see that I was wet and swollen, then trailed my hand down my stomach to cup between my legs.

It didn't seem strange when the Roth growled, nor when his shoulders braced against my thighs and he lowered his head. I cried out when his tongue swept over me, when it probed and found my entrance, when it sank inside me while his shoulders held me open for his plunder, the wide stretch an unfamiliar and delicious pleasure-pain. When my head fell to the side I realised that the Prince had joined us, sitting hot-eyed next to Vesper, his chin cupped in one hand as the black-haired Roth licked and sucked me by turn and my hands found his horns and directed him where I needed it most.

It didn't seem strange at all when my body tightened, then coiled, then was released from its delicious torture in a wave of sensation so strong that my core cramped.

Anna, the Roth between my legs growled, and that wasn't strange, either; it was a promise, a caress, a prayer.

I woke with a start, the sound of my name on his tongue still echoing in my ears, and I realised that the cramp was real, and pain was radiating from my core, all the way down my thighs.

No, I thought desperately, the heady pleasure of the dream fading before the inconvenience of reality. *Oh, please, no. Not now.*

After a five-year battle with gynaecologists, I'd finally gotten a begrudging diagnosis just a handful of months previously – adenomyosis. My periods ranged from *painful* to *downright excruciating*, and the sensation radiating down my thighs was not a good sign. I curled into a ball, then changed position a moment later when that made it worse.

I felt Vesper's eyes on me. 'Anna?'

I didn't answer, trying not to flush as I remembered my dream, rubbing my stomach to try to ease the pain. I got up and went into the wash corner – I couldn't call it a *bathroom* – and cleaned myself up, fashioning a pad from the odd sheets of moss provided in place of toilet paper, shivering in the cool air.

'Anna, what's wrong?' Vesper said, after I'd washed my hands and emerged again. 'You've gone a colour you weren't before. This one isn't as nice as the pink.'

'Got my period,' I said through gritted teeth.

He blinked. 'I don't know what that means.'

'Menstruation?' I said. 'Courses? Cycles? Bleeding?'

'Ah.' He studied me, frowning. 'Starlings don't do that.'

'Good for them,' I said acidly.

'Um,' he went on. 'Is it normally so ... That is to say, you look ... odd. Is there something you need?'

'A heat pack, three ibuprofen, my favourite movie, a block of chocolate, and a family-sized bag of sweet chilli crisps,' I snapped.

His frown deepened; he seemed to consider something. 'I can make this body hot,' he said eventually.

The pain flared and I bit back a whimper, sitting back down on the cot and bending at the hips.

'Anna.' Vesper's voice was soft, softer than I'd heard it before. 'Where do you need the heat?'

'My stomach. My back. My –' I faltered as I remembered the dream-sensation of the black-haired Roth's tongue between my legs '– my thighs.'

'I – ah. I can't come to you.'

I looked warily across at his ankle, chained to the floor.

'I won't hurt you,' he said softly. 'I give you my word, whatever it's worth. Come here, Anna.'

I staggered across the cell. I hesitated when I got within arm's reach – I'd never been so close to him, after all – but pain made the decision for me and I sank to my knees next to him, gasping at the shock of the cold cell floor.

He leaned over and took my hand. I shivered at the contact. 'I'll warm the body up slowly, all right? You tell me when it's hot enough.'

His skin felt just like mine, until it began to warm in slow, slight increments. I waited until it got as warm as my heat pack would, then I tentatively placed his hand across my stomach.

I moaned aloud, but it was a sound of relief, not pain.

'Stars,' he said, sounding alarmed. 'What do organics usually do when something breaks? Should you see a flesh engineer? A – what's the word – *doctor*?'

'I'm ok,' I said through gritted teeth. 'This is helping.' I paused. 'Thank you, Vesper.'

'Come here,' he said again, and pulled me off the floor, arranging me on his lap, my back against his chest, my legs stretched out along his. He rested one hand on my stomach and lay the other across my thighs; I let my head fall back onto his shoulder. It was more comfortable than my bed had been; warmth radiated all around me, relaxing my muscles.

I tried not to think about how intimate it was, and about which bits of Vesper were pressed up against which parts of me. I tried not to think about how good he smelled – like the sweetest woodsmoke – and about how nice it felt to have a strong pair of arms wrapped around me, especially when those arms belonged to someone who looked like him. I tried not to think about how his eyes had flared in my dream, how he'd stared at my nakedness, watching as the Roth pleasured me.

He might have been an intergalactic thief and occasionally an outright dick, but he was an excellent cuddler.

I dozed, letting his warmth lull me back to sleep.

I woke when my uterus decided to start *eating* itself. I twisted on Vesper's lap, unable to get comfortable. His hands were still warm on my stomach, but it wasn't helping; the knife-sharp pain was radiating down to my knees.

'You organics are nothing but trouble. Fleshbag!' he shouted at the ceiling. 'Anna needs help, now!'

I didn't know who he was talking to until I remembered the cameras in the corners. 'Just painkillers,' I whispered. 'I don't need a doctor. I already know what's wrong.'

'I don't think the Roth know what painkillers are, brightness,' Vesper said tightly. 'But they should have a medic on board, and most medics are familiar enough with other species, so he might be able to help. He'll be Roth, so don't trust him, but unless the Prince and his muscly sidekick have medical training they're hiding very, *very* well, you don't have any other options. I don't want to watch you like this.'

'My pain shouldn't be about *your* comfort, Vesper,' I grated out, unaccountably hurt.

He grabbed my chin and gently turned my face until I was looking into his eyes. They flared, golden and glowing, alien and unknowable and so very *beautiful*. 'Anna,' he said quietly; he was close enough to touch, close enough to *kiss*. 'I'm trying to help you.'

My mind went entirely blank.

I was spared the need to answer by two massive arms scooping me off the starling's lap and cradling me against a hard chest. Tall, Dark, and Looming growled something softly; Vesper responded.

'He's going to take you to the medic,' Vesper said tightly. 'Don't let him leave you alone. I don't know what play the Prince and this one are planning, but they've had plenty of opportunity to hurt you, and they haven't. The medic is another matter entirely.' He crossed his arms. 'Bring her back quickly,' he hissed at the Roth.

Tall, Dark, and Looming didn't answer.

The short corridor outside the cell led into a bedroom. The Roth walked too quickly for me to see much, but I still took in the monstrously large bed, covered in a forest-green blanket that looked suspiciously like the one on my cot. When he carried me through the sliding glass door and into the ship proper, I tried to take in more – anything that might help me eventually get free – but there wasn't much to see, just endless hallways of silver and white. I wondered if he was deliberately taking me through empty corridors until I realised that the lights were dimmed, and it was probably the middle of the night.

'Were you asleep?' I said softly.

He didn't answer, though he did glance down. He'd braided his hair back from his face, and the stretch of his cheekbones was gloriously, strikingly harsh. His jaw tightened, and I must have looked even worse than I felt, because he quickened his pace through the white hallways until we reached a glass door.

The Roth growled, and it slid open.

He carried me into a room that held some cupboards, an examination bed, and a wide screen that took up most of one wall. There was nothing else in the room itself, though when I tilted my chin up, I could see that there were a number of fixtures in the ceiling that looked a lot like lights.

He settled me down on the bed.

The door slid open again, and an unfamiliar Roth entered. He was a foot or so shorter than Tall, Dark, and Looming, though he looked to have the same hard muscle, and I wondered if that was just how the species was made. His horns curled back in spirals, and his hair was a salt-and-pepper grey. He stopped short when he saw me; his mouth dropped open.

He spoke in a series of growls to my Roth, who snarled back. Eventually – after a lot of gesturing – they seemed to come to an agreement of some kind; the older Roth – the medic, I assumed – gave me what might have passed for a smile, then did something to the screen to make it light up. At the same time, the room went dark, and light streamed down from the ceiling above me in a series of sweeping lines, as if I was being scanned.

When a picture of my body appeared on the screen, I realised that was *exactly* what was happening. My Roth tapped on the tiny screen on his wrist and said something into it; when I saw a smaller image of the same picture of me, I realised that he was either downloading or streaming the information elsewhere.

'I just need painkillers,' I said weakly. 'That's all.'

The doctor gestured to my abdomen on the image.

'Yes, that's it,' I babbled, wincing as pain bloomed again. 'Adenomyosis. Though I don't know why I'm expecting you to know what it is; I'm fairly sure that half the doctors on Earth don't believe it exists.'

My Roth tapped his wrist again, growling.

'Anna?' Vesper's voice came through a moment later.

'Vesper?'

'The fleshbag has tapped into the camera circuit so I can translate. They don't have anything they can give you straight away. Roth pain responses are very different to your nervous system, and the black-haired one said they use a practice similar to one on Earth – something to do with needles in the skin? – to manage pain. But you don't seem to have the same points to target, so they can't do that for you.' He paused. 'The medic is going to try to manufacture a painkiller, but it might take him a day or so.'

'That's okay,' I said tremulously. 'I'll just go back to sleep. Can I come back now?'

My Roth growled; the medic answered with a lighter snarl.

'The medic wants to check your other vital signs,' Vesper said. 'He's – *don't you dare leave her, fleshbag!*'

I looked at my black-haired Roth, alarmed. 'He's leaving?'

'The medic is insisting. He's saying that there's nothing to worry about.' Vesper paused, sounding as if there was a *lot* to worry about. 'The medic outranks him, lodestar. He has to leave. *But go and get the Prince, you horned fool. Get the being who outranks the medic.*'

My Roth gave me an apologetic look and patted me awkwardly on the shoulder. I hated myself for it, but I clutched at his arm. 'Please don't go,' I whispered.

He looked stricken, his strong features crumpling with worry. He tucked a lock of hair behind my ear with a gentle hand, his eyes scanning my face, then disentangled himself from my grasp. He turned, and clearly had a thought; he removed the screen from his wrist and gave it to me.

'Vess-perr,' he hissed, and tapped the screen.

'Vesper,' I repeated. I held the screen up to my cheek. 'Vesper?'

'I can hear you, brightness. That's all I can do, but I can hear you.'

I took a deep breath. 'Okay.'

Tall, Dark, and Looming gave me one last searching look, his brow creased into a frown, then left the room.

My mouth went dry and I swallowed.

The medic smiled again, then placed his hand on his chest and made a thudding motion with his fist, mimicking a heartbeat.

'Oh, my heart. Yes, here,' I said, and did the same.

He nodded, pleased. He put two fingers on his collarbone and tapped in the same rhythm.

'A pulse? Here,' I said, placing two fingers under my chin. 'And here,' I said again, tapping my wrist. 'Though I can never find it there.'

The medic nodded, and gave a series of short growls.

'He wants to take your temperature, but he has no idea how warm humans are supposed to be, so this is a giant waste of time,' Vesper snarled over the tiny screen. 'He's going to try to listen to your pulse instead. Apparently, the scans pick up the beat, but they can often miss something irregular, and they won't pick up anything odd in your lungs. If he does anything you don't like, poke him straight in the eye.'

I cleared my throat as the doctor pulled out something that looked remarkably like a human stethoscope. It made sense, I supposed, that if you had a similar heart and similar hearing, then you might come up with a similar way to measure it.

He placed the double ends in his ears, and smiled in what seemed to be an apologetic way before he put the flat end on my chest, steering well away from my breast. I relaxed slightly, trying to steady my breathing as he listened to my heart, keeping his body as far from me as he could reasonably manage. I was glad; I hadn't minded being bundled into the black-haired

Roth's arms – or Vesper's – but that didn't mean I wanted to be touched by anyone else.

He gave a soft growl.

'He wants you to turn around, lodestar. He's going to listen to your lungs. He asked if you're comfortable lowering your shirt for him. If you like, I can tell him exactly where to stick his –'

'It's okay, Vesper,' I said hurriedly. I turned around and undid my top buttons, shrugging my shirt off one shoulder.

'Talk to me, Anna. What's he doing?'

Something cold was placed gently above my shoulder blade. 'He's listening now, Vesper. I'll have to be quiet.'

'Tell me the moment he's done.'

I took a steady breath in, then exhaled. My position on the bed was making my cramps worse, but the coolness of the alien stethoscope distracted me from the pain. I took a handful more breaths, and felt the doctor take the chest-piece off my skin.

I huffed a relieved laugh. 'It's finished, Vesper, it –'

Something sharp sank deep into my shoulder, and I screamed.

ALCIDE

I HEARD HER SCREAM from the corridor.

Callan was outside the clinic door, already pounding on the glass. 'He's locked us out,' he roared. 'Alcide, that fucker has *locked us out*!'

'Move,' I said shortly. I had the override code for every room on the ship, and I tapped it in with a calmness I didn't feel, my blood rushing hot around my body, fear boiling in my stomach.

When the glass slid aside, my vision went white.

Dainn had sunk a needle deep into the human female's shoulder; the vial was filled with the distinctive blue sedative used to render Roth patients unconscious. She shrieked and struggled fiercely against him; a feral growl ripped from Dainn's throat as he ducked down and *bit* her, trying to hold her in place. The female cried out in pain and wrenched herself sideways, dislodging Dainn from her skin; his sharp second row of teeth took a strip of pale flesh with them as Vesper's voice shouted from the wrist screen.

My hand was on my sword before I knew what I was doing, and I didn't think at all as I swung it through the air.

Dainn's head hit the floor with a dull *thump*. It rolled in an uneven, ungainly spin, before its horns brought it to an abrupt stop; blue blood leaked out onto the surgery tiles.

'*Anna*?' Vesper shouted from the wrist screen. 'Anna!'

Callan blinked at the doctor's head, then stowed his gun, carefully flicking the safety setting back on. 'Well, that's one way to deal with it. I didn't know you kept that thing sharp. I thought it was only ceremonial.'

'There's no value in a dull blade,' I said blankly, repeating something my father said often. I felt oddly hollow inside; I focused on the red mess of the human female's shoulder. *Anna*, Vesper had called her. *Her name was Anna.* 'She's bleeding. Her name is Anna, and she's *bleeding*.'

Callan threw open Dainn's neatly-ordered cupboards until he found packages of sterilised bandage. He opened one and approached Anna slowly, with his hands in the air. 'It's all right, beautiful. You're safe, but you're bleeding. We just need to stop the blood.'

Anna didn't understand him, of course. She shrank back, shivering, her eyes empty.

'Anna, lodestar, it's Alcide and ... the other one.' Vesper's voice came over the wrist screen, soothing. 'They're not going to hurt you, because if they do, I will find out whether I still have enough energy to go supernova, and *I will take out this ship and every being on it*, dark matter chain or no dark matter chain. They're trying to help you. Someone mentioned blood.'

His voice broke on the last word. 'Blood should be on the inside. If you're bleeding, you have to let them stop it. Let them help.'

She still had the wrist screen clutched in her hand, so tightly it was almost cutting into her skin. She blinked, and seemed to take us in properly. She said something to Vesper, her voice rasping.

'*That fucker did what?*' Vesper snarled.

Anna flinched.

'Dainn tried to sedate her, then bit her, and Anna has a wound on her shoulder,' I said calmly. 'Dainn's head is now on the floor, separate to his body.'

Vesper was quiet a moment. 'If I ever get out of this chain, Prince,' he said, his voice eerily calm, 'be prepared to wear a matching scar.'

'Are you always so exceptionally unhelpful?' I snapped. 'Your feelings don't matter. We need to stop her bleeding.'

I heard him exhale. I didn't think that starlings strictly needed to breathe, but Vesper had taken on several organic qualities in the time he'd worn the humanoid body. I wondered if it was changing his personality as well as his mannerisms.

'Anna, brightness, let them stop your bleeding. I'm sorry I got angry. They're going to stop the bleeding, then they're going to bring you back here, aren't you, Prince?'

I gave a hasty nod as Anna's eyes focused on me. 'We'll take you straight back, Anna, I promise.'

'He promises, lodestar. They'll stop your bleeding, then bring you back. Let them see.'

Anna turned her back to us without saying a word. She pressed the wrist screen to her cheek as Vesper continued to murmur to her, too low for us to hear.

Now that she was still, her shoulder looked worse than before, shining and mangled, her skin messily torn. Callan loosed a deep, rumbling growl at the sight of it, his eyes jet with anger.

'*Cal*,' I snapped. '*Stop her bleeding.*'

Callan approached her slowly. She shuddered when he gently mopped the blood from her skin – it had slowed its flow – and then whimpered when he pressed more bandage to the wound. The sound pulled at something deep inside me; I forced myself to stay still, not to go to her, not to touch her. Her fresh scent had turned cloying with fear; I put my hand to my face, trying to block it out before it made me lose control.

Callan had said that he couldn't take her back to Earth, that he needed to keep her. I understood why, now; forcing myself to stay still was one of the hardest things I'd ever done. Every instinct roared to do the opposite, my chest aching with the need to take her and hide her and care for her, as if it was what I was made for.

Callan kept the bandage pressed in place until her strange red blood soaked through, then reached to gently remove the needle from her shoulder. The vial was full; it looked as if Anna's struggling had prevented Dainn from injecting the sedative within it. My pilot handed the needle to me, and I threw it immediately into the waste chute; a moment later, he gave me the sodden bandage, which followed the sedative, and pressed a clean bandage to Anna's back.

The clinic screen flashed. I went to it, frowning; a comms channel was open. I went still as I realised.

'Dainn was contacting my father,' I said blankly. He hadn't managed to send anything – no text, no recording, no voice message – but I closed the channel and searched his recent files anyway, just to make sure. I looked across at Callan. *Why would he contact my father now?* 'Cal, do you think –'

Callan looked down at Anna, then back at me. 'Put yourself in Dainn's position, Prince. Remember the King's orders. And remember who Dainn is – was – loyal to.'

My father, my father, my father.

Dainn was going to give Anna to my father.

I didn't speak, just stood, listening to Vesper mutter expletives over Callan's wrist screen, and tried not to think about what might have happened had Dainn been successful.

'I think it's stopped,' Callan said softly, after he'd discarded three more bandages.

I nodded tersely. 'Take her back to the cell. Let Vesper look after her, then take her some extra bedding, whatever water Bryn has distilled, and whatever food you can make.'

'Don't you want to see her settled?' Callan asked gently.

I twisted my lips. 'I need to clean up here and throw the garbage out the airlock.'

Callan put his hand on my arm. 'Cide. Let me do that.'

'I killed him.' I took a deep breath. 'I killed my father's friend, my mentor, and our only medic. It's my responsibility.'

'You don't have to do it by yourself.'

I brought my hand up and let it rest on his, just for a moment. 'I do, Cal. Look after Anna. I'll do the rest.'

His lips twisted, but he scooped Anna up carefully, making sure to keep his hands well away from her wound. Anna lay her cheek on his chest.

I looked away, keeping my eyes on the wall screen until the door slid closed behind them.

Dainn's eyes were still open.

Dainn had taught me how to count. He'd looked after my scrapes and cuts and breaks through childhood. When my father whipped me, Dainn had intervened before the King stripped the skin from my back.

But he'd also tried to kidnap Anna and deliver her to a fate worse than death.

'You deserved to die,' I told his body fiercely. 'You are everything that's wrong with our species.'

I thought about the way I'd wanted to steal Anna away, to keep her safe, to protect her. *You're hardly any better than Dainn,* I told myself. *Complicit in kidnap, with your instincts still shouting more loudly than your morals.*

One of the cupboards was full of the moss sheeting that covered the surgical bed. I took an armful and spread it out on the floor, rolling Dainn's cooling body onto it. Blood had soaked everywhere, and by the time I'd wrapped him up, my hands were covered in it. I added another layer of moss for his head, closing his eyes – it was unnerving to see him staring up blankly – then awkwardly folded the moss sheet over his horns.

The nearest airlock was just down the hall. I slung Dainn's body over my shoulder and tucked his head under my arm, thanking the dread gods that it was still in the early hours of the simulated morning. The corridors were usually full of crew moving between the orb's different quarters; as it was, I was alone as I opened the airlock and unceremoniously shoved Dainn inside it, placing his head on top of his body. Moments later, I watched him – and his head – float into the blackness of space, his blood boiling and crystallising behind him.

I thought I'd feel more.

The hall and the airlock had an automatic cleaning cycle, so I added a manual override and went back into the surgery so the bots could do their job. After I closed the cupboards, I did the same thing in the clinic, watching as they mopped up the blood and disinfected the floors and walls. It was almost too easy; other than the missing moss sheeting and bandages, there was nothing out of place, no way to tell what had happened in the room.

I closed my eyes. 'Other than the security feeds.'

I had full access to the feeds, so I logged in from the clinic screen and blanked the entire night for the whole ship, adding a feed of the previous night to replace what I'd wiped. When I was done, I leaned forward on the desk and put my head in my hands.

'*Fuck*,' I said aloud.

I'd killed my mentor – my father's friend – to protect the human female. And if *I* hadn't done it, Callan would have, without thought, without question. And if neither of *us* had acted, then Vesper would have tried to blow up the ship.

I had a feeling that our problems were only just beginning.

CALLAN

ANNA WAS SMALL AND shaking in my arms.

I hated it. I hated that she was hurt, hated that she was afraid, hated the way she was shuddering.

And I hated myself for the way I liked holding her close.

I tried to ignore it, but I couldn't. She fit perfectly against me, as if I'd been born to hold her. Her scent had deepened with blood and fear, but she still filled my senses with spring. I hated that my body reacted with a flood of heat and need, hated that my instincts roared to take her somewhere dark and private to protect her. I hated myself for wanting her, hated myself for *needing* her, and I hated myself for noticing it at all when she was injured and terrified and vulnerable.

I forced myself to refocus, my senses full of sweat and tears and the sweet scent of her hair as I carried her through Alcide's quarters and to the cell.

The starling had been captive for months now, and in all that time, he'd always sat the same way – his back to the cell wall, his chained foot stretched out in front of him, his free foot pressed against his outstretched thigh. When the door slid open, it revealed him kneeling, plucking at the dark-matter chain with angry fingers, as if he glared at it vehemently enough it would simply detach itself from the floor.

Anna stirred in my arms. 'Vess-perr?' she whispered.

'Give her to me,' the starling rasped. '*Give her to me.*'

I paused for a moment. I didn't want to give her to him; I wanted to keep her close. I wanted to feel her warm and safe in my arms and have my nose and mouth full of spring. But Anna reached out to him, so I pushed those thoughts aside and collapsed down to my knees. Vesper held his arms out and I handed her over, careful not to touch her shoulder.

The starling took her up as if she were made of Tirian rose platinum, cradling her with gentle hands. 'Brightness. Talk to me.'

Anna croaked something tiredly, pressing her face into Vesper's neck.

Jealousy stirred, hot and angry in my stomach.

'She wants to know what that fucker tried to do,' Vesper growled. 'She knows it's bad, otherwise the Prince wouldn't have cut his head off. Do I tell her?'

I leant back. 'I don't want to lie to her.'

Vesper gave a short nod, and dropped a kiss on Anna's forehead. Her eyes flew open with shock, then widened again when Vesper said bluntly: 'He tried to kidnap you for the Roth King.'

Anna swallowed, and burrowed further into Vesper's chest. She said something, muffled against Vesper's shirt.

'That's right. You're safe now. It didn't work. And that fucker will never touch anything ever again.'

I got to my feet. 'I'll leave you,' I said awkwardly.

Anna rasped something.

'She said thank you,' Vesper said reluctantly. 'And to tell the Prince the same.'

'I'll tell him.'

Vesper looked up. 'She might thank you, but I don't,' he said, his voice low and furious. 'You think being claimed by the Prince will stop the other males on this ship from thinking the same thing as your dead medic? *Take her home to Earth*, you selfish bastards.'

Anna looked up at Vesper and then across at me, her face pinched with worry.

'I can't,' I told the starling. I turned away from their gaze and strode from the cell; the walls were golden with the furious glow of Vesper's eyes. 'I can't.'

Alcide was in his bedroom. His uniform was crumpled in the corner and he was sitting on the floor shirtless, his sword over his knees. He was cleaning it by hand, and there were several bloody rags strewn around him.

'Cide,' I said softly.

He looked up; his brow was creased in pain. 'He taught me how to count, Cal,' he said, his voice hoarse.

'I know, Prince.' I paused. 'What do you need?'

Alcide was a tall male, as tall as me, but sitting on the floor in nothing but the tight black pants we wore under our uniforms, he looked small. Lost. He dipped his head, staring at his sword. 'Say no,' he said at last. 'Say no, but Cal ... Can you ... Will you ...'

'You can ask for a hug, Cide. Your father isn't here.' I dropped to my knees. 'He's not here, and he won't know. I'll give you whatever you need. Always.'

He gave a strangled half-sob and launched himself towards me, his sword clattering to the floor. He linked his arms around my waist and pressed his face into my neck.

I wrapped my arms around him and held on as tight as I could.

I'd held him like this once before, in our seventeenth year. His mother had died when he was born and he had no memories of her, but his maternal grandmother had raised him in every spare moment the King had allowed, had taught Alcide all the things he needed to know to grow into the worthy male he was. She'd seemed healthy enough to live forever, but just after Alcide's seventeenth birthday, she'd died on a trip outside Scytha City.

He'd been devastated.

I'd held him like this for hours. I didn't remember my parents – I'd been adopted by the military – but I could imagine well enough what it would be like to lose someone I loved. So I'd held on, and Alcide had held back, and after a long while he'd stopped sobbing, then stopped hiccupping, and his breathing evened out to match mine, and for a long time it had seemed as if we were sharing the same breath, and a strange, unfamiliar tension had risen, and Alcide had pulled back, and his eyes had been like the night sky, and something in my chest had wound tight like a spring as he stared at me.

Then Alcide's father had walked in.

The King had torn us apart, roaring, and he'd ordered us both whipped. My punishment had been private, but Alcide's hadn't; his father's Court was never told what it was Alcide had done, just that he'd transgressed.

The King almost killed him. Dainn had stepped in and convinced the King to stop, and had spent the next few months caring for Alcide's wounds until the only thing left were thin grey stripes on Cide's wide back.

I wasn't so lucky – my back was still a mess of scars – but I didn't care. I would have taken the punishment twice over to have Alcide look at me again that way, as if I'd suddenly answered a question he'd been asking for years.

His arms tightened on my waist, and I wondered if he was thinking the same as me.

'Do you want to get off the floor, Prince?'

He gave a small shake of his head. 'Don't want to move.'

'All right,' I said mildly. 'But you're heavy as sin, Cide, and my knees are getting old. You don't have to move, but I'm going to.'

'Your knees aren't –' he started, then bit off the rest of the sentence as I hauled him up and onto his ridiculous bed with its canopy and four posts. It was big enough to sleep four males of my height and shoulder width, as if whoever designed it was expecting their Prince to entertain nightly orgies.

They clearly hadn't met Alcide.

I settled back on the farcical mountain of pillows and arranged Alcide to be more comfortable. He threw one of his legs over mine.

I ran my hand over his hair.

He had incredible hair, Alcide. Like red silk, cut raggedly to fall somewhere between his chin and his shoulders. He'd tied it back, but I teased it out from its messy braid and let it flow through my fingers. He made a low sound so I kept up my movements, gently rubbing around the base of his horns.

'It's all right, Cide,' I whispered.

'Cal,' he murmured, and lifted his face; the air went taut between us, and it was if no years had passed at all and we were striplings again, only now his eyes weren't just full of the night sky – they held the entire fucking universe.

I moved first, because I knew he wouldn't, and I could take the blame if something went wrong. The first brush of my lips over his was gentle, a promise rather than a kiss, a caress that sent heat all the way down to my toes. The second was longer, an exploration, a tasting, a test.

The third was a ravaging.

Alcide surged up against me, taking my face in his hands. He nipped on my bottom lip, hard enough that I shuddered, and thrust his tongue against mine. It was apparent that neither of us had any experience, but it didn't seem to matter; our lips moved in a savage dance and my fingers tightened in his hair until he moaned. His body was hard and hot against mine and I kissed him back desperately, fervently, almost angrily, as if I were trying to devour him whole.

Perhaps I was.

Our horns knocked together and I laughed at how clumsy we were, how desperate. Alcide laughed, too – laughed, until my lips found his neck, and then he was panting, tipping his chin back to bare his throat to me.

I traced the column of it, then mapped his shoulders and chest with my hands, breathing hard. His fingers traced a path over my stomach and down, trailing over my straining cock with a featherlight touch.

'Tease,' I rasped.

He gave a devastating grin and palmed me properly through my uniform, rubbing up and down my shaft until my hips were bucking against his hand. I groaned and returned the favour, finding the hard, thick length of him through his pants, squeezing his swollen head. I was throbbing and leaking precum, and I captured his lip between my teeth as I flicked his buttons open.

He was silky and hot beneath my hand, and for a moment I forgot how to breathe. I traced him gently from tip to base, my fingertips following the ridges of scales and feeling them ripple against my skin, then circling his perfect thickness. I pulled him free so I could devour him with my eyes; he groaned as I bent down and drew him into my mouth.

'Cal,' he grated out, as I took him in and flattened my tongue against his shaft, dragging over the sensitive scales. They pulsed; I swallowed a moan. 'Dread gods, *Callan.*'

I really wished that I knew what I was doing.

'Come here,' he murmured, and pulled me back up for another kiss. 'I need to hold you.' A moment later, his hand was inside my uniform and it was my turn to groan as he palmed me, my turn to gasp as his hand moved, my turn to pant as he tore aside my clothing and we were finally skin to skin, heart to heart.

Mine felt about to burst.

My hips pinned him to the bed; he ground up against me as I traced his lip with my tongue. He was hot against my stomach, his scales rippling against my skin as he bucked. It was fast and clumsy and perfect, and I swallowed his moans when he came, his fingers embedding themselves in my back until I followed him over the edge. When I stopped shuddering and rolled off him, I was a panting, floating mess – and I wanted to do it again.

We lay in silence for a moment. My hand found his and our fingers laced together.

The silence changed, became expectant.

He shifted towards me, splaying his free hand on my chest. 'Callan,' he said, my name like a prayer on his lips. I turned, just in time to see his expression falling. He swallowed. 'Callan, I want to be loyal.'

'You want to be loyal,' I repeated, frowning.

He rubbed his temples. 'Cal, I want to be loyal to my claimed.'

'To your –' I started, and then it hit me.

Anna.

Alcide wanted to be loyal to *Anna.*

The same Anna that *I* wanted. The same Anna that I had stolen from Earth *because* I wanted her. The same Anna that I wouldn't – *couldn't* – return to her home, return to safety, because I needed her close. Coveted her. Because I was fixated by her clear blue eyes, her shining hair, her springtime scent.

I didn't know which of them I wanted more – Alcide or Anna – but it was apparent that I wouldn't be getting either.

I rolled off the bed, catching up my uniform and pulling it on with a speed I'd never managed before.

'Cal, I'm sorry. I –'

'You have nothing to be sorry for, Prince.' I took a deep breath and gathered my courage, knowing this was the end of one chapter before Alcide went forward alone into the next, needing to put what I'd felt for years into words. 'Cide, I just want you to know –'

My wrist screen beeped, alerting me to movement in Vesper's cell. I touched the screen.

'Fleshbag?' Vesper's voice was desperate. 'Fleshbag, *Anna won't wake up.*'

Anna had points of colour burning on her cheeks; her skin had otherwise turned too pale. She was limp in Vesper's arms, unmoving, and sweat was beading on her forehead.

'Help her,' Vesper croaked. 'Her light is wrong.'

'Fever,' Alcide murmured. 'Starling, she's burning up. Let us put her on the bed.'

For a moment, I thought that Vesper would refuse. He drew her closer, his eyes raking over her face, as if he was silently imploring her to wake. When that didn't work, he took a deep breath and held her out to me.

I took her up, then settled her down on the cell's cot; she gave a soft moan.

'Put her on her stomach, Cal,' Alcide said. 'We might need to wash the wound again.'

I turned her over as gently as I could, then stared at the mess Dainn had made of her shoulder.

'Should it ... Should it look like that?' Vesper said.

'*Nothing* should look like that,' I muttered.

'Bandage, antiseptic, water,' Alcide said. 'I'll be back.' He disappeared back outside the cell.

'If she dies, I'm taking this ship down,' Vesper promised. 'I'm fairly certain I'll die, too, but you *definitely* will. As fair warning.'

'What is it you want from her, starling?' I snapped.

'I don't –' Vesper inhaled sharply, then shook his head. 'Less than you, I'm fairly sure.'

Me, who had stolen her from her home planet because I couldn't bear to leave her there, and then delivered her to a male who'd *bit* her.

Guilt wasn't a big enough word for what I felt.

'If you want less than me, then you still want more than you'll get,' I snarled. 'She won't ever be yours.'

His gaze flared golden. 'You've been moping after her with those big black eyes, but you look at the Prince the same way,' he said slowly. 'That can't feel good. If he claims her, you'll still be exactly where you are now. Watching both of them from afar. Forever.'

I swallowed. 'I don't care. As long as Alcide is happy, and as long as Anna is safe, *I don't care.*'

He studied me, so closely that I felt myself begin to flush. 'You know, my twin told me an Earth saying once,' he said. '*Misery loves company.* I can't promise I'll be *good* company, but at least you'll have some.'

I stared at him, blinking in surprise. He looked steadily back, his eyes glowing with fear or worry or something else entirely.

My chest wound tight. 'Vesper –'

The glass door slid open. 'Got them,' Alcide said, holding up a basket of things he must have taken from Dainn's empty surgery. 'Is she in pain?'

'She hasn't moved,' I said; I didn't know if that was good or bad.

Alcide soaked some bandage in water and an antiseptic mixture and began gently swabbing at the angry flesh on her shoulder. 'I have no idea what I'm doing, Cal.'

'I think her temperature being so high is bad,' Vesper offered. 'Before this, she was almost always the same warmth. I can feel that she's hot now.'

'We need to get her to drink,' I said decisively. 'That's a good thing for humans. Right?'

'I will rephrase. *We* have no idea what we're doing.' Alcide dampened his bandage again. 'How can three beings be so ill-equipped to care for the one that needs it?'

'Did you not have an apprentice healer?' Vesper demanded.

'I think you underestimate the Roth body,' Alcide answered. 'We don't get sick. And when we do, we die. That's all there is to it. A ship's medic is like … a diamond. You only have one if you're rich enough to afford it, and it's never entirely necessary.'

'Of all the ships in all the universe,' Vesper muttered, 'I get chained on this one with you fleshbags and *no fucking healer.*'

Alcide leaned back. 'This looks all wrong,' he muttered, frowning at Anna's shoulder. 'Maybe I shouldn't have killed Dainn.'

'Of course you should have,' Vesper growled.

'I think it's clean. Well, clean*er*,' Alcide amended. 'Cal?'

I took the bandage from him and examined Anna's shoulder. It looked better than it did before – Alcide had swabbed away some of the weeping blood and pus – but it was still swollen and shiny and angry-looking, and Anna hadn't stirred. 'It's definitely cleaner. I'm not sure it's better.'

'Maybe she just needs sleep.' Alcide turned to Vesper. 'Will you watch her?'

'How could I do anything else?' the starling answered.

'We'll leave her in peace,' Alcide decided. 'Perhaps she will improve in the morning.'

The Prince went to his bed, though I knew he didn't sleep. I stood outside the cell all night, watching the female I'd stolen – and the other being who seemed equally entranced by her.

VESPER

We watched Anna for hours.

I knew the Roth – *Cal*, Alcide had called him – was outside, standing straight-backed and still, his massive arms folded across his chest. I was troubled by our conversation, and by my reaction to him. It wasn't as if I was a stranger to males – in my experience, they were an easy gender to manipulate, regardless of species, due to their unfortunate tendency to think with their smaller brain – but I was feeling something towards the Roth that I wasn't sure I had a word for.

I liked that he was so loyal to his Prince, and the way his uniform stretched across his shoulders. I liked the way his chest rumbled when he growled and the way his hair settled around his horns. But it was *this* – the way he stood watching over Anna, even though she'd never know it – that troubled me. More accurately, I was troubled by my *reaction* to it, by the way it made the body's chest constrict.

I should have been angry. I should have been jealous. I should have wanted to burn him up with a thought and the smallest twitch of a finger.

But instead, I *liked* knowing he was there, watching over our human.

Our human.

'You're losing it,' I muttered to myself.

You're already lost.

Anna's temperature changed over time, though I couldn't confidently say that the change was a good thing. She seemed to go from sweating to shivering, from being too pink in her cheeks to worryingly pale. Her heartbeat was similarly erratic, speeding up and slowing down as she occasionally tossed her small body around on the cot. She got up twice, stumbling behind the screen to use whatever was behind it, but she seemed barely conscious each time, unresponsive to my questions and falling immediately asleep when she made it back to her bed. The light inside her – the many-layered light that I couldn't stop staring at – flickered in a way that felt *wrong*.

'This isn't working,' I observed.

The Roth cleared the glass immediately. 'No,' he said flatly. 'She's worse.'

'She needs a proper healer. One who knows how humans work.'

He rubbed his eyes. 'We're in the ass-end of the universe.'

'Then take her back to Earth,' I snapped.

'If we take her back, *you* lose her, too,' he returned.

Something twisted inside me, like the body housed another being within it. *Disgusting.* 'Better to be separated by distance than death,' I said, irritated. 'How far from Earth are we now?'

'Further than is helpful,' he answered. 'We need another option.'

'Then tell me what we have, so I can *help*. What is the closest inhabited planet?'

He hesitated. 'Define *close*.'

'By the stars,' I muttered. 'Is there *anything* close? A space station? A ship?'

'The Tirian peacekeeping vessel we've been trailing, and another small ship they seem to be following. It's of Nataran make.'

I stared at him. 'That's it?'

'That's it.'

My eyes flicked to the bed. 'The Tirians would have a healer.'

'Yes. But if we asked to board the peacekeeping ship and the Tirians find out we took her from Earth, they'll fire first and ask questions later. The doctor would need to come to Anna. I don't know if you've noticed, but the entire universe pretty much hates us, so I'm not sure a distress call will work.'

'So we steal them.'

The Roth frowned at me. 'I – *what*?'

'We steal the doctor,' I said, leaning forward. 'We bring the doctor to Anna.'

'How do we do that, starling?'

I raised my ankle. 'If you got this off me, I could have a doctor here in a handful of heartbeats.'

'That's not happening.'

I hadn't expected him to go for it, but it was worth a try. 'Then we'll need to do it the hard way. Get on board the ship and take what we need.'

'How do we get on board a Tirian peacekeeping vessel? We can't just take a scuttler and dock.'

'Well, what else have you got?'

'What else? We don't have anything else.' He tugged on one of his horns. 'Well, except the Darnagh craft in the hold. We picked it up as salvage.'

'The Darnagh ...' I considered it. 'Is it in working order?'

'Perfectly. But they wouldn't just let us board the peace-keeping ship, even in the Darnagh craft.'

'No.' My lips pulled up at the corners. 'But what if we were flying one of their own?'

It was almost too easy.

It was a version of a play I'd used before. A distress signal used as a lure, a trap laid in the dark, a uniform change. Swanning into enemy territory like you belonged there – because they believed that you did. Then taking what you wanted, and hightailing it before they realised that the thing you wanted was missing.

I didn't trust the two meatsuits to pull it off, but I didn't have any other choice.

'You need to watch Anna while we're gone,' Cal growled at me.

'We've overridden the security codes again,' Alcide agreed. 'No one will be getting in. But just in case –'

'I'll watch her, Prince,' I said crossly. 'Though stars know what I'm supposed to do if something happens.'

'Glare,' Cal suggested. 'Or pull the supernova move you keep threatening. Put your balls on the table instead of just talking about them.'

'Put my ... Do Roth actually do that?'

Alcide grimaced. 'Of course not. It's unhygienic.'

'Is that why you two stopped the other night? Hygiene issues, Prince?'

'Why we ...' Alcide's cheeks flushed dark blue before he gave me a fierce scowl. 'Dread gods take you, starling.'

'Why *did* you stop?' I persisted, grinning as I remembered the way their lights had intertwined, the way their heat had flared in a way that was unsurprising, unmistakeable, and unaccountably arousing. 'I was enjoying the show. Your heat signals suggested that neither of you *wanted* to stop, so –'

'Anna,' Cal said pointedly.

'Yes,' the Prince said, drawing himself up. 'We need to go.' He turned his back on me and left, giving the motionless human one last glance along the way.

'No, I mean *Anna*,' Cal repeated, when he was sure the Prince was gone. 'Alcide wants to be loyal. To his *claimed*.'

I stared at him. 'She hasn't said *yes* yet.'

The Roth twisted his lips. 'You don't need to remind me.'

'No. But someone should remind *him* whose arms she crawled into after your healer tore her shoulder to pieces,' I hissed, my hands suddenly burning with fury.

'We both know what happened, starling,' Cal said tiredly. 'We all know what a fucking mess I've made.' He looked down at Anna, and for a moment his face was tight with longing. 'And we know I am what you said. A selfish bastard. Because even now, no matter how much I hate myself, no matter how much guilt I feel – I don't regret it.'

I watched as he walked away. I watched the Roth's heat signals as they went to the orb ship's hold, watched the Darnagh craft flare to life. I watched through the cold black of space as they flew towards the asteroid belt.

Watching them made me strangely nervous, so after they landed the ship, I turned my eyes back to Anna, instead.

ALCIDE

CALLAN LANDED THE DARNAGH ship on the tiny moon
in silence. I wouldn't have been able to fly it – the controls
were very different to our scuttlers – but Callan navigated
it with ease. I sometimes forgot what a good pilot he was; I
was so used to thinking of him as my *friend* that I overlooked
everything else.

I glanced across at him as he flicked buttons to power
down, wondering whether he'd prefer his life without the
complication of *me*. Whether he'd prefer to simply be a
pilot, without having to also look after a prince.

I had the uncomfortable realisation that while my life
would be worse without Callan in it, his life would be *better*
without me.

'We need to talk about contingencies,' he said roughly.

'Contingencies?'

'I am an acceptable loss, Prince. You are not. If something goes wrong, you leave me behind, do you understand?'

I swallowed. 'No.'

'*Yes*,' he insisted. 'I'm a military orphan, Cide. You're the Prince of Scytha. If something goes horns-up, you *run*. I'll distract them.'

'I'm not doing that, Cal.'

'Of course you are,' he said. 'One of us needs to go back for Anna.'

I stared at him, blood rushing in my ears. 'You're asking me to choose between you.'

His voice was flat as he pushed himself out of the pilot's chair. 'You've already done that.'

I didn't know how to answer him, so I followed silently. We cleared the hold, arranging some crates so we'd have something to hide behind, and Callan activated the ship's distress signal.

'Now we wait,' he said.

I buttoned my uniform up to my chin, then stretched my fingers, letting my body push its protective scales through my skin. I watched Callan do the same thing. The shimmering scales crept up his neck and around his face in shades of pearl white and the palest blues and purples, his opaque second eyelid shuttering, making his black eyes a filmy grey.

The Roth were almost unique amongst organic species in the universe in that we could survive in space for several hours without any technological intervention. Our scales regulated our temperature and the pressure from the vacuum, along with protecting us from radiation and space dust, and our second eyelids acted as tiny shields, saving our vision from unfiltered solar rays. We couldn't stay in space forever, though. A special membrane would block our nostrils and throat to remind us not to breathe, but our lungs would only hold enough oxygen for a couple of hours, and after that, we'd have to replenish it or face suffocation.

We wore our scales to war, too, and essentially became almost impossible to kill. There were only a few known materials that could cut through them – Kjidja iron, Illisae crystal, Dvensk titanium – along with our scales themselves.

I took a long last breath, hoping the Tirians would take the bait quickly.

I gave Callan a sharp nod when I was ready, and he pressed a button. The hold of the small Darnagh ship opened, to make it look as if we really *had* run into trouble; the Darnagh couldn't survive in space the way we could, and there was no way they'd open their hold to such a harsh atmosphere. For a moment, I battled to stay standing as the artificial gravity inside the ship flicked off.

Our biology wasn't quite good enough to let us *hear* in the vacuum, though, so Callan gestured for me to sit while he monitored the ship's communication system for indications that the Tirians had received the distress call. I didn't sit, but rather pushed gently off the floor and floated in the low gravity until it eventually pulled me back down.

Callan's scaled lips twitched up.

I wanted to make him smile, so I did it again, managing a number of somersaults mid-air before I sank back down to my feet.

Show off, he mouthed.

You're just jealous, I mouthed back.

He made a face and I laughed. I hadn't been alone like this with Callan – *completely* alone – since we were sent into the desert wilds of Scytha for our mandatory military tests, and even then we were tracked by drone and had no idea which dunes were recording livecasts for the audiences in Scytha City. This was the first time in my entire life it was just me and Callan, with no threat of interruption.

I took a step closer to him.

Cide, he mouthed.

Cal, I returned.

My fingers itched to touch his scales, to trace their shimmering pearlescence. Warmth gathered low in my belly, unfurling through my limbs. There was something irresistible about seeing who Callan really was, about seeing the creature beneath his skin – so dangerous and strong and beautiful.

I took another step, my eyes going heavy with want.

He took in the expression; his jaw tightened and he lifted his chin, his lovely mouth rigid. *Don't play with me, Prince.*

I froze.

Not even a day ago, I'd pushed him away. His cock had still been hard against mine and his skin warm beneath my fingers, but I'd decided to be loyal to Anna.

He gave a sharp nod. *I'm yours, Alcide. Always. But don't be cruel.*

And with that, he turned back to the communication panel, as if nothing had happened.

The Tirians didn't arrive for another handful of hours, so I had plenty of time to feel mortified.

When we finally saw the ships, we took our places behind the tethered crates in the hold. Callan's signal had been accompanied by a message begging for ice, and two of the strange, pod-like craft the Tirians used for short range transport were dragging nets full of the stuff which, I reflected, we should probably try to take back for Anna.

The first pair of Tirians pulled their block inside, and tethered it to the floor, looking around curiously for the Darnagh captain, who should have been present to receive the drop-off. We could tell that they were uneasy; Callan frowned at his wrist screen, trying to send a reassuring message over the ship's comm system, but no sound emerged; I suspected the internal relay was broken, possibly the reason the ship had been dumped for salvage on a small moon in Sector Ten.

We waited until the first pair of Tirians were back in the craft and the second were inside the hold to pounce.

It was all too easy to drag them into the airlock.

They fought, but we had the advantage of surprise and strength. The Tirians were intergalactic peacekeepers because their tech was impressively sophisticated and they were well-organised, disciplined, and bureaucratic, not because they possessed the highest muscle mass. The two in the second pod-like craft were trained – and *well* trained, at that – in personal combat, but Callan overpowered the first within a moment, and politely waited for my scuffle with the second to end a minute later.

We knocked them out and bound them, dragging them inside the ship so they wouldn't suffocate. They'd be cold, but there were blankets and food on board for when they woke up, and I had no doubt that their shipmates would come looking for them – hopefully once we were far, far away. Squeezing into their uniforms was much harder: both of us were at least half a foot taller than the Tirians, and that was *without* our horns. When Callan donned the helmet, I burst into silent laughter; there was a gap of a good few inches between his helmet and his neck, meaning the odd, organic suit that the Tirians wore wouldn't close.

Luckily, it didn't need to.

When we were dressed, Callan took my hand and squeezed it reassuringly. I pressed his fingers back, then held his fist against my chest for a heartbeat.

When we left, I led the way.

The length between the Darnagh ship and the Tirian craft was one of the longest walks of my life. I was tense, every step heavy with the expectation of discovery, adrenaline surging through my body. Callan's hands were balled at his sides, but he strode across the moon's dusty surface like he owned it, and when he reached the empty Tirian craft, it opened under his hand.

I climbed in, saying a silent prayer.

The inside was like nothing I'd ever seen before, an odd mix of machine and organic plant life. I'd heard rumours that the Tirian species had evolved from trees; I'd discounted it as ridiculous, but as I eyed the inside of the tiny craft, it seemed like it might not be so far removed from reality.

Callan settled in the pilot's chair. When the roof closed over our heads, I reached forward and touched his shoulder. He took my hand and squeezed my fingers reassuringly. We couldn't risk speaking – we had no idea what kind of surveillance might be inside the craft – so I settled back in my seat, then almost jumped out of my skin when vines grew around my chest, keeping me securely in place.

Dread gods, I thought. *Let me never visit Tir.*

I calmed down when I realised the vines were staying well away from my throat. Callan pressed a few buttons and we rose smoothly into the air.

The ship clicked and growled; my translator took a few moments to register the language and translate.

Autopilot engaged. Destination: Peacekeeping Ship Number Seventeen-Hundred and Sixty-Three, Title Forest Souls.

If there *was* someone watching us, I wondered whether they'd think it odd that Callan and I were silent. I wondered what Cal was thinking, and whether the tension in his shoulders was my fault, or whether it was for what was to come. I wondered whether Anna was still asleep, and whether she'd gotten better or worse. I wondered whether she was still lying in the narrow bed, or whether she was cradled in Vesper's arms.

I wondered why I didn't feel jealous.

I wanted her. Not just so I could keep her safe, but for *me*. I wanted to be the one who kept her safe, who gave her whatever she needed, whatever she wished for. I wanted to breathe lungfuls of her fresh scent and feel the silk of her hair against my fingers.

When Callan had first brought Anna on board, I'd barely held back from snarling him away from her, from baring my teeth and showing my dominance and forcing him to leave the little human to me, and me alone. The notion of her cradled in Callan's arms, or pressed against Vesper's strong chest, should have made me fly into a rage. But that possessiveness seemed to have faded, even if my fixation with her hadn't. Instead, Anna's injury made me *glad* that she had two other protectors. Something might get through me, but *nothing* would get through Callan. And if something *did* manage it, then I had no doubts that Vesper would make good on his threats and incinerate it without thinking twice.

Anna – our little springtime human, the female that smelled like *hope* – would be safe. And in the end, that was what mattered.

Cal isn't the only one obsessed, I thought, fiddling with the sleeve of the Tirian uniform. The bark was uncomfortable, pressing against my scales beneath it. Roth didn't need so many *layers*. I wondered what it would be like to hold Anna without any layers between us, to feel her soft skin on mine, to lay her hand on my chest so she could feel how hard my heart was beating.

I wondered what it would be like if Callan was there with us, holding her just as close.

I pushed away the image. Whatever I was feeling, I had no right to expect its return – from either of them.

I would never *expect*, but I could still secretly hope, and dream in some dark corner of my heart that Anna would say *yes*, not because she had to, but because she *wanted* to.

And Callan ...

Don't play with me, Prince.

I'd die before I hurt Callan even more than I had already done.

Which was all *without* the chaos that was Vesper thrown into the mix.

What a gods-damned mess, I thought.

Callan tensed. 'There,' he breathed, so softly I almost missed it.

The Tirian peacekeeping ship was made of two large rings, joined by their rectangular docking bay. One giant ring was glassed in, and even from a distance I could see the green of their famous on-ship Forest, the trees stretching taller than they had any business being. We didn't have trees on Scytha, not anymore.

My body went tight with tension.

The ship made its way to the docking bay. My scales rippled their anxiety, causing odd, full-body shivers. They became worse the closer we got, resulting in a deep thrumming sound bursting from my chest as we followed the first pod-like craft into the dock's airlock.

The craft settled gently onto the dock floor and powered down.

'Remember, Prince,' Callan said softly, his voice tight. 'Get in, then get the doctor out. Nothing more. Leave me behind if you have to.'

'Dread gods be with you, Cal.'

'And with you, Prince.' Callan paused. 'And Cide?'

'Yes?' I murmured, tensing as the craft's roof opened.

'Remember why we're doing this,' he said, and climbed out. I swallowed and clambered after him.

The dock was like nothing I'd ever seen before. Its floor was home to a number of different Tirian craft: the small pod-like ships, the larger landing vessels, and some craft that had definitely come from elsewhere, including a Roth scuttler that had seen better days. But the oddest thing was the walls: they were covered with some kind of moss, encasing the huge hanger in a dark, rich green.

Callan cleared his throat, bringing my attention back where it should have been; the first pair of Tirians were heading to a small room encased in opaque glass. A door slid open to admit them, then closed once they walked through. A small light began to glow over the door moments later.

'Decontamination,' Callan whispered.

'Then the doctor will be in there,' I murmured back.

He gave a slight nod. 'Or an assistant, at least.'

I tried to repress my shiver.

We waited outside the door, trying to pretend like the eyes of the Tirians in the hanger weren't on our backs. None came close; they were too well-trained to approach when we might have been exposed to something unknown – or nasty – on the tiny moon. The welcomes and the questions wouldn't come until the decontamination had been completed – but by then we would have our doctor and be on our way out.

Hopefully.

The light went off.

'Here we go,' Callan murmured. 'Courage, Prince.'

When the glass door slid open, I strode in before him.

The Tirian standing inside was handsome, with moss-green eyes and waving blonde hair. He gave us a kind smile. 'Well done on your mission,' he said, his tone deep and smooth through my translator. 'You know the drill.' He gestured to the glass cubicles that lined one wall of his clinic, then moved to focus on a large screen. 'Pick whichever you'd like. Any injuries to report?'

Callan pulled his stunner from beneath the Tirian uniform.

'I know you're saving the debrief for the Captain,' the Tirian started, when we didn't answer, 'but I need to know whether –'

Callan pressed the stunner to the doctor's temple. 'Are you a doctor?'

The Tirian froze.

'*Are you a doctor*?' Callan repeated.

'Yes,' the other being answered. 'Yes. I'm a doctor.'

CALLAN

We watched as the doctor packed his bag.

He was outwardly calm, but I could sense the fear beneath. He knew what this could mean for him – pain, possibly death – but he gathered the things he'd need for his patient anyway. I respected him for that; he was already doing better than Dainn, who clearly hadn't cared a bit for Anna's safety.

He stiffened. 'The female. She's not your species. Is she a prisoner?'

I forced myself not to look at Alcide. We hadn't told the Tirian that Anna was human; a healer might risk themselves for their patient's health, but if he knew we'd abducted her, he might be more inclined to make it someone else's problem, too. 'Not your concern, doctor,' I growled.

He swallowed and closed his bag; I saw him press a distress button, but I let it go. I'd been expecting him to press it earlier.

Everything fell silent when we re-entered the hangar. My scales rippled, every instinct shouting at me to run. I steeled my spine and directed the doctor calmly towards the Pod instead. I'd already disabled its tracker on the way to the ship – Tirian craft were so easy to operate it was almost farcical – and Alcide would have to somehow manage in the back with the doctor on his lap.

One of the Tirians started forward.

'Stay back,' I warned. 'We're taking the doctor, but that's all we're doing.'

Another Tirian called out to him. She didn't try to approach us, but I could see her fingers flicking over her screen.

The doctor took a deep breath. 'Juni, just ... Tell Ashton to stay with the Hamadryad, yes?'

I shifted slightly in surprise. I'd heard of their Hamadryad, beings made of *elya*, heard that they were more goddesses than Tirian. If this doctor knew one, he might be more important than we'd thought.

Which made it imperative that we got him to Anna *quickly*.

The Tirian female stepped forward. 'Doctor –'

'Stay *back*,' I snarled, and fired a shot into the floor.

The entire hangar went still; Tirians weren't stupid.

'Willow!' the female cried.

When the doctor replied, I realised that was his name. 'Tell Maeve she's the one we'll always wait for. Tell her I'm sorry,' he said desperately.

'I'm sorry, too,' I said, and let my fist fall on his temple.

He slumped; Alcide was already climbing inside the small craft. I shoved the doctor in with him, letting Alcide work out how two large males would fit in a space barely designed for one, then slid into the pilot's chair.

The first shot rang out as the Pod roof was hissing closed. I ignored it, initiating the launch sequence, and then the craft's shields. There were a few more shots before the Tirians in the hangar realised it was useless, and by that time, we were already in the air.

'All good, Prince?' I called back to Alcide.

'Mmph,' he answered. 'Dread gods, what are Tirians *made* of? He's heavier than you are, Cal.'

'Just make sure he doesn't wake up.'

'I don't think there's any danger of that,' Alcide said wryly. 'You hit him pretty hard.' There was a short silence. 'Stars, Cal. His blood is *green*.'

'Wait, I made him *bleed*?' I worried. I flew the Pod on a different path back to our orb ship, dodging asteroids in the outer layer of a thick belt.

'It's all right, I think. I'm fairly sure that I can see his skin healing.'

'You can *see* it healing?' I shook my head. 'Gross.'

'I wish Anna healed this quickly,' Alcide said, so quietly I wasn't sure whether he meant for me to hear.

I didn't answer.

In the event of an emergency, the quarters that Alcide occupied aboard the orb would detach from the main ship, forming a second craft. It was the sole purpose I was necessary, and the reason I was able to stay so close to him. While I technically also had a position as one of the co-pilots of the orb proper, the Pilot Prime, Glest, hated me, and used an ancient mechanic called Bowen as his second, instead. I piloted the orb only when I couldn't possibly avoid it – or Glest – any longer, and spent the rest of my time subtly adjusting our course on Alcide's orders.

Glest was too arrogant to double-check his work, which made everything appallingly easy.

Alcide's quarters had their own small dock, so he could entertain dignitaries without them having to move through the rest of the orb. Though Alcide had never used it in that way, it suited our purposes; it was clear when I landed the Tirian craft that no one had even noticed their crown Prince had been gone.

It worked to our advantage, but the disregard some of the crew had for their Prince infuriated me. The King's obvious dismissal of his son meant that some of the older Roth felt they could do the same.

When the old King fell, I'd make it my mission to show them just how wrong they'd been to ignore Alcide.

We got the doctor out of the Pod with some difficulty, accidentally banging his shoulder – and his head, reopening the wound – along the way. Drops of thick green blood fell on Alcide's bedroom floor as we passed through, but the Prince didn't seem to notice, too focused on getting the Tirian to Anna.

She was still lying in the cell's cot. Vesper stood upright, his chained leg angled back, as if he were straining to get as close to Anna as he possibly could.

'What took you so long?' he demanded, as the cell's glass door slid open. 'She's worse.'

I lay the doctor gently down on the cold floor. 'We did the best we could manage, starling. One Tirian doctor, slightly unconscious.'

'Turn it back on,' Vesper said.

'He's organic,' Alcide said, exasperated. 'He doesn't have an on-off switch.'

'Well, how do you make him wake up?'

I strode to the cell's small bathing section and took up one of the cloths we'd left for Anna to use for washing, then soaked it in the bowl of water. Coming back out to the cell, I laid it on the Tirian's forehead.

He stirred.

'We should go,' Alcide murmured. 'We should let him work in peace. We'll only distract him.'

I nodded, then leaned down to stroke the hair back from Anna's face without thinking. She was shivering, cold sweat beading on her brow; I tucked the blanket around her neck, careful with the wound on her shoulder.

Alcide's eyes were heavy on my back. 'Callan,' he said expressionlessly. 'Let's go.'

I hated leaving, but I knew Alcide was right. The doctor would work better without us there – Vesper wouldn't hesitate to call us if the Tirian stepped out of line – and I needed to wash the stress of our trip to the Tirian ship from my skin and my scales.

'I need a day of leave,' I muttered to myself as we stepped outside. I pressed a few buttons on my wrist screen, bringing up the livecast feed of the cell.

'Even if I gave you one, you'd still spend it standing right here,' Alcide said.

I twisted my lips, but I knew he was right.

'Cal,' he said tentatively, 'what do females ... need?'

I snorted. 'You're asking the wrong Roth.'

'There is *literally* no one else I can ask,' he said. 'And I need to know.'

'You're talking about when Anna wakes up,' I said flatly. 'If she agrees to let you claim her.'

He nodded.

I thought for a moment. 'We can start with the basics, I suppose. We know she needs food, water, somewhere to bathe, somewhere to sleep. How do we get her clothing?'

He shrugged. 'We'd need to take some uniforms apart, I think. Even the smallest warrior on this ship is twice her size.'

'Can you sew?'

Alcide wrinkled his nose at me. 'I think they missed that during prince lessons.'

'Lucky you have me, then. I've been stitching my uniforms my whole life.' I paused. 'If she's going to be the princess consort, then she'll need information on Scytha. On our history and our government and the way the monarchy works.'

Alcide gaped at me, then reached up to tug on a horn. 'I haven't thought this through.'

'It will be fine, Cide,' I said soothingly. 'You'll be there to help her.'

'And you,' he said, his voice low.

We opened the door to Alcide's suite. 'I'm here for anything you need, Prince. Always.'

Alcide studied me. For a moment, his eyes flared with warmth – or something else – and I tensed, half hoping he would pull me closer, seize my mouth with his, and continue what we started the other day, complications be damned. Instead, he took a deep breath and gathered himself, turning away.

'Take your day of leave, Cal,' he said. 'You deserve it.'

He slipped inside his room. I stood on the threshold, unable to sort through the mess of feelings tangling inside me.

Alcide was right, as it turned out. I spent my day of leave outside the cell, watching the human on the bed and the starling chained to the floor as the Tirian doctor woke and began to work.

ANNA

Pain pain pain PAIN pain pain pain PAIN PAIN PAIN.

I panted, trying desperately to escape the fire racing through my body, burning through my blood. I was ice and molten lava by turns, my teeth chattering, my throat moaning of its own accord. My vision was blurry, and I couldn't find the strength to turn over, let alone sit up.

An odd collection of sounds broke through the rasp of my too-swift breath; clicks and snarls and tiny growls, then words.

'Vesper?' I croaked.

'Right here, little lodestar.' Vesper's voice was deep and tense. 'Haven't moved an inch.'

I opened my eyes.

They were gritty, so I lifted my hand to rub them. 'I feel ...' I broke off when I saw the being near my bed. 'You're new.'

A fair-haired angel, with wide green eyes. Wide green eyes – *with no pupil.*

Vesper's scent of sweet woodsmoke filled my nose; I cleared my throat softly.

The being smiled. 'I'm new. Greetings. I am Willow. He.'

'Anna,' I rasped, then swallowed. 'Urgh. I don't suppose you have any water?'

Willow passed me a full glass, then carefully helped me sit up to sip at it, avoiding my shoulder, which was sending throbs of pain down my arm with every movement. The water tasted even odder than usual, heavy and metallic, and I wondered whether something had been added to it.

'I feel better,' I said.

'You are far from better. But you are improved,' Willow said. 'Could you manage some food? The starling – Vesper – said that you haven't eaten for days.'

I wrinkled my nose when he offered me something that strongly resembled a protein bar. It tasted just as bad – thick and cloying and artificial – but I managed a few small bites before I went back to the water. I felt eyes on my back the entire time. I glanced behind me at the cell's glass wall, which was transparent rather than black; beyond it stood my black-haired Roth, his massive arms crossed. 'Hello, Tall, Dark, and Looming.'

Beside me, Willow's full lips twitched. 'Is he always that attentive?'

'Always,' I said absently. 'I hated it at first, and now I'm afraid I have Stockholm Syndrome.' I didn't mention that whatever I was feeling, the same thing also applied to the Prince, and that I was feeling some variety for Vesper, too. I had no idea how long I'd been asleep, but I remembered being cradled in his arms, remembered him holding me close to his chest. I remembered how it felt to have my head nestled on his shoulder, and how when I'd breathed, my senses had been full of the woodsmoke warmth of him.

It had felt nice. More than nice. *Safe.* He'd held me not as if I was breakable, but as if I was *precious.*

Willow frowned at me in question.

'It's a human thing,' I said with a sigh. 'Never mind.'

The doctor nodded. 'Humans have a lot of *things.*'

'You know humans?' I said, surprised.

'I know *a* human,' Willow answered. 'Now I know two.'

'Did your human have a nervous breakdown when you met them?'

Willow smiled, an expression full of warmth. I felt a flare of jealousy in my stomach. What Willow felt for his human was evident in that expression; I wanted to see an expression like that directed at *me.* Not from Willow, though, as handsome as he was.

'My human walked on board our ship as if she owned it.'

'How nice for her,' I said crossly. 'I wish I could have done that. Instead I was scared, and then I got *bitten*, and then I got sick, and now ...' I bit my lip and turned to stare at Tall, Dark, and Looming.

Now what? I asked him silently.

He didn't shift a muscle, though his eyes flickered over me, as if checking I was still all there. My chest pulled tight under that close black gaze and the evident concern in his expression. It would be so easy to get lost in those devouring eyes, so easy to feel revered, to feel cherished.

'Were you injured anywhere else?' Willow said carefully.

Were you injured anywhere else?

I wasn't stupid. If the Roth doctor had managed to sedate me and give me to the King, I knew what might – what *would*

– have happened. But the Prince had killed him before he had the chance.

I was still scared, and thinking about what had happened in the doctor's lab made me feel sick. But I hadn't been harmed – at least, not in the way Willow meant.

I cleared my throat. 'Only my mind and spirit,' I said lightly, 'but unless you're a counsellor as well as a medical doctor, I suspect I will need to work through that myself. Or with Vesper,' I went on, giving him a small smile. 'I don't think we will be leaving any time soon.'

The Roth said something in his odd, growling way.

I sighed again, this time a little wistfully. 'I wish I could understand him.'

'You don't have a translator?' Willow said, frowning.

'A translator?'

He turned his frown to Vesper. 'You couldn't do it?' he said. 'I thought starlings could facilitate translation without any kind of techplant.'

Vesper gave a half-shrug, and a wide smile. 'I am a selfish being at heart. I've been rather enjoying having her all to myself.'

I blinked. 'Vesper,' I said slowly, my hands curling into fists as anger began to burn in my stomach. 'Willow better not be implying what I think he's implying.'

Vesper rolled his eyes. 'One moment.'

Vesper's delicious scent rolled through the small room again, making me shiver. I pressed my thighs together under the blanket; it was like being a teenager again, high on pheromones, getting hot and bothered in a moment by something as innocuous as *scent*. I wasn't used to feeling this way, so susceptible, so out of control. I was angry and turned on by him all at once, frustrated at his complete and utter selfishness and simultaneously holding myself back from begging to return to his arms.

I didn't know what to think about it.

'Say something, you big lump,' Vesper said commandingly.

Tall, Dark, and Looming scowled fiercely, his lips twisting. 'Something,' he growled after a moment.

I laughed, shocked and delighted. His voice was deep and rough and lovely, and I wanted to hear more of it. 'Oh,' I breathed. 'I understood that. *Oh*. Thank you,' I went on, my words rushed. 'Thank you. For the blankets and the pillows, and for ... after the doctor ... *Thank you*. And please thank the Prince as well. For the ...' I bit my lip.

'For the beheading?' Vesper said lazily.

I shot him a glare. 'For the *protection*.'

The Roth's eyes lingered on my face. 'I will tell him.'

'Technically, it's his fault you're here in the first place.' Vesper stretched, showing his taut biceps and strong forearms. 'I wouldn't be too profuse in thanks.'

Willow blinked. 'The Roth took you? From Earth?'

I tried to sort through my feelings, but there were so many of them, and I was still so tired. I *knew* that what they'd done was horribly, awfully, *entirely* wrong. The Roth had taken me from my home without consent, and had offered me a choice between a cell and a forced marriage, which was possibly the most rubbish choice I'd ever been given, and they'd dressed it up as *protection*.

It was entirely fucked, whichever way you looked at it.

But.

Neither of them had hurt me. They could have; they could have done a number of unspeakable things. But they *hadn't*. They'd kept me fed, kept me watered, saved me from the doctor. Then they'd brought me another doctor, from some other place – I didn't know where Willow came from, but with his green-tinged cheeks, pointed ears, and pupil-less eyes, he *definitely* wasn't Roth. When I was ill, they let Vesper cradle me in his arms, let him offer what comfort he could.

When I looked at them, I didn't feel as though they'd taken anything away from me.

It felt as if they could *give* me something.

I just didn't know *what* yet.

I sank back down onto my pillows, trembling. Sweat was beading on my forehead again; I must have smelled atrocious, though Willow gave no sign of being uncomfortable. I wanted a shower and would need to use the toilet, so I reconciled myself to the fact I'd have to ask Willow for the most intimate kind of help once I could gather the nerve. 'He took me.'

Willow gave me a sip of water. He watched me drink with a tight expression, closing his eyes for a moment when I was done.

'Willow?'

'Yes?'

'Will I die?' I whispered.

He gave a kind smile. 'Not anymore. Though your recovery may be slow, unless I can fetch more supplies from the ship's medical lab.'

'Slow is better than never,' I sighed.

Willow stood, and had a murmured conversation with the Roth about needing another drip. The Roth was reluctant to let Willow go to the surgery, but offered to fetch what he needed. I snuggled down in my blanket as they spoke, watching Vesper, who was watching me straight back, his jaw tight.

I smiled tiredly at him. 'How's everybody's favourite intergalactic thief today?'

Vesper leaned forward, then stretched so he could touch my foot. 'I –' he began, then frowned, looking past the Roth. 'What in the worlds?' he said.

'Vesp –'

An alarm began to blare.

The Roth's eyes widened. '*Brace*,' he snarled.

Willow threw himself over the bed, pinning me in place. Vesper gave an angry shout, but it was cut off by the sound of a giant *boom*.

ALCIDE

MY FATHER ALWAYS ANNOUNCED himself with friendly fire.

It wasn't his worst habit, but it *was* my least favourite. *It keeps soldiers on their toes*, he told me once, like every being wasn't already balancing on the very tips when my father was in the same galaxy.

What's wrong with a livecast? I wanted to say.

I never did.

The screen in my room flickered to life. The only person who had higher access than me to my ship's security was my father; he could activate anything he wanted from a distance.

I went cold when he appeared.

My father was a brute. Most Roth had horns that curled backwards; his curled *forwards*, making face-to-face conversation a dangerous game. I'd seen him take a soldier's eye out on more than one occasion. His expression was set into a near-permanent sneer, even when he smiled, and he never retracted his second row of teeth, giving the impression that he was always ready to bite.

When I looked in the mirror, I saw his wide black eyes looking back at me; I hated it more than I hated anything else about him.

'Majesty,' I said, bowing.

'Whelp,' he said by way of greeting. 'What *are* you doing?'

I'd been rifling through my uniforms to find something we could tear apart and sew back together for Anna. 'Cleaning,' I said shortly.

'And your ship's status?'

'Everything is as it should be.' I breathed shallowly, trying to keep my heartbeat even.

'Then why can I not contact Dainn?'

'You can't?' I pretended surprise. 'I have not seen him today, but he has been running bloodwork at my request. Perhaps he simply missed your screencast. You know how he gets.'

'How long has he been running bloodwork?'

I gave a nonchalant shrug. 'Some days.'

My father studied me with narrowed eyes. 'Days, you say. Interesting.'

'Is it?'

'Well, yes,' he said, 'given that you threw his body out the airlock last week.'

I froze.

My father snorted derisively. 'You think he didn't contact me the moment your pilot brought that alien on board? You think I am not tapped into my own son's systems? You think I did not watch you slay my advisor – my *friend* – and bring that Tirian onto the orb?' The King shook his head. 'You become more disappointing every day.'

My stomach sank.

It wasn't as if my father hadn't said things like that – or worse – before. It wasn't as if I'd ever been a source of pride for him; it wasn't as if he actually *loved* me. But the derision in his voice made me feel so small, so insignificant.

I wondered if he'd care if Dainn had killed *me*.

'You will send the alien female to me.'

'Send the …' I trailed off. Anger began to burn inside me, deep in the pit of my stomach. 'No.'

My father blinked. 'What?'

'No,' I repeated more strongly. 'No. She's mine.'

My father laughed. 'As if you'd know what to do with her,' he mocked. 'She doesn't have the parts that you prefer.'

I knew that was a swipe about Callan, but I refused to feel shame. 'She didn't seem to like Dainn all that much, father,' I said, inspecting the backs of my hands. 'She fought him so fiercely he couldn't even sedate her. He was too old for her, I suppose. How many years his senior are you?'

He visibly bristled, his scales armouring his neck. I didn't care about a being's age, but my father was touchy about it, as I supposed all Kings were; the pass of every sun reminded them of their mortality. 'Enough of your running mouth,' he snarled. 'I will depart to board *my ship* in less than a click. Have her ready in *my* chambers.'

He meant the suite I slept in. 'You don't seem to be listening, father. I said *no*. My answer has not changed. She is not for you.'

My father settled back in his chair and gave a slow, awful smile. 'So be it. I will take two heads with one sword. Start praying to the dread gods, Alcide. If you do not surrender the female to me, you will not live to see another sunrise.'

I swiped the screencast closed, and tapped my wrist screen. '*Shields up*!' I roared. '*Every single shield!* Soldiers to their stations, *now*!'

'Prince Alcide?' Bryn's voice came through the tiny screen.

'Bryn?'

'We've been hailed by the royal orb, sir. The King is ordering us to stand down and allow boarding.'

'I am giving you an opposing order, soldier,' I said calmly. 'Make your choice. Me, or my father.'

I heard Bryn swallow. His answer seemed to take a lifetime. 'You, sir.'

Triumph flooded through me. A small victory, but I'd take it. 'Excellent,' I said thickly. 'Shields up.'

'Shields are up, sir,' Bryn said a heartbeat later. 'But sir –'

'I'll be on the bridge in a moment,' I said. 'Bryn – how many souls do we need to fly this orb?'

'To fly it *well*, sir?' Bryn considered it. 'Six. To get it from one point to another? Three, if Callan is the pilot.'

'Then while I make my way there, Bryn,' I said, my voice low, 'if there are any soldiers who make a different choice to yours, please do feel free to dispose of them in whichever way you are most comfortable with.'

I flicked the channel closed and opened another. 'Cal?'

'Prince?' he answered immediately.

'This is it. My father is here. The shields are up, but we need to brace for attack. He wants me dead, and he wants Anna.'

Callan loosed a growl that made me shiver.

'I need you on the bridge. And I need to know who we can trust.' I paused. 'Cal, are you with me?'

'Always, Cide.'

'I'm going to ask you to do something that will scar your soul.'

'I know just who to kill first,' he answered. 'I'm not just your pilot, Alcide. I am your sword, and you are my hand. You are my compass. You are my *purpose*.'

I closed my eyes for a moment. 'Remind me to pay you more.'

He snorted. 'What would I do with it?' I heard the soft sound of his scales emerging beneath his uniform, the whisper of the sudden hardness against the fabric.

'We have Bryn.'

'A good start.' He paused. 'Let's find you a new ministry, Majesty.'

'As long as you're part of it,' I said, and cut the channel.

I let my scales push through my skin, then swiftly changed my uniform. My black jumpsuit went on the floor; the pants and boots and high-necked jacket of my rank went on instead. A wooden box in my storage space held my circlet; I adjusted it to sit around my horns, nestled into my hair, then positioned my sword in its scabbard at my hip.

The last thing was my signet ring. I pushed it over my smallest finger, then took a deep breath, adjusting my collar in the middle.

I was their prince, and I would look the part. Even dead.

Callan emerged from the cell as I finished. He gave me a swift look. 'Perfect, Prince.'

A shock ran through the ship as our shields began to absorb my father's attack. I kept my balance, but heard an angry snarl from the corridor outside.

I opened the door with a calm I didn't feel; Callan was tense at my side.

A mechanical engineer ran at us, fully scaled and roaring. He shot wildly, using his nerve ray gun rather than the far more dangerous antimatter weapon, which would have caused the ship irreparable damage within seconds. The nerve rays were absorbed by my scales, my skin crawling underneath; it wasn't a pleasant feeling, but it was a thousand times better than a shot hitting bare skin.

'I suppose you've chosen my father,' I said evenly.

'Traitor,' the engineer spat at me, and raised his gun again.

I spun and struck his head from his shoulders.

'The thing about a sword,' I said to his body, taking his gun for myself and attaching it to my belt, 'is that if you have one made of fused Roth scales and keep its blade honed, it will do what few other things can, and *cut through itself* – that is, cut through our scales. Interesting fact, isn't it? And my father said that studying history was a waste of time.' I wiped my blade on his jumpsuit, then turned to see Callan staring at me, his black eyes hot.

'That was, ah –' He cleared his throat. 'That is to say ... You look good covered in blood, Prince.'

I flushed.

Another two soldiers ran at us before we made it to the bridge; unfortunately for them, they hadn't been trained by the best Roth fighters alive. I took them both down, one with slightly more mess than the other.

I might not have been the best at hand-to-hand grappling, but I'd had a *lot* of time to practise with a sword.

'I'm not strictly necessary right now, am I?' Callan said, his jumpsuit still pristine, his gun still unshot.

'My father is the worst kind of male,' I answered, 'but I suppose I should be grateful for some of the things he taught me.' I flicked him a glance. 'And you are *always* necessary, Callan.'

Darius – a mechanic – was defending Bryn when we got to the bridge, covering him as Bryn worked furiously to return fire on my father's ship. He'd brought it up on screen, so I could see the orb against the black of space, an asteroid belt visible behind it. The Tirian doctor's ship was nowhere to be seen, though I imagined it wouldn't be far; they'd be able to pick up the light exchange from the battle on their far-range sensors and they'd be obliged to investigate.

I ran my sword through one of Darius' adversaries, then beheaded the orb's Pilot Prime while Callan took care of two other officers in a far more brutal, traditionally Roth way – by ripping their throats out with his deadly second set of teeth.

'Urgh,' Bryn muttered. 'Blood on the control panel.'

'You're welcome,' Callan said.

'Is there *anyone* on our side?' I asked.

'Jedys has locked himself in the secondary control room to make sure our systems stay open to us, and us only. And Darius is on our side.' Bryn turned, and gave me a hard look. 'Well, *my* side. He's with me.'

I blinked. 'Of course.'

He turned back, apparently satisfied with that. 'You also have Octus and Taran. They've barricaded themselves in the storerooms to make sure the food isn't spoiled. You have Aristos in the dock; he disabled the airlock so no one can leave. He picked off a few that way, I think. And Ellar is outside your quarters, making sure no one can get to the cell.' He shot me a knowing look. 'If our future queen consort is in there, then the starling isn't enough. Not while they're chained by dark matter.'

Callan swore. 'How long have you known?'

'A while. You're good, but I'm better.' Bryn adjusted a missile trajectory and pressed a button. The ship shuddered as it launched. 'I could tell that there were places the security feed had been cut and looped. You deleted the copies from the servers, but I make my own backups.' He grinned. 'It was impressive, the way you both caught that starling. I watched the casts of him swearing for weeks. He taught me a few phrases.' The screen lit up as our ship absorbed a return shot. 'If it's worth anything, I've been studying this quadrant over the last couple of days. Your father's orb has been tailing a ship – a Nataran personal craft. I have no idea why, but it might be worth keeping in mind.'

'You're dangerous, Bryn,' I murmured.

'Yes, Prince. But if you're a fair ruler, then I'll always be on your side.' He frowned as he prepared a fresh volley of missiles. 'If I can be so bold as to advise you, think about what your father would do – and do the opposite.' He flicked me a glance. 'Males like that are on the way out. Our species is dying. Violence hasn't worked. We need to try something new.'

'As the dread gods will,' Callan murmured.

Bryn snorted. 'If you like. I prefer to put my faith in the things I can see. In *you*, Prince. Make the most of it.' He flicked an image of our orb up on his screen and studied the damage to our shields. 'I saw your grandmother once. It was from a distance, but even still, I knew that she was what a Roth should be. I see her in you.'

I closed my eyes for a moment, feeling the old echoes of grief stab at me from the inside. I pushed it aside with a silent promise that I'd let myself feel it another time, then cleared my throat. 'Want to go hunting?' I said to Callan.

He grinned, his sharp second set of teeth raking over his bottom lip. 'I thought you'd never ask.'

As it turned out, we didn't have to; Callan looked slightly disappointed. Aristos and Ellar had hatched a trap, letting the remaining crew loyal to my father steal themselves a scuttler – which they'd rigged with a timed pulse bomb. It detonated the moment the scuttler broached the ship's shields, taking no fewer than ten Roth soldiers with it.

I didn't care. We had enough souls to fly the ship. Even so, a worry tugged at me – if it was this hard to take a single orb ship, then how hard was it going to be for us to take *Scytha*?

I knew that my grandmother had led a resistance network, a secretive collection of Roth who stood quietly against my father's regime. They were non-violent, so their defiance came in small ways: sabotage of scuttlers and orb ships, missing food deliveries for soldiers, pamphlets left in public areas, graffiti scrawled on walls. I'd never been in contact with them – I was too young when my grandmother died, and perhaps they thought it too dangerous to reach out later – but I hoped they still existed, hoped they were still opposing my father. I couldn't count on it, however, and nor could I count on their support.

I'd have to earn that for myself.

I bit my lip. If – by some miracle – we lived through this, and got back to Scytha, I'd have a mammoth task in seizing and holding power. I didn't particularly *want* to kill – especially not civilian Roth – but I wasn't sure that I could see a way around it, not if there was widespread support for my father. If we were a dying species anyway, we might as well fade from our solar system knowing that we'd tried to end things on a positive note. And if my name was a footnote attached to a description like

The Last Roth Prince in the annals of intergalactic history, then so be it.

Unless I could find another way.

As we made our way back to the bridge, the ship was a continual shiver, the floor beneath our feet unsteady. 'How much longer will the shields hold for?'

Callan didn't answer.

'*Cal.*'

'Not long, Prince,' he said tersely.

'Ah, Callan?' Bryn's voice came from Callan's wrist screen. 'You should see this.'

I wrapped my fingers around Callan's wrist and held it up so we could see. Bryn had focused one of the ship's external cameras on a patch of space full of small asteroids.

But asteroids weren't the only thing there.

'What *is* that?' I frowned at the small white speck travelling between the space rock.

'It's a Pod,' Bryn said.

He was right; it was one of the small Tirian crafts. 'What is it *doing*?'

The Pod appeared to pause. I knew that it wouldn't have – we couldn't see the reverse engine thrusters, and space didn't work that way – but it did seem to take a few moments to decide on its course.

It headed for my father's ship.

'What –'

'I have no idea,' Callan murmured. 'But either way, surely it's your father's problem now.' He took his wrist back and grasped my shoulder. 'Cide. Are you ready for what today could mean?'

'We could all die,' I whispered.

'Or you could be King by sunturn.'

I closed my eyes.

Callan's fingers took my jaw; he lifted my chin. My eyes flickered open, taking in his thick black hair, his wide jaw, his unwavering gaze. 'Alcide. What is your first royal order?'

I took a deep breath. 'What we've always talked about. Dissolve the Royal Cabinet and hold debates to replace the ministers. Disband the Court and establish qualified advisors instead. Make overtures to the Intergalactic Council for help to clean the seas and the skies. Implement immediate plans for sustainable agriculture and aquaculture. Make plans to withdraw our forces and settlers from the occupied planets. Change the laws to allow females to work and hold office once more. Free the females in the Scytha City brothel. Take them back to their home planet and give them reparation.' I swallowed. 'A full overhaul.'

'And you know what will happen.'

It wasn't a question. 'Civil war. Some may obey. Some will revolt.'

'And what do we do?'

'We keep to our principles.'

His eyes bored into mine. 'Tell me.'

'To leave Scytha a better place than we found it. For *all* Roth.'

He released my chin. 'There's my King,' he said softly. 'Now, let's go and watch our shields fail.'

I caught his hand. There was so much emotion churning in my chest and stomach that it was difficult to breathe, but I needed to tell him how important he was. That if this worked, it was down to *him*, not me, to his unwavering belief, to his constant support. I needed to tell him how much he meant to me.

'Cal –'

He squeezed my fingers. 'Come, Prince. We don't have a lot of time.'

When we went back to the bridge, Darius had joined Bryn at the control panel. 'The primary shield is failing,' Bryn said shortly.

'What are our options?' I said.

'Stick it out and hope their shields fail first, or flee,' Bryn said. 'We're evenly matched. Our ships aren't made to fight *each other*.'

'Tell everyone remaining to go to the dock,' I said. 'They can leave now, take a scuttler. The range will be long enough to make it to a nearby system and seek refuge.' I straightened my jacket. 'And get me a channel to the Spire in Scytha City.'

Bryn nodded and made an announcement, his deep, level tones echoing through the ship. 'Cal,' I said quietly, while Bryn was still speaking, 'once I've done this, get Anna and Vesper off the orb.'

He blinked. 'Absolutely not. My place is with you.'

It was my turn to take his chin in hand. He looked back at me levelly, but I could see panic sparking in his eyes. 'Cal. Get her out. Vesper and the doctor, too. Detach my quarters and go. That's an order.'

'*No.*'

'Yes,' I said calmly. 'It's not their fault this is happening; not even Vesper deserves this. Get them off this ship.'

'Cide –'

I leaned forward and kissed him; I couldn't help it. Bryn made a small, surprised sound but I ignored it, gently exploring Callan's mouth, leaving him with a tiny, soft bite on his lovely bottom lip. 'Get them to safety, pilot.'

'Alcide,' he said hoarsely.

'The channel to the Spire is ready, Majesty,' Bryn said.

I sat down next to him. Callan's hand squeezed my shoulder and was gone.

I waited until I could see the King's Room in the Spire. He was absent, obviously – currently occupied with trying to kill me – but many of his Cabinet were there. It wasn't them so much that I wanted to see, but their juniors: the Roth working under them, the ones closer to my age, the ones whose minds hadn't been beaten closed by a lifetime under my father's reign and his heavy-handed insistence on traditions that suited his desires.

'Honoured Roth,' I began. 'I come to you now from the bridge of my ship. Our shields are about to fail, and this may be the first and only time I address you.'

A murmur of consternation rippled through the room.

'My father is the aggressor; he wants something I am unwilling to give him. A female I wish to claim for my own.'

Another murmur; this one unhappy. My father had already claimed multiple females, while most of the males in the room had none. I could play on their jealousies, if not their morals.

'Either his ship will fail, or mine will,' I went on calmly. 'But I wished to see my home one last time. To see my people, whom I have been proud to serve as Prince.'

There was a shout, anguished. I swallowed.

'Should my orb fail, I will remember my people and the planet of my heart. But I also come to you in warning.' Under the control panel, my fingers dug into my thighs, but I managed to keep the rest of my body – and my expression – still. 'If the dread gods will my victory and I return home to Scytha, a new era will begin. Some of you will not like it.' I paused. 'Some of you will try to kill me. But hear me now: if I return, be prepared for change. I want the Roth remembered for their fairness, not the blood they shed. I would have Scytha spoken of in admiration, not fear. I would have our planet replenish and prosper, not turn to dust and crumble. And I will work to make it so. If I live through this, then the dread gods are with me. Keep that in mind if I return.' I lifted my chin. 'For the glory of Scytha is all.'

Half the King's Room repeated the old call back to me before they realised what they were doing. I shut off the cast, then slumped in my chair.

'Nice,' Bryn said. 'But if you want the dread gods with you, then you best start praying.'

CALLAN

Every step away from Alcide felt wrong.

The weight settled in my stomach, making it churn. *Wrong, wrong, wrong*, every instinct chanted. I belonged at my Prince's side.

Halfway to his quarters, I stopped and leaned heavily on one white wall. I was covered in Roth blood, and I left smears of it everywhere.

'I can't do this,' I said to myself. 'I can't leave him. I *can't*.'

I made it to the cell anyway. Anna was asleep, one small hand curled under her flushed cheek. The Tirian doctor was dozing, his head lolling onto his shoulder, his fair hair falling in waves over his eyes. Vesper looked utterly relaxed, letting his head rest against the cell wall.

'Any news?' he said softly, before I'd even cleared the glass.

'We're holding out,' I whispered cautiously. 'Vesper –'

'I take it you have a final warning alarm.'

I swallowed. 'Yes.'

'And if I hear it?'

'I will unchain you, and trust you to jump Anna somewhere safe.'

He tipped his chin down, his eyes flaring. 'Just Anna?'

'If I thought Alcide would go, I'd ask you to take him, too.'

'But not you?'

I took a deep breath. 'They come first. Always.'

'Agreed. And I'm not going to argue about saving my own skin.'

'I didn't think you would.' I crossed my arms. 'I'd be grateful if you saved the Tirian, but I don't know how many you can take, and my priority is –'

'Anna.' Vesper said her name like a caress. 'I know.' He gave me a hard look. 'It would be easier for me if you and the Prince didn't live through this. From where I'm sitting, the universe would be better off if the Roth became nothing more than a memory.' He shook his head. 'But despite that, I'd be ... irritated ... if you perished.' He studied my face. 'Anna comes first, always. But you could try not to die, if you felt like it.' He paused. 'Is *Cal* your full name?'

'My name is Callan,' I answered, surprised. 'Callan Sandborn.'

He gestured at my uniform; I realised he was looking at my badge of rank. 'What does that mean?'

'It means I'm a pilot. Technically, a pilot who graduated in the top section of his class.'

Our eyes locked; the air between us turned heavy. 'Then try not to die, *Callan Sandborn*, pilot-who-graduated-in-the-top-section-of-his-class.' He rolled my first name on his tongue; the sound sent a shiver down my spine.

'I'll do my best, Vesper,' I said softly, and opaqued the glass.

Bryn and Darius were looking decidedly more tense when I went back to the bridge. Alcide was gripping the side of the control panel, his knuckles shadowed where the skin was stretched taut. Every hit to the ship's shields was more evident; I stumbled to the side as a missile exploded uncomfortably close to the hull, the shockwave disrupting the artificial gravity.

'You're supposed to be gone, Callan,' Alcide growled.

'I'll leave your side when my heart stops beating, Prince,' I said. 'And probably not even then, dread gods willing.'

Alcide glanced back at me, his cheeks flushed. I could have been more circumspect, but we were facing imminent death, so I decided not to worry about it.

If you couldn't declare your undying love during a life-or-death space battle, then when *could* you do it?

Bryn cleared his throat. 'I think –'

'Is that the Tirian Pod again?' Darius interrupted, leaning closer to the screen.

I peered over his shoulder. 'That's it. What *is* it doing?'

'Leaving the King's orb, by the looks of it,' Darius offered.

'As intriguing as *that* is, perhaps I could call your attention to our sensors,' Bryn said gruffly.

'Oh, *fuck*,' Alcide said.

I closed my eyes for a moment. 'Two more hits?'

'Two more hits,' Bryn said. He launched another missile; the screen confirmed that there were five remaining in the gun as our ship lurched again, the imperial ship firing wildly towards us. 'Do I sound the final alarm?'

'I –' Alcide started, then froze. 'What the *fuck*.'

'*Brace*!' I roared, as white light flared around his father's ship.

I grabbed the control panel as our orb was hit by a wave of debris. The light from the explosion flared blindingly before swiftly disappearing. I blinked down my secondary eyelids but didn't make it in time; sparks danced across my vision.

'They've disengaged,' Bryn said, astonished.

'Of course they have,' Darius answered dryly. 'They're flying half a ship.' He pointed to the screen. 'Bryn. One more, here. Make sure that fucker can't get away.' He glanced at Alcide. 'No offence, Prince.'

'I –' Alcide started, then stopped as he watched the other half of his father's ship break into pieces.

It was oddly beautiful, really, seeing the flickers of silver and white against the black of the void as the force of the hit pushed the remains of the Royal Orb out in a graceful arc.

'No one's coming back from that,' I breathed. 'Look, Cide. The missile hit the shell near the main bridge. It would have broken up their control room within moments. And the last hit took out the hangar.' I reached out to grip Alcide's shoulder. 'Cide.'

'We need to get out,' Bryn said. 'We can't take another hit. If we get caught by the debris again …'

'Go,' Alcide said. 'Where's the nearest inhabited planet?'

'Far,' Darius said grimly. 'The closest thing to us now is the Tirian peacekeeping vessel.'

'What do we need?'

'Time to patch,' Bryn answered. 'Time to catalogue what's happened and what we need to do to fix it.'

'Then we land on the closest planet we can,' Alcide ordered. 'Preferably one with a compatible atmosphere, but if we can't find that, then just a planet with enough space to land safely.'

He reached up to cover my hand on his shoulder with his own. 'Cal. Will you take the pilot's chair?'

'Fuck, *yes*.' I folded into it with a laugh. 'You might all want to strap in.'

Bryn took the co-pilot's chair; Alcide and Darius sat behind us as I engaged the orb's engines and changed our course, directing us as far as possible from the ruin of the orb ship.

When we were far enough away that my heart had stopped pounding, I looked across at Alcide. 'Dread gods, Cide,' I said hoarsely. 'You're King.'

ANNA

Despite the danger, I slept like the dead.

When I woke, I kept my eyes closed, listening to the sounds of the cell. There weren't many: my own heartbeat; Vesper's too-even breathing as he pretended to sleep; the scuffle of Willow rifling through his bag, then, soon after, his quiet, bored sigh.

I couldn't help but laugh. 'What would you be doing if you weren't here?' I said, poking my face out from my blanket nest.

He gave me a gentle smile. He really was very pretty, once you got past the lack of pupils. The Roth didn't seem to have them either – or perhaps they did, but they were hidden in their wide black irises – but somehow I didn't find their eyes as strange as Willow's glowing moss-green.

'I'd be in my lab,' he answered. 'It's time to give the younglings on the ship their yearly vaccinations. They get annual shots for standard viruses, but I need to tweak it each time for the environments we're most likely to visit in the upcoming year. These ones need to be adjusted for the marine viruses common to Natare. It's a fair amount of prep work, not to mention getting through the shots themselves. Once the younglings are done, I move onto the adults.'

'What is your ship like?'

He described the shape of the ship, and their central Forest – he said the word reverently, like it deserved a capital letter – but skirted over the detail and didn't mention any names, which I could understand. He was in a cell with Vesper, after all, and he knew next to nothing about me. 'What's this ship like?' he said, when he'd finished describing something that sounded like it belonged in a fantasy movie and Vesper had proved that he was definitely *pretending* to sleep by a sniping comment about the size of Willow's ship.

'I haven't seen that much of it,' I said. 'Just the corridors when I was brought on board, and the doctor's lab.' Anger flared in my stomach. 'And the Prince's chambers outside this cell. I don't know why I've been kept in here.'

'My Captain often makes choices for reasons that are not immediately apparent,' Willow said. 'We come to understand in time. She has all the information, after all, and we see only part of the picture.'

'All the Prince can see is the body part he's thinking with,' Vesper muttered. 'Also very probably not enormous.'

'Thank you, Vesper. You seem to have strong opinions about the Prince's body parts,' I said.

Willow turned his face away to hide his smile.

I sat up and smoothed my blankets. The fabric was so soft; it was like petting a kitten. *Oh goodness,* I thought. *I hope this isn't made from space kittens.* 'Do you have a family, Willow?' I asked, mostly to distract myself. 'A partner? Children – *younglings*?' I corrected, remembering what he'd called them.

'No younglings,' he said, though his voice was full of yearning.

'But you want them.' I glanced at the glass. There was no way to tell whether the big Roth was there or not. The healing wound on my shoulder seemed to throb. 'I do, too. But I don't want to be *forced*,' I said, thinking of the Prince's marriage offer. 'I want to have them with someone I love.'

Willow took my hand and squeezed it. 'That is preferable.'

'Do you have someone? Someone you love?'

Vesper straightened, but didn't open his eyes.

Willow gave me a searching look, then – apparently after some consideration – answered. 'I have two someones. Maybe even three.'

I blinked. '*Three?* Gosh. That's ... a lot of personality to keep track of. Most humans can't cope with one.' My eyes darted towards Vesper before I could stop myself.

He sniffed. '*Most* humans seem like fools.'

'Four is a small family for Tirians,' Willow said. 'Most families are seven or more.'

'*Family?*' I repeated.

'A ... A *harem*, I think. A female's group of lovers.'

I gave a shocked laugh. 'Goodness. Lucky female.' I paused, my brain catching up. 'Wait. Does that mean that your some-ones, your ... *family* ... are waiting somewhere, wondering where you've gone? Are they worrying about you?'

Willow looked away. 'I hope they are,' he said. 'Yes. Yes, I think they will be worrying.'

I stared at him for a moment, thinking about how I'd felt when Tessa went missing, how it felt not to know where she was, or who'd taken her, or if she was safe, or if I'd ever see her again.

'Nope at *that*,' I muttered, pushing myself from the bed. My arms trembled and the wound on my shoulder pulled, but I struggled until I was on my feet, then staggered to the glass wall. 'Tall, Dark, and Looming!' I shouted, thumping the glass with my fist. 'I want to talk to you!' The glass cleared immediately, revealing my unnecessarily tall Roth. *Really, who* needs *muscles like that?*

He frowned at me. 'You should be resting.'

'Shouldn't you be *flying this ship*?' Vesper muttered behind us.

'Willow needs to go home!' I said, mustering a shadow of Maeve's imperious command. 'You stole him to help me, and I'm helped. You need to send him back!'

My Roth crossed his arms. 'No.'

I crossed mine, mimicking his stance. 'You have to! You took him from his home, from his family. I understand that you can't send me back, but you can let Willow go!'

My Roth frowned; I frowned back. 'He knows too much,' he said.

'He knows nothing but this cell!' I insisted. 'He knows that Vesper is here, but Vesper really *is* a criminal –'

'Hey,' Vesper protested. 'There hasn't been a trial yet.'

'And he knows that *I'm* here, but –' I steeled myself '– I am stating now, for the record, and for Willow to know, that I have *chosen* to be here, and I will not leave.'

'You *chose* to be here?' My Roth repeated my obvious lie, his eyes narrowing.

'Yes.' I pressed my shaking hands against the glass. 'I am stating that I am here of my own free will. There. Willow knows that you are holding an intergalactic criminal –' I waved a hand at Vesper, who wrinkled his nose '– and you are *hosting* me as a *willing guest*. Let him go home.'

'A guest,' my Roth repeated flatly.

'A *guest*,' I insisted. 'An *honoured* guest of the Prince.'

My Roth stared at me. 'I will ask Alcide,' he said, after a long, tense moment.

I nodded. 'Good.'

'Fine,' he growled, and opaqued the glass.

Willow caught me as I staggered back, then helped me get back into bed, making a *tsking* sound when he saw how my hands were shaking. 'You didn't really choose to be here, did you, Anna?'

'It doesn't matter. You helped me, and now I'm helping you.' I scowled. 'The Prince better pull his head from his royal backside and send you home.'

Willow tucked my blankets around me. 'Even if he doesn't, thank you for trying.'

Exhaustion swamped me, my false courage failing. 'You've always got to try,' I whispered. My eyes fluttered closed, and I knew no more.

I woke some time later to a growl echoing around the cell. Willow was resting his head on my bed, and the Roth Prince was giving us a scowl that had me shivering.

'Prince,' I croaked, my voice rasping, my throat raw again. 'I wish you wouldn't growl at me.'

As soon as I said it, I knew it wasn't strictly true. In fact, if I was honest, I rather wished the opposite.

'I was *not* growling at you,' he said.

His voice thrilled through me; my stomach churned with something like excitement at being able to understand him. 'If you were growling at Willow, then you can turn around and march right back out,' I snapped, taking in the way he was glaring at the other male.

My Prince stared at me, then rubbed his temples with long, strong fingers. 'Things were easier when I could not understand you.'

'Did Tall, Dark, and Looming tell you what I said?'

One auburn brow quirked. 'He told me.'

I took a deep breath, steeling myself. 'Let Willow go, and I'll consider giving you what you want.'

He studied me. 'You will consider it over dinner.'

I blinked, surprised. 'Dinner? With you?'

The Prince cocked his head. 'Is that not an Earth custom?'

'It's an Earth custom,' I muttered ungraciously.

'Then you will have dinner with me.'

'With *just* you?' I looked across at my black-haired Roth, disappointment mixing itself into the churn of emotions in my stomach.

The Prince gave a short, sharp nod.

'*Fine*,' I said. 'I will have dinner with you. But I am still *considering*. It doesn't mean anything.'

His face brightened as he smiled. It was close-lipped, as if he was trying to stop himself. 'I will keep that in mind.'

'Just *please* don't make me eat the chicken again.'

He laughed – a surprised, deep sound that had my core clenching. 'No chicken,' he agreed, his eyes darting to Tall, Dark, and Looming.

'So you'll let Willow go?'

My Prince was silent. He was silent for so long that I started to sweat. In the end, though, he gave a silent nod and turned his back, disappearing out of sight.

'Come now,' my black-haired Roth said to Willow.

'*Now*?' I repeated, alarmed.

Willow gave me a reassuring smile. 'I'm going to leave more antibiotics and painkillers here, and the vitamins, and the food pouches, and a thermometer. Vesper, if she gets hotter than thirty-eight Earth degrees Celsius, give her the painkillers first, then another antibiotic shot. Drink more fluids than you think you need, and keep up the vitamins. Wash the bite clean twice each day with water or an antibacterial spore wash – a gentle spore wash, not an industrial one. Any questions?'

I shook my head. 'Thank you, Willow.'

'You're welcome.' He turned and rifled through his bag, making what seemed like an unnecessary amount of noise, scraping packets against packets and rustling wrappers. 'Do you need help, Anna?' he whispered, the words obscured by the noise he was making.

Oh.

My heart ached, touched that he cared enough to ask. *Say yes*, part of me insisted. *Tell him you want to go back home. Tell him you want to go back to Earth and forget any of this ever happened.*

I glanced at my Roth, and then at Vesper, and I knew that voice was a liar. I might not have chosen to be here, but I didn't want to leave. Not yet.

And I'd *never* forget it. Any of it.

Vesper gave me a small smile, his eyes flaring gold, like he knew what I was thinking.

If I never saw that smile again, my heart would break.

And if Willow brought his people back to the ship to get me out, then my black-haired Roth and my Prince would be in danger, and Vesper would be taken into someone else's custody.

'No,' I whispered. 'No. Not if it means they could get hurt. I'll work something out.'

'I'll flag the ship regardless.' Willow handed me packets of the odd food he'd brought. 'I'll be thinking of you.'

'I wish I could see you again,' I said, mustering a smile. 'I'd like to meet your family.'

Willow smiled back, showing his sharp canine teeth. 'Stranger things have happened. Stay well, Anna.' He nodded at Vesper. 'Starling. I'll forget I ever saw you.'

'That would be ever so kind,' Vesper said. 'But if you happen to meet another starling who looks quite like this, please do feel free to let my twin know that I'd appreciate a rescue at their earliest convenience.'

'I'll keep that in mind.' Willow stood and walked out, giving me one last smile.

The glass blacked, and he was gone.

I sighed. 'I think I just did something incredibly stupid.'

'It did seem to be an uncharacteristically foolish decision,' Vesper agreed. He gave me another small smile. 'But I'm grateful for it.'

I made my way across the cell on shaky legs until I was at Vesper's side. He looked up at me, questioning, his eyes flaring.

I bit my lip. 'I know you only did it before because I was sick, and you don't have to say yes, but would you –'

He pulled me down into his arms and held me.

The Prince didn't sleep on his dinner. He waited a few days – as far as I could tell, anyway – until I could move about without pain and getting tired, and then informed me over the hidden speaker that I would *join him for dinner that night*.

'When is night?' I said to Vesper.

'It's always night somewhere,' he answered perversely.

I could tell he wasn't happy about the dinner, and the ship landing on a deserted planet hadn't helped his temper. Landing hadn't made any difference to me, but Vesper didn't like it; being *on terra* – as he called it – made him cross.

Too much earth, he complained.

I like earth, I'd said.

He'd gotten an odd, pinched look when I said that, and hadn't spoken for some time, which – for Vesper – was extremely unusual.

'So what should I wear?' I said playfully, trying to jerk him out of his bad mood.

His gaze lifted from his dark-matter chain. 'Starlight,' he purred, his eyes blazing.

I flushed. 'Rather short on that at the moment.' I swept a hand down my side. 'What do you think of this delightful, hand-sewn, reclaimed uniform?'

'I think you'd look better in Ketruscan silk, but the uniform is a close second,' he said.

'I think I'll braid my hair. I wish I had a mirror.'

'Leave it down.'

I stared at him. 'What?'

He cleared his throat. 'Your hair. Leave it down. Your hair, it's like ... Well, I don't know what it's like; I always thought that poets were a waste of stardust. But whatever it's like, it's lovely. Leave it down.'

I ran my hands through my hair. It badly needed a proper wash – with actual hair product, not just water and an alien version of antibacterial soap – and was possibly starting to smell. 'Lovely?'

'Lovely,' he agreed.

'Vesper. It's oily. It's knotty. It's full of sweat and probably still some blood. In no universe is it *lovely*.'

'Lovely,' he said stubbornly. 'Leave. It. Down.'

'Bossy,' I muttered, though I was secretly pleased by the compliment. *Delicate*, I was used to hearing. *Fragile*. Not *lovely*. Especially not when I'd been living in too-close quarters with the complement-giver for weeks on end with negligible privacy.

'Will you let him claim you?' Vesper asked, surprising me. He tilted his head back, staring at the cell's black ceiling.

'Do you think I'll have a choice?'

He snorted. 'Of course. If it was any other Roth, probably not. But the Prince? He's a dreamer. He wants to build a better world. If you insisted on going back to Earth, he'd probably take you.'

I chewed on my lip.

I hated being confined in this cell, but I didn't hate being away from Earth. My chest still tightened with sadness at my grandmother's death, and I missed her, missed her presence and her lilac scent and the way that she laughed, but I didn't miss our too-small apartment, or the constant stress that came with being her carer. I didn't even miss Advena as much as I'd thought I would, though I *did* miss Claire and Maeve and Tessa.

Because I'd never done an adventurous thing in my entire *life*, and now I was on a mother-flipping *spaceship*, casually hanging out with aliens.

All of whom seemed to be unfairly handsome.

'Will he take us back to his home planet?'

Vesper stretched. 'You? Certainly, if you don't decide otherwise. Me? No idea. I don't know if he's keeping me out of vengeance, or as some kind of bargaining chip. If it's the latter, then he's smarter than I thought; he could hand me over to the Intergalactic Council in exchange for some kind of favour.' He grinned. 'I am very well-known and important, you see.'

'You mean you are *notorious*.'

'That too,' he said, unfazed.

I adjusted my collar. 'What would you do if you were free?'

His eyes blazed again. 'That depends. What would you want to do?'

I frowned at him. 'Me?'

'Would you want to see the ice planets in Sector Eleven? The electric pink moon of Gyoden? Visit the sugar mountain on Ciatkla? The thousand-year storm of Pholos? The pleasure houses of Intrika?' He wrinkled his nose. 'Meet my twin and see their lover's tentacles?'

'I ... You'd go wherever I wanted?'

He gave a half shrug. 'I should think that much is obvious, Anna.'

My lips parted in shock. 'Vesper, I –'

'Dinner,' my black-haired Roth said roughly, and cleared the cell glass.

I spun and glared at him. 'You have awful timing, you know that?'

His expression didn't change. 'Come.'

'Have fun!' Vesper called after me, his voice bright. Before my Roth opaqued the glass again, I saw Vesper draw his knees up and bury his face in his arms.

My heart hurt.

There was a small window in the tiny corridor between the cell and the Prince's room; I stared outside, fascinated. Vesper said that we'd landed on a mid-sized moon, but it was nothing like Earth's; it looked more like I imagined Mars to be, with rocky, scarlet terrain and no discernible plant life. Nothing stirred in my sight, though my Roth frowned as he glanced outside.

'There's a storm coming,' he commented.

'A storm?'

'We can see it on the radar. Our engineer thinks we'll be safer on terra than if we tried to make it back to dark space, but he needs to fix our primary shields before it hits.'

'Our engineer?' I repeated. 'As in, singular?' I was pretty sure that most sci-fi films I'd seen featured *teams* of engineers.

'There are a lot less Roth on board than there were before.'

'Oh,' I said uncertainly. 'Were they lost in the battle?'

'In a manner of speaking.'

'But you and the Prince are ...' I trailed off. *Safe? Unharmed?*

'Alcide is King now,' he said matter-of-factly.

I blinked. 'I'm sorry. About his parents, I mean.'

The Roth shot me a startled look. 'Why? His father was a monster. Scytha has a chance for the future now.'

'Oh.' I bit my lip. 'I don't understand anything about your planet.'

He studied me; I tried not to flush as I met his black gaze and shivered beneath it. 'Alcide does. What he doesn't know about Scytha isn't worth knowing.'

'That sounds like a good thing for a Pri – for a King.'

'It is. He'll be an excellent King,' the Roth answered. 'If he ever gets the chance to rule,' he added under his breath, so softly that I was sure I wasn't supposed to have heard.

I tensed when he reached towards the door to Alcide's quarters, remembering the last time I was carried through it; the healing wound on my shoulder throbbed in response.

'Alcide would never harm you,' my Roth said softly, sensing my discomfort.

'I know,' I managed, surprising myself when I realised it was true; I felt safe with both of them. 'Sorry.'

He gave me an odd look. 'Why would you be sorry? Roth males are hunters. It is instinctive to be scared. But you need not be. If he hurt you, I'd kill him myself. If I could get to him before Vesper did.'

He didn't give me time to unpack that, pressing his hand to the panel next to the door. It slid open soundlessly, and he ushered me inside.

I gaped.

In my swift trip through to the doctor's lab, I'd seen that Alcide's chamber had previously held a ridiculously oversized bed and some shelves. It had been unusually sparse, though I'd reasoned it down to space travel and restrictions on size and personal belongings, which – I imagined – would be normal for a military ship.

Now it was like fairyland.

The chamber was strewn with greenery, with leaves and branches and flowering vines, all interspersed with tiny lights that twinkled and danced. Candles – or something that looked very much like them – covered the shelves. The ridiculous bed had been draped with swathes of golden linen, curtaining it so the mattress was barely visible, as if Alcide was trying to hide it altogether.

A table had been laid at the foot of the bed, complete with more candles and a golden tablecloth. The plates and cutlery were positioned for a formal setting, and the Prince – *King* – stood next to it, dressed in a uniform of gold and black: a high-necked black jacket with gold buttons in a line from waist to chin and glimmering at both cuffs, with deliciously tight black pants that left little to the imagination, tucked into black boots fastened by a single golden button at the sides.

Alcide's eyes were lined in gold, and his horns were tipped in some kind of gilding; gold glittered on his fingers and cuffed both his ears. His hair was the only normal thing, sitting slightly mussed over his forehead, lending a rakish air to the military uniform that had me swallowing as heat bloomed on my cheeks.

'Anna,' he said politely.

'How did you do this?' I blurted.

He gave a half-shrug. 'Callan and I accessed signals from Earth satellites and did some research. The generators on board did the rest.' He paused. 'Do you like it?'

Callan. I glanced across at my black-haired Roth, who inclined his head. *His name is Callan.*

Knowing his name was like placing the final piece in a finished puzzle; it settled somewhere deep inside me, somewhere beneath my ribs, as if I'd been waiting to know it for years. *Callan.*

I realised that Alcide was watching me, waiting for my answer. 'It's beautiful,' I managed, truthfully. The room was like a grotto, all draped greenery and swathes of translucent linen. I tugged at my unwashed uniform, feeling suddenly self-conscious. Alcide had clearly prepared for this, and I hadn't even been able to wash my hair, though the way he was looking at me suggested he didn't mind.

There was a trolley and tray standing near the table, with a jug of water and some plates of food. One was piled with the charred meat the Roth must have preferred; there were two others, one featuring what looked like an artificial attempt at some kind of carbonara, the other holding two packets of the freeze-dried nutrition Willow had left behind.

'You cooked for me again?'

Alcide grimaced. 'I know you didn't like the last one. We tried again, but you don't have to eat it.'

'I'll try it,' I said hastily. They'd gone to so much effort, I couldn't *not*. 'But I can cook for you, if you have a kitchen. If you'll let me.'

'You cook?' Callan said, surprised.

'I'm a chef. Or, I *was* a chef. I don't know what I am now.'

'What do you want to be?' Alcide said softly.

I flushed. 'I ah, I don't really know.'

I felt Callan study my face from the side. 'What are the options?'

I fidgeted, my face going hot under their combined attention. 'I could go back to cheffing, or maybe something different. A teacher, or ...' I trailed off. 'I guess – if I could do *anything* – I'd go back to university and do further study. A PhD. I've been looking after my grandmother for years, and I needed a job to support us, so I couldn't be a student. An opportunity came up to apprentice as a chef, so I did. I love lots of things about it –

I genuinely love cooking – but it's not what's at the core of my heart.' I glanced at Callan, who was staring at me, his eyes wide.

'You were caring for a loved one, and I *took* you,' he said flatly.

'She died,' I blurted. 'The night you took me. I'd literally just got the call.' I looked down, swallowing against the wave of grief. 'It wasn't ... We knew. We knew it would come one day. Just not *when,* and I wasn't expecting it quite so soon.' I looked back up at the two sets of black eyes fixed to my face. 'Willow asked if I needed help. I said no.'

'Anna,' Alcide said, aghast. 'You should have said *yes.*'

I pulled out a chair at the table and slumped into it. 'I don't want to leave Vesper.' *Or you*, I thought, but I didn't say it out loud.

Alcide and Callan exchanged a look. Callan pulled out the other chair, then brushed a hand over Alcide's shoulder when he sank into it. 'I'll leave you,' he said gruffly.

'Thank you, Callan,' I called after him. He nodded as the door slid closed behind him.

Alcide and I sat for a moment in silence. I looked down at my cutlery, adjusting my fork. 'Did you have to make these, too?'

'Yes,' Alcide said, giving a half-smile that made my heart beat hard. 'We made everything. Callan and I aren't engineers or mechanics. We can't help with most of the fixes the orb needs. So we did a lot of cleaning, and then we made this.' He looked around. 'I'm thinking of keeping it, to be honest.'

I smiled. 'You should. It's lovely.'

This was where a human trying to seduce me would say *so are you*, but Alcide missed the cue completely. I didn't mind. 'How are you feeling?' he said instead.

I answered, glad that my period had finished and the only pain in my body was in my still-healing shoulder, and we fell into silence once more.

He sighed when it became awkward. 'I'm no good at this,' he said bluntly. 'I'm too nervous.'

I eyed his six-foot-six-*at least* frame. 'Nervous? You're a King, and twice my size.'

He snorted. 'And do you know the last time I spoke to a female?'

I shook my head.

'When I was seventeen turns old. She was my grandmother. Then she died, and I've not spoken to a female since. I have no idea what to say to you.'

'I'm sorry,' I said softly. 'My mother died when I was young, too.'

Alcide lifted his glass and drained it dry. 'What was her name?'

'Arabella,' I whispered. 'I used to think she was a princess. She had hair down past her waist, and eyes so blue they almost glowed.' I toyed with my fork. 'It was why I liked my friend Maeve straight away. She has the same eyes.'

'My grandmother was fierce. She shaved her head and she had black eyes, like all Roth do, but she was strong and graceful. She could fight with knives, and she taught me everything she thought I needed to know.' Alcide smiled. 'I am lucky to remember her. Callan has no memory of any of his family.'

'How long have you known him?'

'Since before I can remember. He was a military orphan; one of the generals gave him to my father to raise as my companion. It's the best thing that ever happened to me.' His lips twisted. 'I'm not so sure it was the same for Cal.'

'He seems very loyal,' I said. He seemed more than that, but I could have misinterpreted, and either way, I wasn't about to out Callan. Maeve had told me once how awful it was; a friend had outed her to her mother when she was a teenager, and she'd said that it felt like being suddenly stripped naked.

'The most loyal,' Alcide answered simply. He picked up his fork, studied it for a moment, then stabbed a piece of charred meat with a controlled, savage grace. I watched him put it to his lips and take a small bite; I couldn't tear my eyes from his mouth, his lips full and beautifully shaped, the corners tilting upwards as he chewed.

His eyes met mine, and I flushed and looked away, taking up my fork and attacking the carbonara. I shoved a forkful in my mouth.

It was ... not awful.

Alcide raised an eyebrow at me. 'How is it this time?'

I considered, letting the creamy taste flood my tongue. There were pieces of something that did an admirable job of pretending to be pancetta, and the garlicky, buttery taste was not unlike a pasta you might order at a club. 'It's ... good.'

He blinked. 'Really?'

I swallowed and laughed. 'No. Not by my standards. But it's edible, which is better than the last one.'

'It has all the same *vitamins* the Earth dish has,' Alcide said, carefully drawing out the syllables of *vitamins*.

'There aren't very many in this,' I said. I took another mouthful. 'It's made with eggs and cheese and butter and all the good things. As long as there's still carbs, I'm happy.'

'*Carbs* make you happy? What else?'

'Garlic, olives, stuffed peppers,' I answered, closing my eyes for a moment. 'Blue cheese, quince paste, sesame crackers. Chocolate, honeycomb, marshmallow –'

'Are all those things *foods*?' Alcide interrupted.

'I haven't finished yet. Smoked salmon, buttery potato mash, eggs Benedict, fresh banana bread –'

'All right, all right,' he said with a laugh. 'Food. I understand. Food makes you happy.' He paused. 'Anything that *isn't* food?'

'Reading,' I said shyly.

'What do you like to read?'

'On Earth we call them *Classics*. Books that have been around for hundreds of years.' I cleared my throat and flushed. 'I like romances as well. It's silly, I know, but –'

Alcide frowned. 'Why is it *silly*?'

'It's ...' I cast about for how to explain it. 'There are lots of different genres, but romance is one where the largest readership is women, and many of its authors are, too. Humans are patriarchal for the most part, and often things that interest women are seen as frivolous, less serious, not academic. Romance is one of the most popular genres – *the* most popular in terms of sales – but often people won't admit they read it, for fear of seeming frivolous themselves.'

His frown deepened. 'But is romance not something every being – every *human* – seeks? Even in Roth culture, we revere the concept of a soul tie, a bond between equals that cannot be broken. Well,' he went on, a line appearing between his brows for a moment, 'we used to revere it.'

'How is a ... *soul tie* ... different to a normal relationship? To –' I tried to remember the word that Vesper had used '– to *claiming*?'

'It is ... more. Something instinctual, something unbreakable, something that knows, somewhere deep and secret, that you are made for your partner and they for you. Tirians call them *mates*.'

'Ah. Tessa made me read those books. Too much growling for my taste.'

Alcide gave a husky, rasping chuckle. 'Is that why you told me to stop? You've been abducted by the wrong species if you don't like growling. Have you *heard* Callan?'

I laughed. My shoulders – previously tensed and bowed forward – relaxed and rolled backwards as Alcide turned his attention to his pile of ... whatever it was.

'Why did you ask me to marry you?' I blurted.

My back straightened as he put down his fork and turned his full attention to me. Having his full focus was unnerving; he looked at me like he was strategising an attack, like he was trying to see through my skin to pinpoint what made my heart beat. 'Why do you think?'

'Nope.' I took a mouthful of water. 'I asked you first.'

His lips quirked. 'Fine. When I first asked, it was because I believed – and still believe – that it is the best way to keep you safe.' His hand came up; he pulled on one of his horns before he caught himself and lowered his fingers.

'When you *first* asked?'

One long finger tapped on the table. 'It's still that. You're safer now – safe enough that you can have full run of the ship, now that we've removed the bloo – *cleaned* it, but I can't pretend that the risk is nil.' His eyes were on my face, pinning me in place. 'But it's also because I want you.'

I flushed and shrank back in my chair. 'You want to *protect* me. Because I'm fragile. Breakable.'

He studied me. 'Yes, I want to protect you.'

My stomach sank.

'I want to protect you until you have the freedom of *choice*, and then I want to watch what you will do. And while you're doing it – whatever *it* is – I want to be the safety net to catch you if you fall. But first, I want to see you soar.' He lifted one shoulder in an elegant shrug. 'But I did not obfuscate. *I want you.*'

I stared at him. *I want to see you soar.* I'd never thought about *soaring*; for years, I'd been focused on the practicalities of getting one foot in front of the other. Of simply *walking*, getting from one day to the next.

'You don't know me,' I blurted.

He cleared his throat. 'No,' he said. 'I don't. Not really. And you don't know me.' He paused. 'I have not spoken to a female in *eleven turns*. I have never so much as *touched* one since the last hug my grandmother gave me. What I feel for you may have begun from nothing more than instinct, than fascination. But regardless of how it started, Anna, I can tell you how it will finish.'

I swallowed. 'How?'

'If you let me, I will pledge you my loyalty. My trust. My support. My fidelity.' His eyes were black pools and I had the uncomfortable notion that I was drowning in them. 'Scytha will have my head, but I will promise you my heart.'

'It's too soon to be talking about hearts,' I protested weakly. Mine was thudding in my chest, its beat much too swift.

'Is it?' Alcide cocked his head. 'What are the human rules?'

'No hearts on first dates.'

He grinned, and my breath caught. The food was forgotten on the table; my world narrowed to Alcide and his smile. Despite the differences between us, his smile was almost human, his canines only slightly more pointed than my own. 'What about on *second* dates?'

I shook my head. 'Not until at least the third.'

'The third,' he said musingly. 'I'm not sure there are three places on the ship I could take you.'

'You'll think of something,' I said. My breath hitched as his gaze dropped to my lips. He leaned forward, and suddenly we were a whole lot closer than we had been before; I didn't think I was imagining the sudden heat pouring off his body, and I *definitely* wasn't imagining the throb between my legs.

'Anna,' he breathed, and I found myself swaying forward, unconsciously trying to bridge the distance between us.

He sat back, breaking the spell, then stood to refill my water. I put my hands under the table to hide their trembling. His own were steady as he took up the carafe and then my glass; my back stiffened at how close he was. My fingers itched to reach out and touch him, to brush across the exposed skin of his strong wrist.

But I didn't.

Living with your grandmother in a tiny apartment and working nights didn't exactly lend itself to dating easily. It had been years since I'd touched someone, years since I'd been kissed. And while I wasn't a virgin, the sex I'd had in the past didn't exactly make me want to rush out for more.

I didn't know what I was doing.

'Anna, you're shaking,' Alcide said softly. He looked down at me, then stepped back, awareness dawning in his expression. 'Oh, dread gods. You're *frightened*.'

'No,' I protested. 'No, Alcide, that's not –'

He strode to the door and opened it. 'I will never harm you,' he vowed. 'Never. I know you have no reason to trust me – not after what we did – but I swear that you will never be harmed. Not while I draw breath.'

'Alcide –'

'You don't need to explain, Anna. I understand.'

'*You don't,*' I said hotly. I stood, my fingers bunched by my sides. 'I'm not afraid of you. I know you won't hurt me. *I'm not shaking from fear.*'

His face took on a bemused expression, so at odds with his fierce appearance that I almost laughed. 'Why else do humans shake?'

I want to see you soar.

I bit my lip and gathered my courage. The steps between the table and the door seemed like an insurmountable distance; every second like an eternity. Somehow, though, I made it there, made it to Alcide, stepped close enough to see his eyes widen in surprise, hear the exhale when I placed my hands on his shoulders.

I felt him tremble when I rose on the tips of my toes and brushed my lips across his.

I'd expected them to be different for some reason, but they were as soft as mine. I brushed over them again, hesitantly, closing my eyes as shivers spread from my mouth down my body.

Alcide's hand came up; he cupped the nape of my neck, loosely holding me in place. 'Do you shake because you want to be kissed?' he murmured.

I shivered.

He nuzzled my cheek, so softly my knees went weak. 'I need a *yes* or a *no*, Anna-love.'

I swallowed. *Why was it so damn difficult to ask for what I wanted?* I thought of Maeve, and tried to channel her fearlessness. It still came out as a whisper.

'Yes,' I breathed.

Alcide's lips were on mine in the next heartbeat. They were soft, gentle, his mouth encouraging me to move as I wanted to, to *explore*.

So I did.

I'd been in their cell for weeks, but I'd kept myself locked inside for far longer than that. I'd kept myself in a tiny box in the face of my grandmother's needs, kept everything that was *Anna* pushed down deep inside. The box had been made *for* me, made of what was practical, made of *necessity*, but *I'd* made myself the lock. No one else could let me out; I held the keys. I had to trust myself enough to know what was best for *me* – what I wanted, what I needed, what my future could look like.

I didn't regret that it had happened, but I knew that it was time to come out.

Something inside me shifted, and hunger rampaged through my body.

I didn't know what to do with it, so I let instinct take over. My lips wanted to press harder, move faster, so I let them. My tongue wanted to explore, wanted to flick against Alcide's, to taste him, so I let it. My hands wanted to bunch in his hair, so I let my fingers trace his strong shoulders and his neck before they buried themselves in his shining red mane. My breasts wanted to press against his chest and the ache between my legs wanted something to rub against, so I pulled him closer and let one of his thighs come between my own.

'*Anna*,' he groaned, but it didn't seem to be in a bad way, and his hands slipped down to cup my ass. The movement sent a fresh wave of heat rolling through me, so strong I felt lightheaded. I made a mewling sound against his mouth and froze when he gave a deep, guttural growl.

I thought I'd done something wrong, but a moment later he'd picked me up and walked me to the bed, not once breaking the kiss. I barely noticed when he settled me down on the silky-soft coverlet, too intent on the way his tongue was dancing with mine.

I paid attention when his weight pressed down on me, though. A warmth I'd never known stole over me; I felt encased by his bigger body, wrapped in his heat. My legs came up of their own accord, anchoring themselves around his hips to match my arms weaving about his neck.

He broke our kiss, breathing hard, but his lips didn't stay away for long. He trailed them over my jaw, down my neck, and across my collarbone, pausing only at the neckline of the altered uniform. His fingers found the odd zip and stayed there, hesitant.

I put my hand over his and pulled it down.

 ALCIDE

Anna's fingers guided mine as we pulled her zip down together.

I'd worried about *her* trembling, but I was the one shaking now. The zip ran from just under her collarbone to just below the odd pucker of flesh on her stomach. Her skin was smooth and tinted pink, and I shuddered as the uniform revealed more of it, inch by inch, along with the swell of her breasts and the dips and ridges of her ribs and the plane of stomach.

Dread gods.

Roth females were made of muscle the same way we males were; Anna was rounder, softer, and her skin had no shadow of scales beneath. I didn't care about the difference; she wriggled until her arms were free of the uniform and she was bare to the waist.

My mouth went dry. 'I've never seen anything so lovely,' I blurted, then immediately cursed my clumsy tongue.

Anna, however, flushed and tried not to look pleased, so apparently it wasn't the worst thing I could have said.

I kissed her again, because I thought – between Callan and Anna – that I had almost worked that part out, and she seemed to like it, if the noises she was making were any indication. I worried gently at her bottom lip with my teeth, listening with great satisfaction to the mewling sounds coming from deep inside her throat and revelling in the way her body pushed upwards, seeking contact with mine. I leaned my weight on one forearm, and used my free hand to brush my fingers over her neck, then her collarbone, following the path my mouth had made.

But there was no material in the way now.

I slowly mapped out the soft swell of her breasts, giving her time to pull away. She didn't, so I explored further, brushing my thumb over her nipple. She made a small sound of surprise, followed by a deeper moan when I rolled the hardening peak between my fingers.

'*Please*,' she said thickly. 'Oh, goodness. That feels – that feels … *Please*, Alcide.'

I did it again, then made sure I didn't leave the other one out, swapping between them until she was writhing beneath me.

I found that I liked her writhing.

I gave into the urge to taste her skin again, moving my mouth down the path my hand had made, licking and nibbling and kissing all the way. Her skin was softer on her breast than it had been on her jaw, I found, but it was harder on her nipple, and the peak of it harder still, the shape of it perfect to wrap my long tongue around.

'*Alcide!*' she gasped. Her hands found my horns; her fingers gripped them.

My horns weren't sensitive, but the *action* – the notion that she was taking control of me, directing me where she wanted me to go, *using* me – sent every drop of blood that wasn't already resident in my cock rushing down. She was moaning softly, her hands urging me to give her nipple more attention, so I did, feeling an unfamiliar swell of pride when she panted my name again.

My fingers traced her stomach, finding gentle ridges of muscle under its soft curve, before they came across a hip. The bone shifted below her skin as she moved, arching her body beneath me.

I slid my hand down.

She whimpered as my fingers ran through the short, coarse curls between her legs. 'Is this all right?' I whispered, stilling my hand, giving her time, but she made an impatient sound and pressed up.

'I'll tell you if it isn't.'

I moved my fingers further down. 'Gods below,' I breathed.

She was hot, almost hot enough to scald my fingertips. Her flesh was swollen; I skimmed over the bud at the top of her sex until I found the wetness below, silently thanking Bryn for his hurried and intensely awkward human biology lesson. I explored gently until I thought I'd found everything I needed to know about in the first instance. I didn't attempt to press inside her, just collected her moisture and brought it up to circle her bud.

She mewled again.

The sound caught at me and I sat, using my free hand to tug the uniform down until it bunched around her feet. I bit the inside of my cheek as I stared at her. I could have stared for hours on end and still not had my fill; she squirmed beneath me, flushing.

'Anna,' I said hoarsely. 'I –'

'If you don't finish what you started, then *I will*,' she said. She took one hand from a horn and slid it down her body, two fingers framing her clit.

That's not exactly a threat, I thought as her fingers moved. Anna had surprised me a number of times: fighting back against Dainn with an unexpected savagery, standing up to Callan with hidden bravery, and now *this*, taking charge of her pleasure – taking charge of *me* – even while spread out, vulnerable, beneath a male twice her size. I realised that this was *her*; she might be quiet and gentle on the outside, but assuming that was *all* there was – or underestimating her – would be beyond foolish. Watching her touch herself – watching her eyes flutter closed and her lips part, watching her back arch and her thighs tremble, watching her vary the speed and the pressure she used – was possibly the most beautiful – and certainly the most compelling – thing I'd ever seen. I stroked up her thighs as her fingers worked, then traced over her wetness.

'*Alcide*,' she moaned. 'Alcide, I'm –'

I lowered my mouth and licked straight up her slit.

She mewled, throwing her head back, her toes curling against the blanket beneath her. Her taste spread over my tongue; I gave an embarrassingly needy groan at her salty sweetness, my cock throbbing in response. I licked again, more greedily this time, trying to lap up all the moisture I could, then moved up and added my tongue to the frantic motions of her fingertips against her swollen clit.

Anna shrieked; she pulsed beneath my mouth as her body shuddered. Her remaining hand tightened around my horn, encouraging me to continue what I was doing, an encouragement I was only too happy to act upon. I flattened my tongue and worked her gently through the throes of her climax, taking my cues from her slowing fingers. When she stilled, I moved down, and licked her thighs and her slit until I could taste nothing but her moisture.

'*Cide*,' she sighed. Her eyes were still closed, as if she didn't want to come back to herself; I had the sudden, heart-wrenching wish that Callan could see her like this, splayed out naked on my bed, her body relaxed from her climax, her fair lashes shadowing her cheeks. 'That was ... I didn't imagine ... That is to say ...' She took a deep breath; I watched her chest rise and fall with the motion. 'Thank you.'

'Thank you?' I echoed.

'For ... that. For all of it. I didn't know it would feel that way.'

I frowned. We weren't the same species; perhaps I'd done something wrong. 'Was it ... different? To how it feels with humans, I mean.'

She swallowed, squeezing her eyes shut tighter. 'I, um, don't know how that feels with humans,' she said. 'I've never come with someone else before. But that was more than I ever imagined.'

'You don't know ...' I trailed off. 'You haven't done that before?'

She bit her lip. 'I *have*, it just wasn't ... good. And that ... That *was*. Good, I mean. Better than good.'

I collapsed down on the bed and laughed.

The movement made her finally open her eyes, a shadow of hurt flickering across her expression.

I gathered her up and nuzzled at her cheek. 'I've never done any of that before. I was terrified that I was doing the wrong thing.'

She blinked at me. 'You *definitely* did not do the wrong thing.'

'Dread gods be praised,' I said, running a hand through my hair.

She wriggled against me, kicking the uniform onto the ground, freeing her feet, then sat up. 'I don't think we're finished yet.'

'Not finished ...?' I trailed off as she kissed me once more, my mind entirely blank of anything but her.

I hadn't even removed my jacket, fully clothed next to her delicious nakedness; Anna ran her hands down my chest and then began to push the stiff coat from my shoulders. I sat and helped her; she gave me a shy look, then cupped my cheeks with her hands and bent to kiss me again.

When my jacket was crumpled in a heap next to her uniform, she worked the hooks of my shirt to bare my chest, pausing only to examine the first clasp before her clever fingers made short work of the rest of them. I was panting by the time she finished, my skin alight with the pleasure of her stroking it, my mouth devouring hers at every available opportunity. I couldn't get enough of kissing her; I felt as if I was drowning in her kiss, slipping beneath her clear blue gaze, never to resurface.

When she tentatively touched my cock through the barrier of my pants, I groaned again, falling back and fisting my fingers in the blanket so she could do whatever she wanted with me. She traced the shape of me as I all but shook with the effort to stay still.

'Don't do anything you don't want to, Anna,' I rasped. 'There is no expectation, no pressure.'

She grasped me through the sea-cotton then moved her hand up and down; I lost my mind.

'I *want* to,' she said fiercely. She fiddled with the clasp of my pants while I silently tried to convince my cock not to explode on the first brush of her fingers.

There was silence when I was finally free.

Anna stared at my cock, flushing a deep, lovely pink. 'Um, Cide,' she said weakly. 'What is that?'

'Which part?'

'Um,' she said again, reaching out to brush her fingertips over one of the ridges of soft scales reaching from my base to my head; there was a similar line reaching from my base up my stomach, ending an inch or so beneath my ribs, and another lining my spine. My scales rippled gently in response to her touch; her eyes went wide. 'They, ah, *move*?'

'We have scales beneath our skin,' I said softly. 'They armour us. But they are always present up our spine, and ... well, *there*. When we become aroused, they ripple.'

'They're soft,' she said wonderingly. 'They don't feel like scales at all. Just ... bumps.' She shivered. '*Moving* bumps.' She straddled my thighs; my mind went blank at the sight of her naked and spread open and in charge of me. She stroked my cock up and down; I threw my head back, every muscle in my body cording as I fought not to thrust up into her hands. When she explored my head, precum began to seep from my slit, sending tremors through my body.

'Anna,' I said hoarsely, 'I'm sorry, but I don't know how much longer I can hold on.'

She blinked at me. 'Why are you trying to hold on?' she said softly, her voice reasonable. 'I want you to feel the way you made me feel. I want you to feel good.' She gripped my shaft; my scales rippled against her warm palm. 'I think we should learn these things first, don't you? I want to *know* you, know *all* of you. I want to know what feels best for you. I want to learn to swim before I jump in the deep end.' She gave a nervous laugh. 'Besides, I haven't done this for a long time, and I ... um. You're ... big. I'll need some practise first, I imagine.'

'Whatever you want,' I said hoarsely, *honestly*. Her hand began to move and pleasure thrummed through me with every pump of her fist, burning through my body, radiating from my core. It gathered at the base of my spine; my muscles tightened and I growled her name before the sensation broke and I saw white, spilling thick cum all over her fingers and my own stomach.

'*Oh*,' she breathed. She kept her hand moving until she'd emptied me completely, then she lifted her fingers to her mouth.

And licked.

'Dread gods,' I said thickly. My cock twitched at the sight, blood rushing back down as it started to harden once more. It didn't help when she licked again and moaned.

'I didn't think it would taste like that,' she said breathlessly. 'Sweet and spicy.'

'Ah,' I said, my mind entirely empty of everything but Anna licking my climax from her skin with her lovely pink tongue.

'Cide?' she said tentatively.

I inhaled. 'Anna?'

'I think I changed my mind.'

She sucked her bottom lip between her teeth and wrapped her hand back around my cock, working until I was throbbing again, my scales rippling against her fingers, then shifted forward, bringing her warm wetness so close to my cock that my brain shorted. 'I want to jump in the deep end.'

I snarled, a long, low sound before I could stop myself, then took her waist, swinging her onto the bed. She gave a surprised laugh before her knees came up and she wrapped her legs around me, pinning my weight against her. I rolled my hips, rubbing the head of my cock against her folds, then angling so I became drenched in her wetness.

'God,' she gasped, throwing her head back.

'You're sure?' I said hoarsely.

'I think you can feel that I am,' she said tartly.

I nuzzled her cheek. 'Say *yes*, Anna,' I whispered with mock-sternness. 'Say *yes*, or you get nothing.' I pushed against her slightly, her swollen flesh yielding to my hardness.

'*Yes*,' she chanted. 'Yes, yes, *yes*.'

'Dread gods be praised,' I said, and rolled my hips again, groaning as my head dipped inside her tight, divine heat.

A knock came at the door. 'Majesty?'

I froze.

'No,' Anna moaned. 'Don't stop, Cide.' She pressed up, angling so my head dipped further in.

'*What is it*?' I snarled at the door, the sound promising a swift death to whoever stood behind it.

'Ah. The storm, King.' I recognised Bryn's voice.

I dropped my head to press my brow against Anna's. 'What about the storm, Bryn?'

'It's here.'

Anna squirmed beneath me. 'Cide?'

I closed my eyes. 'No. The gods wouldn't be so cruel.'

'Cide.' Anna placed her palms on my cheeks and tilted my head up. 'Open your eyes.'

I reluctantly did as she ordered.

'It's all right,' she whispered. 'There will be other times.'

'Is that a promise?' I growled.

She laughed; my heart constricted at the sound. 'Given what's happened to me recently, no,' she answered. 'It's not a promise. But it is a wish.'

I snarled wordlessly, and brushed my lips over hers one more time, pulling myself from her wet heat and rolling off her to catch up my clothing. I hated every moment that put more distance between us; I was twitching with the need to touch her, to crawl back between her thighs and stay there until she was so wrung out by pleasure that she couldn't walk away. I cleaned myself up then stuffed my feet angrily back inside my pants, willing my cock to calm down, though it didn't seem inclined to listen.

'Will you stay?' I mumbled.

Anna sat up, hugging her knees. 'Stay?'

'Here.' I almost tore my shirt to pieces as I wrenched it across my chest. 'You can go wherever you want on the ship now, but this room will be the safest place on board during the storm.'

She studied me for a moment, then reached for her uniform. 'Vesper doesn't like being on the ground.'

I stilled in the act of buttoning my jacket. 'You'd prefer being in the cell with him to staying here?' I couldn't keep the hurt from my voice.

'No, Alcide,' she said gently. 'I'd prefer not to leave Vesper alone when he's already uneasy.'

'He's a notorious criminal.'

'He's chained to the floor,' she said, a thread of anger in her tone. 'Where he's been for *months*, apparently. I don't doubt that he's done some bad things, Alcide. But he's still a *person*.'

'No, he isn't,' I countered. 'He's a starling. And he's stolen from countless beings. He has no remorse.'

'How do you know that?' she shot back. 'Have you asked him?'

I met her eyes and held them. 'He doesn't deserve your compassion, Anna.'

She straightened her ill-fitting uniform with the poise of a queen. I swallowed.

'He has it regardless,' she said softly. She turned away from me. 'I'll be in the cell, Majesty.'

VESPER

THE TINY WINDOW SHOWED no stars.

I tipped my head back, looking at it upside down. I wasn't sure whether the different view made it better or worse: all I could see was impenetrable red dust. The wind howled outside the ship, louder than a thousand Lupine wolf warriors coming together to sing; even so, I could hear the dull *thunk* every time a rock or piece of earthen debris hit the ship's shield.

'This is not ideal,' I told the window.

It didn't answer.

'Fine, be like that,' I muttered, trying not to shiver. I hated not being able to see the sky; the red veil of dust was making me nervous. I looked at my arms; they were covered in tiny bumps. I poked at them curiously.

The cell door made its quiet sliding sound; I didn't bother to look up.

'If you're here because Anna is with the King and you're bored, turn back around, Callan. My schedule is full today.'

'It's me, Vesper.'

My nostrils flared.

Anna's springtime scent hit the back of my tongue, but it was different. She smelled like –

'*Roth*,' I snarled, looking up. She stared at me, her lovely blue eyes going wide. I dragged in another breath. 'Your scent. You're covered in *Roth*.'

She flushed a beautiful pink. 'I –'

I stood up.

I hadn't been upright very often in the last few months, and not while Anna could see. She took a step back, her lips parting. It was the first time I really noticed how small she was: her head would rest squarely on my chest. I noted it, but it wasn't my pressing concern.

'Come here,' I said quietly.

Starlings didn't have senses as strong as the Lupine, or cephalopods, or Kjidja, but our noses were better than most species. Anna was covered with a scent that was not un-pleasant – some kind of masculine spice – but that wasn't important: the important thing was that *the scent wasn't mine*. I breathed in again; it didn't have Callan's musk.

'*Alcide*,' I growled, reaching out to her. 'Anna, *come here*.'

She stepped forward tentatively, her brow creased, the brightness beneath her skin wavering, unsure. I realised I was scaring her and lowered my hands to my sides. I waited until she was within arm's reach, then took her by the waist, pulling her against me. She gave a squeak of surprise as I lowered my head.

Then trembled as I rubbed my cheek against hers.

In our trueforms, starlings had no need to scent mark. When two starlings paired, their stars intertwined and shone only for each other; it was like seeing two brilliantly bright magnets come together, the force pushing everything – and every*one* – else far, far away, until there was nothing left between them. But Anna wasn't a starling, and I was wearing an inconvenient flesh suit, so I didn't have any other choice. I had to let Alcide know that he wasn't the only one staking a claim.

His scent was *everywhere*.

She stood still as I ran my nose down the column of her neck, following the trail. He'd kissed her soft skin, tasted it with his tongue, so I brushed my lips over Alcide's scent and nuzzled over her pulse, which beat frantically as my hands skimmed her shoulders.

'Vesper,' she said weakly.

'Shh, little lodestar,' I purred against her collarbone. 'I need to fix this.'

Her breath caught as I fell to my knees, reaching for her zipper. The strongest scent wasn't on the garment, so it became irrelevant; I pulled the zip down slowly, waiting for her to protest, waiting for her to stop me.

She didn't.

Heat flared through me as my movements revealed a triangle of smooth skin. Anna was careful about the way she moved around our small, shared space; the screen was always in place when she showered, and apart from when she was sick, I'd never seen more of her than a graceful bare arm. I'd tried not to imagine it, both because I had no interest in torturing myself and through a vague sense of respect, but I regretted that now: the sight of her skin made my mind blank and every nerve in the body I wore fire to attention.

Scent, I reminded myself.

I pushed the uniform over her shoulders, stifling a groan.

Anna was beautiful.

I could see why Alcide had touched her *everywhere*. Her collarbones and hips made intriguing angles under her skin. Her stomach stretched in a smooth arch, bracketed by the equally lovely curves of her waist. She had a constellation of sun kisses just below her collarbone and I bent to kiss her there, following the path of those freckles to the rise of her breasts. Alcide's scent was strong; he'd clearly spent some time paying attention to her nipples, so I did, too. Her nipple was an intriguing counterpoint to the smoothness of her skin elsewhere, pebbling with one pass of my tongue, peaking with another, then hardening as my mouth fastened over it and I sucked.

Anna moaned.

The sound caused my skin to heat further, so I did it again, then swapped to the other one, making sure to trail my cheek over every inch of her skin along the way.

'Vesper,' she panted, when my tongue stroked her. 'Vesper, if you stop now, we can pretend this never happened. If you're only doing this because of Alcide –'

I stilled. 'If you want to stop, then say so, Anna.' My hands spanned her waist, then tugged down her uniform until it pooled at her feet and she was entirely and gloriously naked. 'But I haven't fixed it yet.'

Anna shuddered. 'I'm not sure what's happening,' she said thickly, 'but I don't want it to stop.'

I wasn't about to admit that I seemed to have finally fallen over the precipice dividing sanity and – well, *not sanity*, so I helped her step out of the garment, flinging it into the corner when she was free. I rubbed my cheek over her stomach, taking hold of her hips when my mouth decided to roam lower. I brushed my nose over the short, coarse curls on her mound, breathing in a mouthful of Alcide's scent.

He'd been everywhere.

I followed the scent to her lower lips, listening as she gasped. Her body began to tremble more violently, so I guided her hands to rest on my shoulders and my own held her tightly by the waist, keeping her upright when I nuzzled at her core and her shaking knees threatened to give way. I took one of her legs and hooked it over my shoulder, which didn't help her stability but spread her open for my mouth.

And this body liked that. Very, *very* much. It liked it even more when my tongue licked a stripe up the centre of her and she mewled, her hips flexing of their own accord. Alcide had paid attention to the bud at the top of her sex, so I did, too, sucking it gently as Anna made a stream of incoherent noises.

I rather liked my little lodestar losing control.

'There?' I murmured, though I suspected I didn't need the confirmation.

She whimpered in response, which I took to mean *yes*.

My scent was mingling pleasantly with Alcide's now, his spice and my woodsmoke settling deep into Anna's skin. For a moment, I wondered what it would be like to have Callan's musk there, too, a steady base to the richness of the other two male scents.

I worked Anna steadily, flattening my tongue as her fingers tightened on my shoulders. Sex wasn't new to me: intimacy opened doors like nothing else. It was amazing what beings would do for you after a few selflessly-given climaxes and the right mix of adoring words, delivered with a well-practised, hesitant smile. Researching the right target, shifting into their desired form, and applying the formula of an orchestrated chance meeting and whirlwind courtship had always been one of my favourite plays; it required nothing from me but time, and time was something I had *plenty* of.

I didn't seem to want anything from Anna, though, which was a new experience, and one that troubled me. She didn't own anything I could steal; she held no secrets to use, no valuables to be sold on, no deeds of ownership to be transferred. And this body liked touching her very, very much; but even worse, I liked the way it felt to be with her in this form. I didn't need to change anything for her to desire me, and the organic suit I wore desired her right back. It was *pleasant* to feel her hands tighten on me, pleasant to taste her with this tongue, pleasant to run my fingers over her skin and lose myself in its silken softness.

I wasn't pretending, I realised. That was what was different. I wasn't faking my need to make her shatter, wasn't faking my enjoyment, wasn't faking how badly I wanted her.

I wasn't faking *anything*.

Her fingernails dug into my shoulders and her body tensed; I realised she was nearing her end, and doubled my efforts, holding her tightly upright as she cried out. Her body shook and she pulsed under my tongue; I couldn't repress a groan as her taste flooded my mouth and her scent became stronger, sweeping to the fore and clouding both Alcide's and my own.

'Vesper,' she sighed, once she was still. 'What the *heck*.'

I carefully manoeuvred her leg back down, my arm circling her waist so she wouldn't fall. I folded to sit, stretching my own cuffed leg out, and took Anna with me, cradling her in my arms and increasing my heat slightly when she shivered. She pressed her face into my chest; I heard her give a soft, incredulous laugh, and moments later, she was asleep.

I buried my nose in her hair.

Mine and Alcide's scents were equal now, but for some reason, that didn't quiet the feelings raging inside me. They were all new, to be fair, so I ignored the ones that made this body's heart constrict and concentrated on the ones I'd felt before. Jealousy, possession, desire. I'd only ever had those feelings for *things* rather than *beings*, but they were similar enough that I could recognise them.

Anna gave a sleepy murmur and shifted in my arms; I held her closer. The longer I sat there holding my human, the more certain I became.

My twin, with their multiple lovers, had it wrong. Starlings didn't share. The thoughts I'd had about Callan and Alcide didn't matter. The *desire* I felt for them didn't matter.

The human in my arms did.

This was just another play. I could be patient and wait until the time was right.

And I would have Anna all to myself.

CALLAN

I STARED AT THE screen, my hands bunched into fists.

I shouldn't have watched, not when I realised what was happening. I should have closed the livecast when Anna stepped towards Vesper. I should have turned away when he stood, when he dropped his mouth to Anna's neck.

And I *definitely* should have walked away when he slowly unzipped her uniform. I should never have seen him push the garment off her shoulders, should never have devoured the sight of her smooth back, marred only by the still-healing scars of Dainn's bite. My blood should not have caught fire when Vesper uncovered her nakedness, and I should not have started to growl when he hooked her leg over his shoulder. I should not have groaned to see him working between her thighs, his hands tight on her waist to keep her upright and in place for his mouth. She'd come apart swiftly, her head tipping back, her fingers digging into the starling's shoulders with enough force to hurt. He hadn't seemed to care, scooping her up when she'd recovered, cradling her in his arms like the precious thing she was.

I should never have watched. And my heart shouldn't have pounded, not for *both* of them.

'Callan?'

I started, blanking the screen as I turned. 'Bryn?'

He frowned at me, politely ignoring my flushed face and probably blatant arousal. I couldn't do anything about either, so I crossed my arms and waited, mustering an imitation of self-possession that I was sure the engineer could see straight through.

'The radar says that the storm should pass within the next hour or so, but we've got a new problem,' he said.

'Alcide is the one you want for problem solving.'

He winced. 'I wanted you to see this first.' He held out a small hand screen. 'I managed to keep the signal to Scytha through the storm by hacking into a Darnagh space station. It's ... not *good*, Callan.'

I stared at the screen.

It was very definitely not *good*. In fact, it was everything we'd feared. The screen's feed was of the King's – *Alcide's* – room in the Spire, and its floor was covered in pools and splatters of blue blood. A banner hung above the huge throne, painted with characters spelling out the word *TRAITOR*.

I looked at Bryn. 'Are there feeds from anywhere else?'

Bryn grimaced. 'I set one up to my family's house. They've barricaded themselves inside, but they're still connected to what's remaining of the planet's network. My father said ...' Bryn took a deep breath. 'My father is ...'

'An older Roth male, I suppose,' I said, when he trailed off. 'I imagine he does not support Alcide's proposed changes.'

'Nor Alcide himself,' Bryn agreed reluctantly. 'He has ordered me to do everything I can to kill him.'

I went still. 'And will you?'

'Of course not. He also ordered me to bring the human female home as my claimed, and I have no inclination to do *that*, either. But Callan ... I'm not sure that Alcide has the support right now to survive if we were to return. I spoke to my brother. He said that those who want to side with Alcide are frightened. We've always heard rumours about a resistance, but there's been no word from them, if they even exist. The military is firmly set against the new King and Alcide's supporters do not have the power to push back.'

I tapped the side of the screen. 'Who is commanding the military?'

Bryn paused. 'Fiach Redhands.'

I closed my eyes for a moment. 'Of course he is.'

Fiach was a few years older than Alcide and I, a distant cousin to Alcide's father. He was power-hungry, charismatic, and utterly ruthless. He had extensive military training, and I had no doubt that he would employ his knowledge – and his skill – in a single-minded pursuit of his goal. Which, in this case, meant Alcide's throne – only attainable if Alcide was dead.

And I'd die myself before I let *that* happen.

'I realise I'm not a political advisor,' Bryn said carefully, 'but it seems that Alcide will need to find some outside support if he ever wishes to return.'

'Bryn, right now you are a systems engineer, First Officer, co-pilot, staff liaison, security guard, spy, political advisor, and campaign manager. Plus anything else you wish to take on; there are plenty of openings to choose from. What you say is right. I won't let Alcide go back if death is the likely outcome.'

'So what do we do?'

I twisted my lips. 'You've already said it. We need to find support. But who in the universe would support *us*?'

Bryn rubbed a hand over his horns. 'We need to find someone who sees it the same way we do. That Alcide on the throne can only be a good thing – both for Scytha, and for the entire universe.'

I froze. 'Willow said his ship was headed to Natare,' I said slowly. 'There was a comm we intercepted from an Illisae ship months ago that said they were *also* heading to Natare. For a *peace summit*.'

Bryn's eyes widened. 'I'll find out whatever I can.'

I brought up the navigation system. 'And I'll plot a course for Sector Six.'

Bryn and I explained what the engineer had found. Alcide's face darkened when we mentioned Fiach, and hardened even further when he saw the livecast from the throne room.

'Set a course to Scytha,' he said immediately. 'We must go back.'

'Going back right now would be suicide, Majesty,' Bryn said. 'Going back would be exactly what Fiach wants. He'll let you land, storm the ship, kill everyone on board, and drag you before a crowd for a messy public execution.'

Alcide shook his head. 'Then I will go back by myself. I do not fear death.'

'Yes, but who helps the Roth if your severed head is propped up horn-first outside the Spire doors?' Bryn said patiently. 'What happens to your vision? Callan and I are impressive males,' he went on, without a hint of sarcasm, 'but we follow *you* because you're the dreamer, Majesty. You're the visionary, the one pushing for change. Scytha under Fiach's rule would be no different to Scytha under your father. But Scytha under *your* rule?' Bryn shrugged. 'That's why I'm here. And I won't get that if you race home and find your chest suddenly full of holes.'

'What are you suggesting instead?' Alcide said, less patiently.

Bryn's black eyes flickered to me. 'There's a cross-Sector peace summit on Natare in a few weeks' time. It's supposed to be focused on the *Roth issue*.' He gave a fleeting grin. 'What if we went?'

Alcide blinked. 'The Tirians would shoot us down the moment we arrived in the *quadrant*, Bryn. They wouldn't let us *near* Natare, peace summit or no peace summit.'

'So we don't tell them we're coming, and once we get there, we present Scytha's new King – and *Queen*,' Bryn answered. 'We introduce the summit to our beautiful, very *non-Roth* Queen, who makes a pretty speech about how happy she is with her beloved husband, and how *concerned* she is about the civil war tearing her new planet apart, and the plans that she and her husband have to not only keep the peace on Scytha, but to *sign the Intergalactic Pact and commit to halting the Roth's policy of expansion*, something that *no other Roth ruler has ever done*.'

Alcide went so still I could imagine even his heart had stopped beating.

We waited.

'Do you think that would work?' he said eventually, his voice barely a whisper.

Bryn shrugged. 'I have no idea. But I think our chances of emerging alive are better in this scenario than they would be if we rushed home.'

Alcide's eyes flickered to me. 'I'd need to claim Anna soon.'

'Now,' Bryn said.

My stomach sank. 'Has she agreed?' I said gruffly, not really wanting to know.

Alcide closed his eyes. 'We didn't talk about it. But I am ... hopeful.'

I turned away.

There was a trick I'd been taught during military training. Take a breath, then take a mental step to one side, and leave your feelings behind. When you were part of a unit and commanded to do something that invoked emotion, you took that step to the side, and it allowed you to do things you never would in your normal life. Like discharging a weapon, or hurting your own kind, or planning an attack that would wipe out a town.

Or, in this case, reconciling the fact that the male you were in love with would claim the female you were fairly sure you were *also* in love with, and that you would have no part in their relationship.

I took a deep breath. I closed my eyes. I took a mental step to the side.

I opened my eyes, and turned back around. 'All right then,' I said calmly. 'What do we need to do to make it happen?'

Alcide straightened. 'I need to ask Anna again. Explain the situation.'

'Darius trained at the temple,' Bryn said, surprising me. 'He can officiate. There can be no question of the ceremony's legitimacy.'

Alcide gave a sharp nod. 'That's all we need.' He swallowed. 'I would have liked it to have been special.'

My nostrils flared and I took another mental step to the side. 'It *will* be special, Cide. You respect Anna. You'll give her everything she wants and needs. It won't just be special – it will be *remarkable*.'

Alcide gave me a look I could not read. 'All right,' he said, after a moment's silence. 'Cal, will you get her, please?' He leaned over the control panel and pressed the comms button. 'Darius? When you've finished the task at hand, will you come to the bridge?'

I stared at him. '*Now?*'

'There's no time like the present,' he said tightly.

'You're going to claim her ... *now*,' I said slowly.

'Callan –'

'*Now*, now. As in, *here. Now.*'

Alcide adjusted the already-perfect collar of his jacket. 'We've established that. Only if she agrees, of course.'

I took a breath, and another step. It was both mental and physical; I stepped back from Alcide. It didn't work, though; hurt bloomed in my chest, as tangible as any real injury. I'd lost both of them – *and I'd never had either of them to begin with.*

My hands clenched into fists. 'As you wish, Majesty,' I said, and I turned on my heel and left the bridge.

I barely saw the corridors as I stormed through them, and I ignored Taran's startled glance when I brushed past him without apologising. It seemed only a heartbeat later that I was at the cell and stepping inside.

Scent washed over me: Vesper's woodsmoke and Anna's sweet, fresh spring. I braced against it as Vesper looked up from where he cradled Anna's naked, sleeping form.

'Hush,' he scolded. 'She needs to rest.'

'She can't,' I said bluntly. 'She's getting claimed.'

Vesper cocked his head. 'Is she?'

'*Now*, starling.'

His lips tugged up. 'Well, well. Look who's grumpy all of a sudden. Been watching the cell's live feed, Callan?'

I didn't take the bait. 'Alcide needs to claim Anna. Now. *Anna*,' I called softly. 'Anna. Wake up.'

She stirred, and glanced over her bare shoulder. 'Callan,' she said thickly, then flushed the most delicious pink I'd ever seen when she remembered she was naked. 'What –'

'We need your answer. Will you let Alcide claim you?'

She blinked and shifted upright in Vesper's arms. 'What, *now*?'

I kept my gaze rigidly on her face, feeling my own cheeks heat. 'Now.'

'Perhaps someone should explain to Alcide that patience is a virtue,' Vesper drawled.

Anna ignored him. I expected her to protest; instead, she tilted her head to one side, mirroring Vesper as she studied my face. 'This is about Scytha, isn't it?'

I nodded. 'It's not ... It's not looking good. We have a plan, but the plan involves a queen. Alcide needs you, Anna. But the choice is yours.'

She was silent for a moment. She turned around to look at Vesper; he kept his eyes trained on me, though they flared brighter under her stare.

'All right,' Anna said eventually. 'But I need to get dressed. And I want Vesper there.'

'I –' I blinked. 'What?'

'Vesper,' she repeated patiently. 'I want him uncuffed, and at the … *claiming*.'

'Absolutely not,' I said immediately.

Anna turned back to glare at me. 'That's my only request, Callan. I'm not asking for a ceremony at sunset with a string quartet and a designer dress, or for a two-hundred-head, four-course waterside reception and a European honey-moon. All I'm asking is that I can have a moment to put my uniform back on, and that Vesper is there.' She paused. 'I hope that you will be, too, in case that wasn't clear.'

Something twisted in my chest. 'I'll check with Alcide,' I said gruffly. 'But I wouldn't hold out hope.'

I stepped outside the cell and tapped on my wrist screen. 'Did you hear that?'

'Yes.' Alcide paused. 'What do you think?'

'No,' I said. 'Absolutely fucking not.'

I could almost *hear* Alcide thinking. 'She has a point though, Cal.'

I pushed aside the odd truce that had crept up between me and the starling; I pushed aside the way my stomach tightened when he smiled, the way that the air between us seemed to go tight when we were in the same space, how I'd felt watching him with Anna. 'He's a *criminal*, Cide. That's why he's in there. He's charmed Anna like he's charmed hundreds of beings before her. Who knows what he's plan-ning next?'

Alcide paused. 'You think he's just using her?'

No. I'd seen his face when she was hurt; if he'd faked that expression, I'd eat my own hand. 'I don't know. And not knowing is what makes him so dangerous.'

There was another pause. 'Do it,' Alcide said decisively.

'I – fucking *what*, Alcide?'

'Do it. Uncuff him and bring him with you. I won't begin my partnership by denying my claimed the single thing she asks for.'

My claimed. An overpowering, cloying, hateful mix of jealousy and envy wrapped its fingers around my throat, dampening my voice. 'It's your call, Majesty,' I responded, my voice terse. I tapped off my wrist screen before Alcide could respond, and stormed back inside the cell.

'Get on your feet,' I snapped at Vesper. Anna gave me a startled look as she zipped up her uniform, her deliciously smooth skin disappearing. I felt a pang of loss, but ruthlessly pushed it aside; in a matter of moments, Anna would be my *Queen*. She'd be for me to obey, not worship. Her skin would be for Alcide to touch, to caress, to lick as she trembled. I'd never be so close to her again.

I stepped forward, the words pushing up my throat as if I'd choke on them if I didn't let them out. 'Anna,' I said hoarsely. 'I'm so sorry that I took you from your home. I'm so sorry that I brought you into this, sorry for the mess I made. I know that this was all my fault, and I hope you can forgive me. One day.'

She blinked at me, and her expression went soft. Her springtime scent filled my nose and I fought the urge to touch her. 'Callan,' she said gently. 'I've already forgiven you. Despite the way this began, I can't regret it.' She reached out; I held myself rigidly still as her fingertips brushed over my arm. 'You gave me an adventure that I never would have been brave enough to take for myself.'

There was a moment as we stared at one another, a moment that stretched and seemed to thicken, heavy with the things I felt but couldn't say, tense with emotions I imagined flickering in her eyes. Her fingers stayed on my arm, and it was as if they were grounding me, tethering me, *tying* me to the tiny human I'd stolen but would never get to keep.

I swallowed, armouring myself against the feeling, stepping back and breaking the moment, then fishing under my uniform for the darkmatter key.

It was an odd thing. The metal made me uneasy, so I'd wrapped it in layers of thick linen and encased it in a small, thin box made of Tirian steel. My uniform was full of secret pockets, intended for hiding different weapons, and the box was settled in one against my hip.

Vesper regarded me solemnly as I took it out and opened it. When I unwrapped the key, he hissed.

Anna took his hand.

I knelt and fit the key inside the cuff. I didn't like the thought of Vesper chained, but I didn't exactly want him free, either. He was a potential danger to Alcide and to Anna, and therefore he was a danger to everything I held dear. I paused for a moment before I turned the key; the silence in the cell was so thick I could have cut it with a knife.

There was no sound as my wrist twisted. The only noise came from the cuff as it fell with a *thunk* onto the cell floor.

I tensed, waiting.

Vesper gave a dark laugh; he stretched his arms above his head. Light streamed into the cell, into *him*, and his skin began to glow from within, his golden eyes brightening. The air around him heated.

'By the stars, that's better,' he muttered. He poked a long, glowing finger into my chest. 'You do know how that thing works, don't you? It blocks starlight from our forms and *starves* us.' He stepped forward, uncomfortably close, and fisted his hand in my hair, holding me still as his lips brushed across my mouth. He kissed me gently once, twice, before my lips parted and he kissed me *properly*, his tongue flicking against mine, his teeth raking my lip, his fingers so tight in my hair that my eyes smarted. Fire spread through my body and I went rock-hard as he pressed up against me; just as I reached back – just as my hands curled around his hips, as my teeth sank into his lip, as I felt his cock hardening against mine – he pushed me away.

I stared at him, bemused, struggling to control my ragged breath and the way my chest tightened.

He gave me a wide, taunting grin, so beautiful my heart gave a painful thud. 'Thanks, handsome. It's been fun.'

Light swirled into the cell; I threw up my arm as my eyes burned. 'Anna!' I roared, staggering back. I blinked down my second eyelids, shading my eyes with my hand as the flare began to die down.

Vesper and Anna were nowhere to be seen.

ANNA

I SCREAMED AS MY *body tore itself into a million tiny pieces, but no sound emerged. I was rushing upwards and there was light all around me, keeping my pieces together as I moved at a speed I couldn't fathom. I could see nothing but light and darkness, feel nothing but the rush of distance past me. It was terrifying and exhilarating all at once; a deep chuckle rumbled through the black, and a voice wrapped around whatever was left of my mind.*

'I knew you'd like it, lodestar.'

I couldn't answer, but I knew the voice was right.

'Wake up, Anna.'

I moaned wordlessly.

'Anna. Wake up.'

I roused myself enough to give a slight shake of my head.

'You have to help me out, lodestar. I don't know where we are.'

'Vesper,' I said breathlessly. 'Vesper, I'm going to –'

I leaned to the side and vomited.

'I swear by the stars, I have marooned beings for less than that.' Vesper's voice was wry. 'Why must organics persist in being so surprisingly disgusting?' Gentle hands stroked my hair back from my cheeks and held it away from my face. 'I suspect there's more coming. I'll try not to judge you, brightness, though I make no guarantees.'

My stomach heaved and I vomited again.

'How did your species ever live long enough to evolve when you do ridiculous things like this?' Warm fingers stroked the nape of my neck. 'It can't be a sensible reaction to *anything*.'

'Poisoning,' I said weakly. 'Bad food. Being around things that are bad for your body. Indulging in too much –'

'All right, all right, it serves a purpose. A *disgusting* purpose, but a purpose. I think you need one more, love.'

'I don't –' I started, then retched onto the pale stone beneath me.

Pale stone?

'*Qu'est-ce qui s'est passé?*'

The question came from an unfamiliar female voice, shocked but quiet.

I frowned and looked upwards, blinking.

A woman – *a human woman*, with curly brown hair and lovely hazel eyes currently wide with shock – rushed towards me. She took a bottle of water – *human water, in an expensive glass bottle* – from her handbag. '*Es-tu malade?*'

I stared at her. French. She was speaking French. She offered me the water; I pushed myself up, looking around for the first time.

Pale stone buildings. A pale stone road beneath me. Cool, fresh air. A view to die for, looking out across at more buildings made of pale brick, dotted with greenery, and fields stretching for miles around.

I whimpered.

'*Tu vas bien*?' she said.

'*Je vais bien, merci*,' I said weakly. French had never been my strongest subject, and I stared blankly as she quick fired something more complex at me. 'Vesper?'

His woodsmoke scent settled around me. I breathed in deeply, and let it do its work.

'Where did you come from?' the woman demanded, pulling her coat tighter around her. 'First you were not there, and then you were there, and then you were *vomiting*, and –'

'Thank you for your help,' I managed. 'I just stumbled. Vertigo. We were trying to get a good photo.'

She frowned at me, no doubt taking in my strange, ill-fitting uniform, and my decided lack of camera or phone. I took a mouthful of water and offered it back to her.

'You keep it,' she said. Her eyes flickered to Vesper, and she stared, her cheeks flushing a deep pink as she took him in. 'You sound ... English? American? Where are you staying?'

Jealousy stirred in my stomach, threatening to upset it again. 'Australian. We're not sure if we are,' I said shortly. I staggered to my feet; Vesper caught me around the waist and tucked me against his side. My heart thumped unevenly.

'Ah, headed back to Avignon, then?'

'Mmm,' I answered noncommittally. I glanced around me, my eyes falling on a sign that read *Château de Gordes*.

I closed my eyes. We were in freaking *Provence*, the subject of multiple teenaged-Anna mood boards before I realised just how much it would cost to get there. *Here.* 'We just wanted to see the Sénanque Abbey before we left. Could you point us to a taxi?'

The woman smiled, and gave us some directions, then left only after I thanked her profusely and said pointedly that we didn't want to keep her. Her evident interest in Vesper made me unaccountably angry, and as I was piecing it all together to get a picture of what had happened, I became downright *irate*.

'We're on Earth,' I whispered furiously. 'You brought me back to *Earth*.' I took another swig of water, both to cleanse my mouth and so I would do something with my hands that didn't involve punching Vesper square in the face.

He looked down at me in surprise. 'Of course I brought you back to Earth.'

I willed myself not to throttle him. 'Vesper,' I said, as calmly as I could manage, '*I didn't want to come back to Earth.*'

He blinked his golden eyes. 'But Callan *took* you from here.'

'He did,' I agreed carefully, 'and I'm still angry about that. But it doesn't mean that I *regret* it.'

'But you *must* regret it,' he said, his brow furrowing.

'Vesper,' I said tersely, 'I like you very much. But if you *ever* tell me what I *must* or *must not* feel, I will turn around and walk away from you, and I will not be coming back.'

'Anna,' he said, his hand cupping my cheek. 'You're not thinking straight. Callan *abducted* you. You were *assaulted*. You were in constant danger, including during a *literal space battle*. You were put in a position where you couldn't say *no* to Alcide —'

'And I was still happier than I was here!' I shouted, push-ing his hand away. 'Don't *patronise* me, you dick! I know the beginning wasn't ideal, but I *did* have a choice about Alcide, and I *made* it! *And it was one more choice than I was given about my recent life on Earth*!' I glared at him, my chest heaving. 'Do I wish Callan had *asked* rather than just *taken*? Of course I do! But if he'd *asked*, I would have been scared, and I would have said *no*, and I never would have met *you*! Or met Alcide, or known Callan! Are you going to take that away from me, Vesper? Are you going to take *them* away?'

He stared at me in shock. 'I thought you'd want to come back,' he said weakly.

'Well, you thought wrong, starling!' I snapped. 'Why would I want to be here without Callan? Without Alcide? Without *you*?'

He swallowed. 'Without me?'

I swept my arm out to encompass the beautiful town. 'What are you going to do on Earth, Vesper? I give it a month be-fore you're bored, and two before you leave for some kind of *crime-for-crime's sake* play and never come back.' I pushed at his chest; he didn't move. 'I know I was probably just helping to pass the time for you –'

'Anna,' he said, horrified. 'Anna, *no*. That's not –'

'And the moment I'm not the only available being, you'll –'

'Who's making assumptions now?' he snarled. 'Will you just –'

'No I *won't just*!' I shrieked. We were amassing a whispering audience now, but I couldn't help myself. 'I will *not* let you make choices for me, Vesper! Not when I was *only just beginning to make them for myself again*! I –'

He took my face in his hands and kissed me.

Perhaps I'll let you make this particular choice, I thought, before my eyes fluttered shut and I found myself kissing him back, desperately. He slipped an arm behind my back and arched me beneath his body, devouring my mouth, despite the fact I must have tasted horrendous.

'Anna,' he said a moment later, nipping at my bottom lip. '*I think I'm in love with you.*'

I opened my eyes and stared up at him in surprise.

'Just in case that wasn't clear,' he said, echoing the words I'd spoken to Callan just minutes before.

The crowd around us clapped dutifully.

I pushed myself out of his arms. 'You're in love with me, Vesper? Then *prove it*.' I slapped my hand against his chest. 'Find us a hotel room so I can have a shower, get me some food, find me some clothes, and then *take me back to my wedding.*'

I didn't know how he did it, and I wasn't about to ask. All I knew was that a bare handful of moments later, Vesper had secured the kind of credit card I'd heard of but never seen in real life, had pulled me down a street and charmed the staff at the fanciest hotel I'd ever seen into getting us a *suite*, and I was standing in one of the most beautiful rooms I'd ever had the pleasure of being in, looking into a sumptuous bathroom that had not only and bath *and* a shower, but a view over the gorgeous town that made the breath catch in my chest. The staff had eyed me dubiously; Vesper had tucked me into his side and given an indulgent smile.

'My wife's belongings were lost on the way here,' he said. 'I need to replace some of them for her. I'd like to refresh my wardrobe, too. Where would be best?'

The hotel's gift shop had some options, as it turned out, so I left Vesper to it and followed the porter through the building to our suite, gawking at the huge bed and intricate wallpaper before pushing into the bathroom. When I finally picked my jaw up from the floor, I stripped off my uniform and filled the bath, dumping most of the bottle of bubble bath in with the water.

I sank into the hot water until it covered my ears, cocooning myself in silence. I could hardly believe that I was back on Earth, let alone in *France*, and in a particularly beautiful part of it, somewhere I'd always wanted to visit. Not only that, I was with one of the handsomest males I'd ever seen, who'd swiped someone's credit card to pay for a place I never would have dreamed of staying. I hoped he'd taken the credit card from a tourist, rather than a local, and from someone who wouldn't miss it, but I thought that Vesper had quite enough experience to choose his marks carefully.

I let myself feel guilty for a moment, but the hot water soaked the feeling away far more swiftly than it probably should have.

I scrubbed every inch of my body twice, then took advantage of the amenities provided to deal with my nails and to shave my legs and under my arms. I got out reluctantly, then spent about ten minutes brushing my teeth until I was fairly sure the scent of spearmint overpowered the smell of soap. When I was done, I turned around and got straight into the shower.

I'd been in a cell for *weeks*. I was allowed to have both.

I shampooed four times and conditioned twice, then wrapped a huge, fluffy towel around my body and blow dried my hair. When Vesper returned, looking unnervingly *human* with his arms weighed down with bags, I was curled up on a couch, wearing a robe and reading the only book I could find in English on the built-in shelves – *Vanity Fair*.

Vesper made a small noise of surprise as he took me in, and I realised that he'd never really seen me looking – well, *clean*. Callan had snatched me during the tail end of a seven-hour shift in a hot kitchen, and it had gone downhill from there. He dumped the bags and stalked towards me, his eyes flaring gold. 'Anna.'

'I'm still angry with you,' I warned, putting out a hand – otherwise, I knew, I'd let him pull me into his arms and kiss me, and if he did that, I was likely to forget how irritated I was.

'I thought you might be. I ordered us some food on the way back up.' He paused. 'I didn't know what you'd like the best, so I got the chef's recommendations. Is that all right?'

I sniffed. 'I suppose.'

His lips curved into a wide smile. 'I like it when you're angry. You're fierce.' He paused, tipping his head back to look at the ceiling. 'I thought about what you said.'

'And?' I enquired, when he didn't continue.

'And I believe I may have done the wrong thing.'

'You very definitely did the wrong thing, Vesper, though I think you did it for a good reason.' I paused. 'What else?'

'*And* I'm sorry for it,' he said eventually, with evident reluctance; I wondered how often he'd said the word *sorry* before. 'I'll ask what you want in the future.' His eyes lowered back to my face, glowing brightly. 'What is it that you want, lodestar?'

'Food,' I said, somewhat mollified. I hadn't expected an apology at all, let alone a *good* one.

He made a dismissive noise. 'No, what is it you *want*? In your ...' He put his hand over his chest. 'Meat pump?'

'*Heart*,' I corrected, biting my lip so I wouldn't laugh.

'Heart, then. What does your *heart* want?'

I looked down at the book in my hand. While *Vanity Fair* was a satire rather than a love story, no one could say that Becky Sharp hadn't gone for what she wanted.

I considered Vesper's question. Barely a few months ago, I wouldn't have been able to answer it, too weighed down with what I *needed* to do, rather than what I *wanted*.

But now?

Now, I wanted to see things I'd never seen before. I wanted adventure. I wanted to see what else the universe held. I wanted to *fly*. To *soar*.

And I *wanted* in a different way, too. I *wanted* in a greedy, possessive way I hadn't known I was capable of feeling; it was all new, all surprising, all overwhelming, in the best possible way. Though I'd never bought the one-man-one-woman romance our society sold as the ultimate prize, I'd also never considered that I might desire something different.

But I did. Part of my anger at Vesper bringing me back to Earth was the sudden absence of Alcide and Callan. If *they'd* taken me away from Vesper, I'd feel the same. I wanted all three of them close; *wanted* so badly it was turning into something else entirely. With Alcide and Vesper, I knew that feeling – or some of it, at least – was returned; I wanted to discover whether Callan felt the same burning, whether he wanted to slide his fingers over my skin the same way I wanted to be held in his arms again, whether his actions would match the intense promise in his eyes.

It didn't mean that I'd forgotten my grief for my grandmother. It didn't mean that I wasn't still angry about being kidnapped. It didn't mean that I thought Callan stealing me was right, or validated by the fact that I had feelings for my captors.

But being human meant having all sorts of conflicting emotions, all at once, all the time. I could grieve my grandmother while my heart bloomed with new love. I could recognise that my kidnapping was wrong while that place beneath my ribs ached to be close to Callan. I could resent being held in a cell while being grateful that my freedom from it brought me choices I never would have had otherwise.

I could be angry with Vesper about taking me away while melting inside at his reasons for doing so.

'I want to see new things,' I said at last, running my fingers over *Vanity Fair*'s thick spine. 'I want to meet new beings, live in a different place. I want to learn new ways of doing things, new ways of seeing things, and I don't want someone telling me that's not what I want, not what I need.' I looked up at Vesper; his eyes were burnished gold, glowing brighter by the moment. I swallowed my fear. 'I want to see new things with *you*, learn new things with *you* – but not you alone, Vesper. What I feel for all three of you might just be enforced proximity. It might just be lack of choice.' I rubbed a hand over my chest. 'But that doesn't make it any less real. I won't choose between you.'

Vesper gave a sharp nod. 'All right.'

I blinked. '*All right*?'

He shrugged. 'I thought you might say that. And I like them. If that's the only way I get to keep you, then that's what needs to happen.'

I stared at him. 'And that's it?'

He frowned. 'What else is there?'

'I thought you'd argue.'

He snorted. 'It goes against my nature to share. I won't promise to be good at it, but I *will* promise to try. Plus, you gave a very good ultimatum. I don't want you to walk away, brightness. I like touching your light.' He looked out the window at the sun. 'Is there anyone here you need to contact?'

I'd thought about trying to find a library to email Claire and Maeve – and our boss, Jessa – but got caught up on what I could possibly say. *Hi, I'm so sorry I didn't contact you – also, I won't be back*? Was that better or worse than not knowing? Better, I thought, but how could I possibly justify it? Tell them that I'd simply left, rather than been kidnapped – *by aliens*? Leaving without telling anyone was so impossibly out of character that my friends would never believe it, and nor would Maeve accept an explanation like *I've fallen in love but I can never see you again*. She'd call the police, thinking I'd been coerced, the search would continue – I assumed there'd already been one – and I'd leave them with as little resolution as they had now. Unless I could contrive to visit them somehow in the future – but then, what would I say when they asked where I'd been, and what I'd been doing?

There was no good answer; I'd hurt my friends either way.

I swallowed, sorrow blooming in my stomach. 'I don't think that's a good idea.'

He turned back to study me. 'Are you sure?'

I nodded, unable to speak.

'Then I give it two more of your Earth hours before the man I swiped the card from realises it's gone; he'd consumed rather a lot of that alcoholic red water, but I assume he can't keep drinking it forever. We should be ready to leave at short notice.

I didn't know what kind of clothing you wanted, so I got a few different choices.'

I uncurled my legs and crossed the room, rising on my tip-toes to press a kiss to his cheek. 'Thank you, Vesper.'

The air around him heated as he cleared his throat. 'I'd steal the sun from the sky if you asked for it.'

I smiled. 'I'd prefer to keep the star I have.'

I didn't think Vesper could blush, but he could certainly be rendered momentarily speechless. I enjoyed it for a moment before I picked up the bags and went into the bedroom to change.

The sizes he'd chosen varied wildly; I didn't know whether to be offended that he didn't grasp the size of my body, or pleased that he hadn't seemed to notice it. The things he'd chosen were lovely regardless; I settled on a rose-pink shift dress and a cream sweater so soft I couldn't resist rubbing it on my cheek. He'd remembered shoes, too, and after discarding a few pairs two times too large for me, I found a pair of supple tan leather ballerina flats that fit perfectly.

He raked his hands through his hair when I walked back out. 'You look ...' he began, then trailed off. His clothing had changed, too: he'd clearly noticed what some of the human men had been wearing and made himself something new to mimic it. I silently thanked whoever he'd modelled from; he looked like an indie musician in tight black jeans and black collared shirt, matching black leather boots laced half-way up his calf.

'You look nice, too,' I said shyly.

'I'm not sure *nice* is the word I'd use for you,' he said, and took a step towards me, his eyes burning. 'You look *edible*.'

I flushed as I remembered the way his mouth had felt between my legs. 'Vesper –'

There was a knock on the door. 'Room service,' a voice called.

When Vesper said he ordered the chef's recommendations, it turned out he meant *all* of them. There were four entrées, six mains, and four desserts, along with paired wines and a charcuterie board piled with meats, local cheeses, pâté, and fruit. It was the kind of food that cost a fortune, and I wished that Alcide and Callan could have been with us so I could show them what human food should be. As it was, Vesper watched me eat curiously, accepting small bites from my fork only when I pushed him to try it, and I lamented that it could be a long time before I'd have such an excellent meal again.

'I'm going to vomit this straight up when you take me back, aren't I?' I said glumly.

Vesper picked up a grape and examined it. 'Very probably. But I'm glad you got to eat it, anyway.'

ALCIDE

I PACED BACK AND forth before my bed, tugging on handfuls of my hair.

'I'll kill him,' I burst out passionately. 'I'll find him and *kill* him.'

You would have done exactly the same thing in his place.

I ignored my inner voice of reason, though I had a sneaking suspicion it was right. My formal jacket pulled tight across my shoulders; I rolled them, trying to get comfortable and ignoring the pain in my chest.

'Calm down, Cide,' Callan said levelly. 'You're not killing anyone, today at least. Stop and re-evaluate. What do we do now?'

I stopped still and rubbed my temples. 'We're lacking our Queen. The Queen our plan *needs*. Quite apart from ...' I trailed off, unable to put into words how unsettled I felt without Anna on the ship, and how my need to find her and bring her back here – bring her back to *us* – was all but overshadowing my concern about our home planet. 'Quite apart from everything else.'

'The Queen we *think* our plan needs,' Callan corrected. 'What do we do now? Ignoring ... *everything else.* Just for the moment.'

I thought for a second. 'Bryn's idea is still the better one, Queen or no Queen,' I said reluctantly. 'If we go home to Scytha right now, we'll very definitely die. If we go to the peace summit on Natare, we only *might* die.'

'The peace summit, then.' Callan stood from where he'd been perched on the side of my mattress, and stretched his arms above his head. Desire thrilled through me as his uniform went tight over all the right places. I pushed it aside; if Anna was still on the ship, I'd be in the middle of a claiming ceremony right now. I had no right to be staring slack-jawed at my pilot.

'The peace summit,' I agreed. 'Will you set a course for –'

The light in my bedroom swirled in an all-too familiar way; the corners darkened, then burst with brightness.

'*Anna*!' Callan shouted hoarsely.

Anna, dressed in human clothing that looked impeccably clean, her hair floating like a fair cloud around her shoulders, fell to her knees.

I stepped towards Vesper, with every intention of my fists connecting with his perfect cheekbones.

'Get a bucket, King,' the starling said wearily, tenderly gathering Anna's hair back from her face, his free hand on her back. He eyed my clenched fingers and shook his head. 'Do that later, if you absolutely must.'

Anna shook her head as her cheeks took on a green tinge. 'I won't be sick,' she gasped, closing her eyes and taking a deep breath. 'I *refuse* to waste that food. I *refuse*, Vesper.'

'I believe you,' the starling said mildly. 'But we'll get you a bucket just in case.'

Callan disappeared and came back a moment later with a cleaning bucket, thrusting it under Anna's nose and then backing away.

I glared at Vesper. 'Where did you take her, starling?'

'Where do you think?' he answered, his eyes on Anna. 'Earth. Turns out, that wasn't where she wanted to be.' He looked up, returning my glare, his eyes glowing. 'I will always take her where *she* wants to be, King. She chose to come back here.'

Anna made a concerning heaving sound, but sealed her lips tightly together and shook her head.

Vesper rubbed her back. 'Humans are awfully impractical, aren't they?' he said musingly.

Anna turned to glare at him.

'And beautiful, of course,' he added hastily. 'Captivating, actually. Even when they make those heinous noises.'

Anna's expression softened slightly. 'You're impossible, Vesper.'

'My presence here would suggest the opposite,' he answered. 'I am inherently and entirely possible.'

Anna shook her head again, smiling slightly. She closed her eyes, taking one more deep breath. 'Okay. I think I'm okay. There's no way that salmon is going to waste. And that crème brûlée.' She tipped her head back, her lips parting, and the three of us froze, mesmerised by her mouth. 'It had lemon in it, did you notice? I need to try to make it. Divine.'

'Divine,' Vesper echoed thickly, clearly gathering his scattered wits more swiftly than Callan or myself could. He let Anna's hair fall from his grasp; I watched it, utterly entranced.

Anna got to her feet. Her blue gaze settled on me, taking in my formal suit, the gilt on my horns, the gold lining my eyes. She swallowed, flushing. 'I believe I'm late to my wedding. I'm ready now.'

There was a moment of silence.

'Ah,' I said, my stomach churning. I considered borrowing Anna's bucket for a moment, before I realised it was *nerves*, and I tried to push them down. 'Anna –'

'I'll get Darius and Bryn.' Callan slipped outside.

I tried to rally, offering Anna my arm. 'We thought it might be nice to say the words on the bridge,' I said, my tongue feeling suddenly too large for my mouth. 'You can see out of the ship, and there's a pair of eclipsing binary stars within observation distance. One is burning so hot it's blue but the other is cooler and red, and ...' I cleared my throat. 'Well. It looks nice, is what I'm trying to say.' I paused. 'Purple.'

Anna bit her lip. 'I like purple. And the bridge sounds nice, Cide.'

I looked down at my feet so I wouldn't stumble as we walked. 'Bryn had an idea. He thought we could record the ceremony and bounce an edited version to Scytha as proof. Would that be all right?'

She thought about it for a moment. 'Yes, I think that's fine. I assume you're not livecasting in case anything goes wrong.'

'You mean like Vesper changing his mind again?' I said wryly.

She squeezed my arm. 'He won't.'

'How can you be so sure?' I growled.

Her lips tugged up into a small smile. 'I think, King, it's for two reasons. Firstly, he knows that I will *eat him* if he tries to do that without my permission again.'

'And second?' I prompted, when she didn't continue.

Anna brushed her lips over the back of my hand. 'We had a talk, and he seemed to come around to the thought of *sharing*. I'm counting on his curiosity, if nothing else.'

I stopped still, trying to work out what she meant. 'Anna –'

She blinked innocently at me. 'We'll be late, Cide. Come along.' She flicked a glance back at Vesper, who was following nonchalantly behind us, examining the white corridors with interest; I realised that it was the first time he was seeing this part of the ship. When I met his eyes, he gave me a slow, knowing wink.

I flushed and stumbled along beside Anna, wondering exactly when our tiny human prisoner had become our captor instead.

'She kept talking about an imaginary human called *Becky Sharp*,' Vesper whispered loudly. 'I can't tell whether she's had a revelation, or whether her skull computer broke.'

Anna reached back and, without looking, tapped him lightly on the arm.

Everyone left on the ship was waiting on the bridge. They'd changed into their formal uniforms and had somehow found some cloth-of-gold to make ceremonial sashes. Darius had evidently upended a vine growing in one of the common areas to make a wreath; Bryn beamed at him proudly, and I wondered how I ever could have missed the warmth in the engineer's eyes when he looked at his love.

Someone had found a sash for Callan, too. As my second, he'd painted gilt up the sides of his graceful horns, and lined his eyes with gold. He was so handsome my breath caught; I shook my head slightly at my selfishness.

Don't play with me, Prince.

Vesper accepted a sash from Octus with a bemused thanks, clearly not expecting to have had any part in the ceremony. As Darius arranged us, though, Vesper found himself standing to Anna's left, with Callan to my right, the four of us lined up before Darius like naughty bairnlings.

It wasn't how the ceremony went, but it didn't feel wrong.

'Usually, your intended would begin by painting your horns in gold, Majesty,' Darius said to Anna. 'But as you don't have horns, we will skip that part.'

She started at being addressed as *Majesty*, but rallied swiftly. 'What about my nails instead?' she said, holding out her hands, palm down.

Darius blinked. 'That could work.'

He'd set up a small altar just in front of the wide window of reinforced glass; upon it sat two small bowls, one of gilt, and one of blessed blood. Darius dipped a small brush in the gilt, then offered it to me.

I trembled as I took it, my fingers shaking as I cradled Anna's hand in mine. She gave me a reassuring smile. 'It's all right, Cide,' she whispered.

I brushed the gilt over the nail of her pointer finger, trying to keep it neat and even, though a tingling spread over my skin at the contact. I switched to her other hand, trying to ignore the way my body was heating and my cock stirring at the clean, fresh scent of her.

When I'd finished, she took the tiny brush back, smiling, and offered it to Callan.

Callan frowned in question.

'Your turn,' Anna said.

Darius' face went blank with shock. 'Ah, Majesty,' he said carefully, 'that isn't the way this usually goes.'

Anna turned her face to me. 'I know we didn't talk about this, and I'm sorry for that. But I think this should be all or nothing, Alcide. It might be a disaster, but I'll have everyone I want, or no one at all.' She turned back to Callan. 'You stole me for a reason, Callan. I'd like to find out what that is.'

My body flushed with heat again, but this time it was because of her words. *All or nothing.*

I'd pushed Callan away because I'd wanted to be loyal to the one I claimed. Even then, I couldn't stop myself from looking at him, from craving him. But if I claimed *both* of them ...

Could I have Anna – and Callan, too?

I straightened, a sense of calm settling over me as I realised that this was the answer. We'd taken Anna's choices away from her at the start, but she was choosing now, and it was *right*. We'd been caught by her as much as she'd been caught by us, as if she'd tied ropes beneath her ribs, and fastened the other end beneath our own –

I inhaled.

Soul tie.

Something instinctual, something unbreakable, something that knows, somewhere deep and secret, that you are made for your partner and they for you.

You stole me for a reason.

I had no idea whether it was possible, but I *wanted* it to be. Because I knew that Anna and Callan were mine and I was theirs, already knotted beneath my ribs, the ropes never to be broken. I had no idea what might lie between me and the starling, but there was room for Vesper, too, if he wanted it.

This was going to happen. And everything I'd planned on giving Anna – my devotion, my support, my *heart* – I could share between the three of them.

I looked up, meeting Callan's gaze over Anna's head, aware that the next words that came out of my mouth would change my life. 'This is the way it goes today, Darius,' I said quietly. 'Your Queen-to-be wishes it. I wish it, too.'

Callan inhaled and turned away. I watched his shoulders tremble as he exhaled, watched his fingers clench into fists by his side.

Anna put a hand on his back. 'Only if you want to, Callan. It's your choice, too.'

He took another shuddering breath and turned to face us once more. His eyes were pitch-black; when they fell on me, I realised it was with *hunger*.

I swallowed, trying to push down an answering flood of desire.

Anna offered Callan the brush for a second time.

He took it, unable to resist. His palm engulfed hers, but he held her gently, bending so that he applied the gilt to her middle nail with care. When she offered her other hand he swallowed, his cheeks flushing, his fingers trembling as he finished. He glanced at Anna's face, then, without a word, offered the brush to Vesper.

The starling's eyes went wide. 'Um – Anna?'

'Only if you want to, Vesper,' she repeated, softly.

Vesper recovered, his shocked expression splitting into a grin. 'Well, this is unexpected,' he drawled, taking the brush from Callan. 'I've never had a *wife* before, or *husbands*. My parents will be *thrilled*.'

Anna merely smiled and let Vesper paint the nails of her fourth fingers with gold.

When he was done, she took the brush from him, and finished off her thumbs and smallest fingers herself, then admired the shine in the low lights of the bridge. 'Do I get to paint the males, too?' she said to Darius.

He blinked. 'Not right now, Majesty. You may do whatever you please later.'

Vesper snorted.

Darius placed the bowl of gilt back on the altar, then took up the blessed blood. 'You are here today by the will of the dread gods, and you stand under their all-seeing gaze. Alcide, son of Sever, do you stand here willingly?'

'I do.'

'And this is the partner you wish to take as your own?'

I glanced at Anna, then at Callan, then Vesper. 'She is. They are.'

Darius blinked at my answer, but kept going. 'Do you vow before the gods to protect them, to fulfil their needs, and to keep any young they might provide you safe from all harm?'

'I vow it,' I said.

'And Anna, daughter of ...' Darius trailed off.

'Arabella,' Anna supplied.

'Anna, daughter of Arabella –' Darius' gaze flickered to Callan and Vesper '– and Callan, and Vesper, do you vow to obey the male beside you in all things, to act as a partner should to preserve his reputation, to bear his young, and raise them in accordance with Roth custom?'

Anna frowned, then turned to me. 'Absolutely *not*,' she said. 'There is no way in *any* world that I am vowing that.'

'Anna –' I started.

'Is that *it*?' she demanded. 'Are they the only vows?'

Darius nodded warily.

'Where is the promise of *love*, Alcide? Of cherishing? Of support and communication and offering comfort in hard times? Why do *you* protect, and I – *we* – obey?'

'Anna –' Callan began.

'Nope,' she said, shaking her head. 'You said something different the other day.' She placed her hand over my heart. 'What is it that you *feel*?'

'I –' I swallowed. There were so many things I was feeling that it would be impossible to name them all. There was one thing I was sure of, though. 'I want you.'

'And what do you *want* to vow?' she said fiercely.

'I –' I took a deep breath. 'I want to vow to make you happy every moment I draw breath. I want to promise that I will respect every decision you make. I want to vow to provide you with everything you need and want, so that every choice is always open to you, and I promise my support down any path you choose to follow. I vow to help you fly.'

Anna gave me a brilliant smile; it hit me square in the stomach, and it was an effort not to stagger beneath the force of it. 'That,' she said, her voice thick. 'I vow that. I will try to make him happy in every moment we share. I will support him in his choices, and respect his decisions. And when I fly, he will fly with me.' Her eyes flickered to Callan, and then behind her to Vesper. 'We will fly together.'

'Together,' echoed Vesper, the corners of his lips curling up.

Callan swallowed audibly.

Darius stared at her, then turned to Bryn. 'We'll need to edit that part. Well, we'll need to edit *everything*.'

'Already on it,' Bryn muttered, fiddling with a hand screen.

'As an ordained priest of the dread gods, I accept your vows,' Darius said, dipping a finger in the blessed blood and anointing my forehead, then Anna's, followed by Vesper and Callan. 'This union is sanctioned; this union is sacred. This female belongs to you –' Anna glared at him '– and you to her,' Darius added hastily. 'And ... you to the others, and the others to you,' he went on, glancing at Callan and Vesper. 'I have no idea how you're going to work this out, but that's your problem, not mine. The claiming is complete.'

'Not the strong ending it could have been,' Vesper muttered. He poked at his forehead. 'By the stars, what is *this* sticky nonsense?'

Anna laughed, a clear, joyful peal that had my throat closing over with emotion. 'Do we kiss now?' she said, giving me a heated look from beneath her fair lashes.

'Kiss?' Darius said, startled. 'At a *claiming*?'

Anna laughed again, then threw her arms around my neck and brushed her lips over mine. I wrapped my arms around her, keeping her pressed against me, and returned her kiss eagerly, snarling softly when she bit my bottom lip. She gave a hum of satisfaction and slid down my body, turning in my arms to pull Vesper in closer with a fistful of his shirt.

'How do starlings get married?' she murmured, before she seized his mouth.

His hands came up to cup her cheeks, his fingertips brushing over her cheekbones as he kissed her with more gentleness than I would have given him credit for. 'We don't,' he said unevenly, when she let him up for air. 'We exchange light.'

'I don't think I can do that,' Anna said breathlessly.

Vesper gave a lazy grin. 'Oh, little lodestar. You'd be surprised.'

On my other side, Callan was edging away, his throat working convulsively. I took Anna by the waist and spun her around, setting her between me and my pilot, who was about to bolt. She took his hand; he froze, then looked down at where their fingers were intertwined.

'Where do you think you're going?' Anna enquired politely.

'I –'

'I hope it wasn't *away*.'

'Anna –' Callan started, his voice anguished.

'I want you,' she said simply, looking him straight in the eye. 'Do you want me?'

Callan swallowed. 'Yes,' he answered roughly. 'Every moment, always.'

Her lips curved up. 'Then it's time to show me, Tall, Dark, and Looming.' Her free hand found his cheek; her thumb skirted the planes of our pilot's face before she rose up on her toes and guided him down to her slowly, giving him every chance to turn away before she brushed her lips gently over his.

Callan groaned, his free hand spanning across Anna's back. He returned her kiss tentatively, then with more eagerness when she arched against him. When they broke apart, they were panting.

Anna glanced back at me. 'Please tell me we're going to bed now.'

'We're supposed to –' I started.

'You go to bed now,' Darius interrupted. 'Your priest declares it so. We'll bring you some food later. A lot later,' he added. 'Bryn and I will work on editing the recording, while you ... Well, I really don't want to know.' He eyed Vesper warily. 'Have fun.'

'You heard the priest,' Vesper drawled, and swept Anna into his arms. *'Bed.'*

ANNA

VESPER LAID ME SO gently on the bed that tears pricked in my eyes; I might have cried, except he ran one of his hands down my back and ended the caress with a cheeky ass squeeze. I laughed and pulled him down for a kiss; he kissed me softly, almost nuzzling at my lips, before stepping back and pushing Alcide forward.

Alcide's eyes were obsidian with intent; his lips went straight to my collarbone, then dragged up my neck as I gasped. He left a trail of kisses along my jaw before he seized my mouth, kissing me until I squirmed, his tongue finding mine in a dance that made my entire body catch alight. My hands met his shoulders and I pulled him onto me; he tried to hold his weight off, but I dragged him mercilessly down. I wanted to feel his weight, wanted to feel encased by him, surrounded. My body was lit with feeling: shivers from his touches, from his kisses, anticipation, nerves.

Alcide rolled and took me with him, hauling me to sit up-right, straddling his thighs. 'You have too many clothes on, Anna,' he said sternly.

My hands went to the hem of my sweater, intending to tug it off, but another pair of hands got there first. Callan took hold of the soft wool and inched it up, carefully pulling it over my head, his chest like a bank of heat behind me. My breath caught at the thought of it, at the feeling of having both of them so close; I turned and watched him fold the sweater carefully at the foot of the bed, placing it down with a reverence that made my heart hurt.

Vesper perched on the side of the bed and grinned. 'Is this usual for a human wedding?'

In truth, I had no idea how it was going to work between the four of us, but I reasoned that I didn't have much experience of how it worked between two people, either, so it wouldn't make much difference either way.

'This is *not* usual for a human wedding,' I said breathlessly, as Alcide's hands settled on my hips and Callan's heat was be-hind me again, his fingers on the zip of my dress. Vesper's eyes burned, but he made no attempt to join in, just leaned against the post of Alcide's bed and watched us like we were his own personal entertainment for the night.

Which we might have been, I supposed.

Callan brushed a tentative kiss over the shell of my ear, then tugged my zipper down with excruciating slowness; I heard him inhale sharply when the cooler air of the bedroom hit my bare skin, then didn't hear him breathe again, not until I turned and looked at him over my shoulder.

'Anna,' he said thickly. 'Anna, I ... Cide, you have to tell me ... I don't know what you want from me here.'

Alcide sat up, cradling me, and reached out to Callan. 'There's no expectation, Cal. What do *you* want?'

Callan's eyes darted between Alcide and I, his face anguished.

'Too much choice,' Vesper said. 'He wants you both the same, don't you?' The starling grinned. 'You know this won't be a one-time thing. That there will always be an ebb and flow. This time might be about Alcide, but the next time might be about you.'

'No,' Callan said, his voice wavering with pain. 'No, I don't know that. This might seem like a good idea at the time, but then morning will come, and the excitement will fade, and regret will grow, and I ... I've never done this before, starling,' he finished up fiercely. 'I don't know what I'm doing.'

'Callan,' I said, turning properly to face him, my back against Alcide's chest. I reached out to touch his face. 'Neither has Alcide. And what I've done wasn't great, and only with one person, so we'll all learn together.'

Vesper blinked. 'Alcide hasn't ... And Anna, only with one being?' He tipped his head back, looking at the ceiling. 'Anna, brightness, have you ever heard the expression *you need to float before you fly*?'

'We're jumping in at the deep end, Vesper,' I said stubbornly.

Vesper frowned at me. 'They sound like *opposite* things, lodestar. Sometimes you need ground rules.'

'Ground rules?' Alcide said slowly. 'The starling who stole half my treasury is telling us we need *rules*?'

'I'm a criminal, not a fool,' Vesper said with a wave of his hand. He fixed us all with a golden stare. 'First. No one does a single thing they don't want to do, and you communicate how you're feeling at all times.'

I bit my lip.

'Second, Anna comes first. Always.'

I opened my mouth to protest, but Callan nodded, his expression serious, and I felt Alcide echo the movement behind me, and I decided I wouldn't complain.

'Thirdly ...' Vesper trailed off, thinking. 'It doesn't matter what happens outside this room. Inside it, you are all equal. It doesn't matter who is king, or queen, or otherwise. In here, you are Callan and Anna and Alcide.'

'And Vesper,' I added quietly.

'And lastly,' he went on, giving me a hot look that made my core clench, 'you will all get jealous at some stage, no matter how much you try not to. Accept that it will happen. When it does, *talk about it*,' he said, his gaze shifting to Callan. 'You won't get what you need if you don't ask for it, and we can't help you if we don't know.'

'That's very ... thorough, Vesper,' Alcide said. 'Have you used these rules before?'

'Why? Are you jealous?' Vesper grinned. 'I assure you that I've never been *claimed* before, so you don't have to worry, *husband*. Little lodestar,' he continued, 'are you happy where you are?'

I squirmed on Alcide's lap, rubbing myself against his hardening cock, then shivered at his answering moan. 'Yes.'

'And you'll tell us if that changes?'

Alcide pressed a line of kisses down my throat; I arched back against him, my arms twining up around his neck. 'Yes.'

'I'm going to assume that Alcide and Callan are as happy with the situation as I am,' he continued, 'though they only need to speak up if not. So: second rule.' His grin widened. 'Anna comes first.'

'You're already putting me first,' I said, gasping as Alcide's hand moved up to span my ribs, brushing the underside of my breasts through the cotton of my dress.

'Oh, no, brightness,' Vesper purred. 'Anna *comes* first. Callan, I believe that both Alcide and I have already experienced that heaven, and you seem well placed to take your turn.'

I blinked up at Callan. 'Cal –'

Alcide tugged my dress down over my shoulders, exposing me to the waist.

Callan gave a deep, guttural groan. 'Fuck,' he muttered.

Alcide pushed the dress down, encouraging me to tilt upwards so he could slide it under me, where Callan took it in hand, tugging it down my legs until I was free and entirely naked.

Underwear hadn't been included in Vesper's bags of new clothes, so I'd gone without, and when I saw Callan's expression, I couldn't have been happier about it. In fact, I'd consider making it a habit.

Callan stared at me, his eyes blacker than night. I should have felt self-conscious, but he looked ready to devour me, and the only thing I felt was a whole lot of wishing to be devoured.

'Start at the ankles, Cal,' Alcide murmured, cupping my breasts with both hands. 'Start at the ankles and work your way up.'

Callan's fingers wrapped around my ankles and spread my legs, baring my most private places to his gaze, and to Alcide behind me and Vesper to the side. He groaned again, his eyes fixed on where I was hot and swollen and getting wetter with want. Without breaking his gaze, he lowered his head and lifted one foot slightly, pressing his lips to my ankle bone, and keeping the other leg pinned wide open.

Vesper let out a deep, rumbling purr as Callan worked his way up my calf, leaving a rush of sensation with each press of his lips. The kisses would have been chaste, had I been less naked, and had Callan been devouring the exposed sight of me with less hunger. Alcide's fingers found my nipples, brushing over them until they peaked, then gently pinching and pulling and plucking until I could feel an answering echo of each movement deep in my core, and I was writhing under his hands.

'Be still, Anna,' he murmured, 'or Callan will stop.'

I froze immediately, but Callan huffed a breath against the inside of my knee, sending shivers up my thigh. 'That's asking quite a lot of Callan,' he muttered, swirling his tongue over my skin.

I moaned.

Vesper leant over me and pressed his lips to mine, swallowing the sound. 'You look so lovely spread out like this,' he murmured against my mouth. Alcide tweaked my nipples and I whimpered in response. 'Callan and Alcide might have pinned you down, but you know who's in charge here, don't you, lodestar?'

'Me,' I gasped.

'You, brightness,' he agreed. 'Always you.' He slid a warm hand over my belly, moving tantalisingly close to my core, close enough that my hips thrust up of their own accord, searching for the pressure of his fingers. He chuckled. 'I wouldn't dare ruin Callan's fun,' he said, skimming his fingers through the short curls. 'But I think your handsome Roth is wearing too many clothes, don't you agree?'

I made an incoherent sound and watched helplessly as Vesper slid off the bed and took his place behind Callan, skimming his hands over my pilot's broad shoulders before undoing the fastenings of his uniform and tugging it down. I moaned again, partly because Callan had licked a stripe up my thigh, and partly because Vesper was tearing Callan's uniform off, revealing the muscles shifting under his pearlescent skin. Callan worked his way higher, until he was running his nose over the tender skin of my inner thigh, breathing in a deep lungful of the scent of my arousal.

'Fuck, Anna,' he groaned.

Vesper had him stripped to the waist; the starling gave the Roth a sharp rap on the shoulder, then took his mouth in a punishing kiss as he divested Callan of the rest of his uniform. Callan looked shocked for a moment, before his hand came up to twine through Vesper's dark curls and he returned the kiss in a way that left me breathless and desperately hungry. Behind me, Alcide shifted, making a low noise as Vesper reached down and unceremoniously wrapped his fingers around Callan's long, thick, and clearly very hard cock.

'Oh my goodness,' I whispered.

Vesper broke the kiss and pumped his hand, watching as Callan panted. The starling didn't seem surprised by the raised ridges of scales beneath his palm, nor by the way they were rippling frantically beneath his touch. 'I think you've teased enough,' Vesper purred. 'I want to hear Anna screaming your name. Can you do that, Callan?'

Callan moaned, then seized Vesper's chin in his hand and dragged him in for another kiss. I watched, breathless. They were so much rougher with each other than they were with me; so much more careless of their strength, of where their teeth went, of what their hands found. Alcide ground against me, growling; his thick length was pressed to my back and I felt him there like a brand.

'Callan,' he grated out. 'If you don't make Anna come, I'm going to do it for you.'

My black-haired Roth pulled away from Vesper and looked down at us, his gold-lined eyes gleaming. With his horns curling back and the unreal lines of his muscles he looked closer to a demon than to human; he was so beautiful my heart thudded against my ribs.

'Callan,' I whispered.

That was all it took; he folded between my legs, pushing my knees wide with his shoulders, just as he'd done in my dream. He didn't bother with his fingers, diving straight in with his tongue, giving a swipe up my slit that had me bucking in Alcide's hands. Either his instincts were supernatural or someone had told him how human females worked, because he narrowed in on my clit immediately, flattening his tongue and working it with small, firm licks that made my whole body tense.

Vesper ran a hand down Callan's spine, watching as the Roth's body responded with an arched back and a moan that vibrated against my core and almost sent me through the roof. My knees tightened on his shoulders and my fingers bunched in the blanket beneath me, my body deliciously pinned between the two Roth.

'Dread gods,' Alcide breathed, as Vesper ran his hands over the perfect globes of Callan's ass.

'Tell me when to stop, Callan,' Vesper murmured.

Callan didn't answer.

I couldn't see where Vesper's fingers disappeared to, but I *could* see the muscles in the pilot's back tense, and feel the deep, guttural moan that ripped from his throat. He doubled his efforts and a few moments later I was arching in Alcide's hands, shrieking Callan's name as release tore through me and

I throbbed against his mouth. He growled against my swollen flesh, his tongue lapping up my climax.

Vesper and Alcide exchanged a look over our heads as I panted and Callan writhed; the waves had barely stopped tearing through my body when Alcide lifted me up into his lap and positioned me over his cock.

'Anna?' he said hoarsely.

'Oh, goodness, yes,' I babbled as he pushed his head against my core, my moisture making us both slick.

'Stop,' Vesper said sharply. Alcide and I froze. 'Anna. What do humans use for contraception?'

'Oh,' I said, my stomach flipping at how careless I'd been. 'I'm not on anything. They put me on the pill to try to manage my adenomyosis, but I got super depressed and stopped taking it. I was thinking about an IUD but since I wasn't seeing anyone, it didn't seem to matter.'

Vesper nodded, though I wasn't sure how much of that would make sense to him. 'What would you do if we were on Earth?'

'I'd use condoms,' I answered. Technically, we should have used them regardless of whether I was on birth control or not, but in the heat of the moment, I'd forgotten entirely. *Twice.*

'Right.' Vesper stopped doing whatever he was doing to Callan, who made a noise of disappointment. The starling pointed at me. 'Stay *exactly* where you are.'

He disappeared in a swirl of star-lit darkness.

'I know he said not to move,' Alcide said carefully, 'but Anna-love, this is ... I'm very close to losing control.' He shifted his hips, the tip of his cock nudging between my folds. I could feel the heat of him at my entrance, feel the ridged scales on his head ripple, so close to where I wanted them, and it took all my willpower not to start sinking down.

'That is the sweetest sight I've ever seen,' Callan said roughly.

I shifted my hips back, so I wasn't in danger of forgetting myself *again*, my thighs trembling as I held the position. 'Callan,' I whispered, and held my arms out to him.

He came into them tentatively, which I hated, but when I drew him down for a kiss he returned it with so much enthusiasm I started panting against his mouth. I bit his lip, tasting myself on his skin, then pulled away with a soft moan; Alcide and Callan stared at each other for a moment, then their mouths crashed together like planets colliding, drawn to each other by a thousand unseen forces, every one of them impossible to resist.

'Goodness, yes,' I panted, pinned between them, surrounded by their heat and their strength. It was everything I'd never known I'd wanted, and I shifted my hips again, dangerously close to sinking down without waiting for my starling to return.

'That's more like it,' Vesper purred, reappearing in a swirl of darkness just in time, dropping a small box on the bed. 'I think I made it to your country this time, though if you ever want to go back to that particular city, I might need to make a different body. Apparently it isn't usual for naked humans to materialise from thin air and shout "*Condoms!*" at the top of their voice, although I will say that it got fairly swift results, even though I was near some kind of odd lake, and nowhere near a shop.'

'Vesper, you *didn't*,' I started, but broke off with a whimper as Alcide reached between my legs and gently pinched my swollen clit.

'Focus, Anna,' he said sternly, and my body lit up at his tone; apparently I liked Alcide's *king* voice quite a lot.

Callan picked up the box, eyeing it warily. 'How does this work?'

I giggled. 'You open it, for starters.'

Callan frowned at the box, then tore it open with a twist of his massive hands. The long line of foil fell into his lap.

'Then you tear one off. Carefully.'

He picked up the foil, and with deliberate concentration, tore along the perforated line to separate one condom from the rest.

'You need to open it,' I whispered, transfixed by his strong fingers. 'Close to the edge, so you don't damage the condom.'

He did as I said; a line appeared between his black brows as he took the condom out.

'You find the top,' I managed, my voice even softer. 'And you pinch it, so you can roll it down ... So you can roll it down ...' I swallowed, then clambered off Alcide. 'You start at Cide's head, and it –'

Callan's expression cleared. 'Ah.' He met Alcide's gaze; the air between them was so charged it might as well have been electric. Alcide sank back on his elbows, a blatant challenge written across his face as he waited for Callan.

Callan surged forward without warning, snarling softly as he wrapped his hand around Alcide's thick cock. An answering growl ripped from Alcide's chest as Callan squeezed his shaft, just beneath his head, then fit the condom over and rolled it slowly down the hard length. I could see his scaled ridges still rippling under the latex, and an embarrassing whine escaped my throat before I could stop it.

Vesper frowned at the remains of the box. 'Lucky they fit,' he muttered, then his frown deepened. 'Anna, there's *only ten condoms in this box*.' He looked up. 'There's *three* of us. I'm going to have to get more, aren't I?'

'Vesper, there's only *one* of me. Unless you're using them with each other, if you think you're going to need more than ten *tonight*, you have another thing com –' I shrieked as Callan swept me up into his arms, stealing the sound with a kiss. He turned me around and settled me in his lap, growling against my neck as he spread my knees.

Alcide ran his hands up my thighs, then touched his fingers to where I was wet and swollen. He seized my mouth in a passionate kiss, dipping the tip of his finger inside me. It was the first time he'd done that, and I arched my back in response, moaning as he worked his way in. Callan reached down and pressed lightly on my clit, making small circles with his fingertips as Alcide withdrew and gently added another finger. I could feel the stretch and I whimpered slightly, my hands finding Callan's biceps and my nails digging into his skin.

'Make her come, Cal,' Vesper said sharply.

I cried out as Vesper fixed me with his glowing gaze and Callan's mouth dropped back down to my neck, his breath hot on my skin, his lips a searing caress. I stared at Vesper as Callan circled my clit and Alcide stretched me, pumping his fingers slowly.

'Come, little lodestar,' Vesper purred, and I did, falling apart with a whine as Callan took my earlobe between his teeth and gently nipped.

'Dread gods,' Alcide breathed as my core gripped his fingers. '*Anna.*'

I collapsed back against Callan, boneless.

When my internal muscles would let him go, Alcide withdrew, licking his fingers with evident pleasure. Callan sank back on the bed and took me with him, arranging me on my side, my back against his broad chest, the column of his hard cock pressing against my ass. Alcide settled before me, throwing an arm over both of us, showering kisses on my cheeks.

'Perfect,' he breathed. 'You're perfect, Anna-love.'

I hooked my knee over his hip and drew him closer, taking his face in my hands as his cock nudged against my entrance.

It still hurt when he worked his way inside, even after two orgasms. Alcide went slowly, carefully, stopping when I cried out; a hand stroked my hair. When the stretch became too much, Callan reached between my legs and toyed with me, bringing me to the edge again, and my body did the rest, taking Alcide's length inside greedily as I throbbed around him. His ridges rippled in answer, pulsing against my internal walls in a flowing wave that had me shuddering with pleasure at the relentless sensation. Alcide groaned as he bottomed out, resting his forehead against mine, then began to move in small, gentle thrusts. Pleasure spread from my core with his every movement, with every fluttering ripple of his ridged scales; I threw my head back, panting, sure that I could take no more.

'So beautiful, Anna,' Vesper crooned, and I realised it had been his hand stroking my hair all along. 'You look so beautiful with Alcide buried inside you, so lovely stretched around his cock.' He trailed a finger down my cheek and around my lips. 'One more time, lodestar. Come one more time, then you can rest.'

'Vesper, I can't –'

'Of course you can,' he purred, and Alcide changed his angle, and a moment later I was crying out incoherently as the scales reaching up his stomach rippled against my clit and my climax crashed through my body. My core gripped Alcide, who groaned, thickened inside me, and followed me over, thrusting deeply as he came.

He took my face in his hands and kissed me while Vesper continued to stroke my hair and Callan buried his face in the back of my neck.

'Love you,' I croaked to no one in particular, and fell asleep.

CALLAN

When I woke up, I was … warm.

I was never warm when I woke up.

I was comfortable, too, even though one of my arms had gone dead. My nose was full of a delicious mix of scents – spring and spice and woodsmoke and sex – and an arm was heavy on my waist.

I opened my eyes. The ship was still in the night cycle, but its artificial morning was beginning.

Anna was lying in front of me, her head pillowed on my bicep. Her lashes fluttered as she dreamed.

I inhaled.

She was so fucking beautiful, with her lips curving slightly, her breath fanning my skin. Watching her put herself – put her body – in our hands had made my heart hurt; she trusted us to give her pleasure, trusted us to keep her safe, even after everything I'd done.

I will never betray your trust, I vowed silently. *Never again.*

She stirred, as if she'd heard the words. 'Callan,' she sighed softly, smiling.

'Anna,' I whispered.

She inched forward and brushed her lips over mine, her eyes still closed. 'I dreamed of you.'

'Of me?'

She gave a slight nod. 'It's not the first time.' She kissed me again. 'They're very good dreams.'

'If you tell me what they are, I'll make them come true.'

Her eyes blinked open slowly, then fixed on mine. 'I don't doubt that for a moment, Tall, Dark, and Looming.' Her hand came up, tracing over my cheek. 'What made you take me, Callan?'

I froze, but her voice was curious. 'You smell like spring,' I blurted.

She looked startled. 'Like *spring*?'

'Like ...' I tried to search for the right words. 'Your scent is blossoms, and hope, and rebirth, and ... I can't really explain it. But I knew that I wanted it, that I had to be near you, that I couldn't walk away.' I reached out and touched a lock of her hair. 'I know it was wrong, Anna. But everything about you feels *right*.'

'You needed me,' she said softly. She seemed to think about it for a moment. 'Alcide and Vesper did, too, in different ways. I suppose I don't mind,' she went on with another smile, 'because I think I need you right back.'

I stroked her cheek. 'That's lucky,' I said. 'I've been yours since the moment I saw you.'

Vesper sat up suddenly behind her, stretching. 'I slept,' he said in surprise.

I took in his dishevelled curls, the deep flush on his cheeks, the way his eyes were glowing.

I'd never seen him look *unguarded* before, and it took my breath away.

But I realised something else, too.

I'd gone to sleep cradled around Anna's back, with Alcide facing her. But Vesper was where Alcide had been, which meant that the warmth behind me and the heavy arm slung across my waist was –

Lips pressed to my shoulder, then brushed a line up my neck. 'Morning, Cal,' Alcide murmured.

'Cide,' I croaked.

His hand splayed over my stomach, then stroked the line of scales there. I lay beneath his touch, still with surprise.

I *couldn't* be this lucky, with my springtime human in front of me, Alcide behind, and Vesper's eyes hot on my skin. Anna had talked of *dreams*, and surely I was still asleep.

'Mmm.' Vesper watched Alcide's hand make its way up my chest to spread his fingers across my collarbone. 'If you promise to wake me up this way, I'll sleep more often.'

Alcide held me gently in place, his teeth scraping down the back of my neck. 'I think I like claiming,' he said softly.

'I think I like being claimed,' Anna murmured, her eyes a slit of light blue as she watched us.

Alcide's free hand trailed down my spine; my scales rippled beneath his touch. 'Do you want me to stop?'

I shook my head, trying to keep myself from trembling.

Alcide's hand quested further down. 'I've wanted to touch you like this since we were striplings,' he breathed. He pushed a knee between mine to open my body to his caress.

'Don't let me stop you now,' I grated out.

His fingers found my entrance and traced a circle around. Vesper had touched me there last night, seeming to read my desires from my mind, and it had lit a flame of craving inside me.

'You're wet for me,' Alcide whispered.

'I – *what*?' I said, pulling away.

His hand pressed against my collarbone, keeping me in place. 'Shh,' he murmured. 'I read about this in a history book. Roth males self-lubricate, just like females do. They just stopped teaching us about the way our bodies work.' He pressed inside; I groaned at the feeling, pulling Anna closer as he moved, stretching me. 'So hot, Cal,' Alcide breathed. 'You're so hot here.'

He withdrew. I protested wordlessly until the pressure returned, wider and flatter than his fingers, and *moving* against my sensitive skin as his scales fluttered.

'Oh, fuck, Cide,' I said, as I realised what he wanted.

'Yes or no, Cal?'

'Yes. Yes, yes, yes, *yes*.'

'I think he said yes,' Vesper said dryly, his hand sliding down to cup between Anna's legs.

Alcide's hand slid from my collarbone to my jaw; he turned my head back so that his lips could meet mine, and he pushed himself slowly inside me.

I gasped as I stretched around him, my body yielding beneath his gentle, shallow thrusts.

'Breathe, Callan,' Vesper said; Anna whimpered as his fingers worked. 'Breathe and relax. Alcide has you.' He dipped his head and whispered something to Anna.

'Oh, god, yes,' she said wildly. She reached down and found where my cock was rock hard and weeping precum, wrapping her fingers around me. 'Cal. Do you want this?'

'Mnph,' I groaned. 'Yes, very much yes.'

'Okay. My hand, my mouth, or –' she flushed '– would you like to be inside me?'

'I think you broke his skull computer,' Vesper said, when I didn't answer. 'Too many good choices.'

'Inside you,' I managed, as Alcide pushed in further, his pants harsh against the shell of my ear. 'Unless you're sore.'

Anna wriggled down, slinging a slender leg over my hip. 'I am sore, but I don't care.' Her hands worked between us, rolling a condom down over my length. She positioned me against her hot slickness, then wriggled until my head slid inside. 'Oh, goodness, those scales,' she breathed, closing her eyes. 'They're divine.'

I groaned as Alcide pushed deeper and my cock sank into Anna.

'Again, Alcide,' Vesper said softly. 'Callan's ready, aren't you?'

'Ah,' I managed.

Alcide thrust one more time, seating himself fully inside me. Anna squeaked as the movement pushed me deeper inside her, as deep as I could go. Alcide's scales rippled in rhythmic pulses, adding pressure in all the right places; my body clenched in response.

For a moment, we were still; I held my breath.

'*Breathe*, Callan,' Vesper growled. He rubbed a hand through his black curls. 'By the stars, look at you all.' He dipped his head to kiss Anna, swallowing her shocked moan. 'Alcide, you're flying this. Talk to each other.'

'Callan?' Alcide rasped, brushing a kiss over the top of my spine.

I closed my eyes, reaching for Anna's waist. 'Fuck me, Cide.'

Alcide withdrew, then pushed back in.

My cock echoed his movement inside Anna.

Anna whimpered.

'Again,' I demanded. 'Fuck, Alcide. *Again.*'

I gave myself over to my King, sensation coiling tight at the base of my spine as his control slipped and he drove deep inside, snapping his hips with a snarl. Anna cried out, her divine tightness clenching around me; Vesper's fingers quested back down and worked her bud in tight circles, his knuckles brushing my stomach. Alcide's hand found my hip and held me in place, finding a rhythm that flooded my body with heat as his scales rippled, stretching and pushing and pressing until every thought fled my mind.

'Let go, lodestar,' Vesper whispered to Anna.

Anna shook her head, her eyes squeezed shut. 'Don't want to,' she panted. Her hand found my chest; she splayed her fingers across my skin as she pressed her foot against my thigh, drawing me closer. 'Too good. Want it to last.'

'It will last,' Vesper murmured. 'This is your life now, brightness. Putting up with three obnoxious males and having more orgasms than you thought were possible.'

'The – other two – aren't obnoxious,' she gasped, but she evidently listened; she threw her head back as her body went taut and her core clenched tight and hot. 'Callan,' she moaned, her body gripping my cock in rhythmic pulses. '*Callan.*'

My name on her lips sent me over the edge; my fingers sank into her waist as I came, pressing my forehead against hers and emptying myself inside her. With Alcide inside me and Anna speared on my cock, I lost myself for a moment, lightheaded and floating as Alcide gave two punishing thrusts and filled me with hot spurts of release.

'Cal,' he whispered, and showered kisses on my shoulder. He made to withdraw, but I held his hip in place.

'Not yet,' I said, closing my eyes. 'Not yet. Why are good dreams always too quick?'

'So I should work on my stamina?' Alcide said dryly.

'No!' I protested, at the same time Vesper said: 'Yes, obviously. Both of you should.'

Anna laughed softly, then buried her face in my chest.

'Glad to see claiming hasn't changed you, Vesper.' Alcide took my chin and gave me a slow, drugging kiss. 'I'm going to pull out, Cal. I don't want to make you sore.'

'I rather think he'd *like* to be sore,' Vesper observed, watching my face flush.

I narrowed my eyes at him, but it was true. I wanted my body to remember every thrust, every grip of fingers, every nip and bite.

'What do we do now?' Anna said, her voice muffled.

Alcide ran his hand down my body, his fingers circling the base of my still-hard cock, my scales rippling against Anna's internal walls. 'We have a shower and we find whatever food Darius brought for us,' he answered, his fingers tightening, 'and then we do that again.'

VESPER

I'D BEEN INTERESTED TO see how Callan and Alcide would
navigate sharing Anna, but as it turned out, I had nothing to be
concerned about. They shared her with an almost strict equity,
swapping her between the two of them so naturally it was as if
they'd been doing it for years. I wondered how long it would be
before they realised they didn't have to swap – that they could
share her *together* – but thought that was rather Anna's business, and I wasn't about to offer the idea if she hadn't mentioned
it.

I'd assumed I'd be jealous, watching them, but the most con-
suming thing this body felt was desire. Even though the dark
matter chain was gone, I'd kept the same form, knowing they
liked it, but it was easier to wear now that I could eat again,
and it felt comfortable in a way that only my trueform had felt
before. Now that I could move properly, I liked the way my
limbs felt, the way my skin could touch and be touched, the

way my stomach tightened with hunger when I watched Anna and my Roth. My body was shinier, now; no matter how hard I tried, I wasn't able to contain the glow coming from beneath my skin. Anna glowed, too, the light at her core so bright I was surprised the Roth couldn't see it. Their lights glowed in response, reaching out to her, and to *me*, something I'd never seen before; I'd thought it was only starlings who glowed for their partners. I loved watching it, watching the way that the Roth would brighten the moment they stepped into the same space as Anna, lighting up the dark.

I assumed I'd have to wait a few weeks for them to remember I was there, but I didn't mind. I was more than two millennia old; a handful of days was nothing. Especially when I had so many delicious things to watch.

But I hadn't counted on my little lodestar.

I hadn't gone back to sleep with the others, just closed my eyes and rested my back against the head of Alcide's ridiculous bed. When a small body curled around me, I gave a contented purr, then froze when her hand began to stroke across my stomach and move down.

Anna didn't speak, just straddled my thighs and pulled the blanket to pool around her waist. I'd expected her to be tentative, but she was confident and sure, taking my rapidly-hardening cock in hand and stroking my shaft, then running the pad of her thumb over my sensitive head. The feeling was exquisite, and I gave myself fully into her control, letting her play with me however she pleased, her arousal dampening my thighs. She toyed with my cock until I was painfully hard and gasping beneath her, rocking slightly as she whimpered under her breath. I hadn't known this form could experience such strong sensations. I had to hold on with all my willpower as she bent and flicked her tongue over my head, then swallowed me further, her lips sliding back and forth over my shaft.

When she rolled a condom over me, positioned herself, and sank down, my throat released a sound I hadn't known my body was capable of making. I hadn't fucked another being in months, and I'd never known a human; the way her internal muscles clenched my cock as she moved sent pleasure striking up my spine. She was almost divinely hot, and my body responded, heating up beneath her until sweat beaded on her chest and trailed over the delicious swell of her breasts.

Her efforts eventually woke Alcide and Callan, who watched with heavy eyes as she rode me, then put some kind of oil to good use as they trapped their cocks between each other's hard bodies and left a glorious mess of sweat and cum smeared across both their stomachs. Anna barely noticed, too intent on her own pleasure as my fingers found her clit and I worked her as she moved, so I resolved to make them repeat the performance another time, when she could watch how beautiful they looked together, how strong and powerful and savage. I held on as Anna reached her climax, barely making it through her hot core milking my cock with strong pulses, then lifted her off me before the pleasure in my body concentrated at the base of my spine and I came. I was glad I did; my cum dissolved the strange plastic sheath – as I'd suspected it might – and I was left with a mess to clean up. I dissolved and re-formed to deal with it before I realised that Anna hadn't seen my trueform properly before, and I was greeted with a shocked gasp when I dropped back onto the bed.

'Um,' she said breathlessly. 'Vesper, was that ... Was that *you*?'

I nodded curtly, feeling uncomfortably vulnerable. It wasn't a feeling I was well-acquainted with – vulnerability was another emotion a thief couldn't afford – and I couldn't say I enjoyed it. 'I'm sorry if I frightened you.'

She shook her head. 'I was just surprised,' she said, reaching up to stroke my cheek. 'You're lovely. You look like the sky.'

I stared at her. 'Stars, Anna,' I said at last. 'I think I'm definitely in love with you.'

Callan snorted. 'You think?'

I raised my eyebrow at him, then voiced something I'd been thinking about but hadn't yet raised, not wanting to spoil the fun. 'How does this work when we get to Scytha? I'm assuming not all Roth will be as accepting of *this* –' I waved a hand to encompass the bed and the naked beings lying on it '– as the ones currently on board.'

Alcide took a deep breath. 'I've been considering that.' He rolled onto his back and stared at the ceiling, rubbing his temples. His hair was flowing in all directions and he was somehow *more* handsome like that, relaxed and messy and clearly well-fucked. 'The first option is that we hide it. It's the easiest way, and the way I like least. Anna is my Queen, Callan continues as my pilot, and Vesper pretends to be –'

'Your security advisor,' I said, nodding seriously.

Anna made a strangled sound into a pillow.

Alcide tried not to laugh. 'Certainly. That sounds ... believable. We pretend to be professional, and everything else is hidden.' He paused. 'Second – we *don't* hide it. We don't even try. We let Scytha deal with the fact that its King is ... is ...' He cast about. 'I don't even know the word for it. Our language doesn't even *have* one.'

'You don't need to explain yourself, Cide,' Anna said softly. '*You* are the only being who needs to be comfortable with it.

And if you need a word to be comfortable, then we can find you one.'

'I'll always need to explain myself,' Alcide said, his expression turning stiff. 'For everything I do.'

'Then explain once, and ignore the rest,' Callan said, wrapping his arms around Alcide's waist and nuzzling his neck. 'When you take the throne, announce it, and move on. A fresh start, Cide. A blank slate. A new Scytha with a new King, a new Queen, and two consorts. I don't want any official title – I want to be what I have always been.'

'More than what you have been, I hope,' Alcide said, drawing Callan's arms tighter.

'Personally, obviously.' Callan nipped Alcide's ear. 'But professionally, I want to stay your pilot. And Vesper … Well, that's up to Vesper.'

'I like the sound of consort,' I said, my lips tugging up at the corners. 'I don't need anything else. And if you announce it publicly, then I can stay close.'

'To Anna,' Callan said.

'To all of you,' I answered, and, deciding I'd had quite enough emotion for one day, dissolved into my trueform, closing my eyes and ignoring any further conversation.

After I'd left my parents and twin, I'd never stayed long enough around other beings to care about them; in fact, I'd deliberately done the opposite. You couldn't let yourself *care* for a being you were about to steal from, someone you were using as a diversion, as a scapegoat, someone you were setting up to take your fall. Being a thief didn't exactly mesh with having a family. I'd been ruthless, cutthroat, selfish, and I'd *liked* it that way. When I was hurting other people, there was no way *I* could get hurt, not really. I'd been in control, always.

But now Anna had her fingers wrapped around my heart, and I'd made myself vulnerable to her and our Roth. I wasn't used to the feeling, and I didn't like it, but my want for her, and for them – my *need* for her, and for them – outweighed the sense of danger. The tiny human had captured me, *vanquished* me, and now she and her horned abductors were changing the very fabric that made me *me*.

And I wasn't even sorry about it.

We stayed in Alcide's room for three days, leaving on the fourth morning after Bryn sent a terse cast saying he was sick of running the orb and would the King kindly come back and do his job. I'd gone back to Earth for more condoms – asking for directions from Anna this time – but Callan decided that it was too risky – not to mention impractical – for me to keep going back. We didn't have a doctor to offer Anna a more long-term solution, but we *did* have a generator, and, after a few failed attempts, Alcide managed to make something from a malleable plastic that did the same job, but with the benefit of not dissolving the moment my cum touched it. Anna whispered to me one night as the Roth lay sleeping that while she *did* want children, she wanted them in the future. My twin had always wanted younglings, but I thought it might take a while for the notion to sink in for me; I was happy to wait for Anna to come around to it.

Alcide and Callan returned to the bridge while Anna and I explored the ship, finding all kinds of interesting storerooms and empty quarters where I took every opportunity to slip my hands inside her clothes. My shy little lodestar had a hidden exhibitionist streak, and was more than happy to let me press her against the wall and lose myself between her legs with doors left precariously open and glass not opaqued, where anyone might walk in or notice what we were doing. I liked the time that was just for us, but Anna's light glowed most brightly when the four of us were together, even if all we were doing was eating or listening to Alcide talk about Roth history.

I liked that, too.

Bryn had hacked into the communications channels used by the Intergalactic Council, so we had up-to-date news on the peace summit. Even a full Earth month out from the summit starting date, delegates were beginning to arrive, though the cephalopod Queen was refusing permission to land on terra until the agreed date. Alcide thought it was a power play, but Anna pointed out how hard it was to plan a big event, and commented that the Queen might simply not have been *ready* to host hundreds of guests.

As we would be turning up without an invitation, it wasn't really an issue either way.

Bryn also kept Alcide updated with what was happening on Scytha. In no sense of the word could it be called *good*. In Alcide's absence, his cousin was beginning to consolidate power, starting with the military and a brutal, impressive coup, before moving onto the Dread Order – the Roth priesthood. The religious organisation was, surprisingly, a harder skull for Fiach Redhands to crack, obsessed as they were with the notion of divine order and Alcide being the gods' representative made flesh. The fact that he'd killed his father only *strengthened* his claim; apparently Roth kings had a long history of impatience with their patriarchs and a penchant for taking the throne in interesting and violent ways. It was seen not as a disruption of divine order, but rather an emphasis of it; the gods, the priests argued, always had a plan, and sometimes that meant sons murdering their fathers over a family lunch. Fiach had a few pet priests who were cobbling together an argument that the gods preferred him, but the Dread Order as a whole were stubbornly resisting that notion. Alcide, they were arguing, was the gods' weapon, their tool, and he was a shining light representing a new dawn; Darius was supporting that notion by sending the priesthood curated updates emphasising Alcide's kingly nature and aptitude for ruling.

'We can play on that,' I said musingly, having turned off a rather lengthy sermon cast we were listening to one morning in the control room. 'If they think Cide is the shining light of a new era, we can dress him accordingly.'

Callan blinked at me. 'Like the Sun King,' he murmured. 'A king from a few millennia ago,' he went on, when I cocked an eyebrow in question. 'You might remember him. His reign coincided with Scytha becoming a Category-2 planet, and he oversaw an explosion of new technology and exploration of our galaxy.'

'Perfect,' I said, though I flicked his shoulder in punishment for the *you might remember him* comment. 'Did he do anything particularly awful?'

Callan frowned. 'Not that I remember,' he said. 'He had three consorts and a number of children. He's one of our few kings who managed to die of old age.'

I tapped my bottom lip with my finger. Callan tracked the motion, his eyes narrowing. I pretended not to notice. 'What did he wear?'

'What do you mean?'

'If he was called *the Sun King*, what did he wear?'

'Not golden armour,' Callan said with a snort, his hand finding my hip. 'Though the tradition of gilding our horns comes from him.'

'We can work with that.' I turned to face him, winding an arm behind his back and bringing him closer. 'We can gild Alcide's horns, and the pommel of his sword, and keep the golden makeup –'

'*War paint*,' Callan growled, pressing his hips forward so I could feel his growing hardness against my thigh.

'War paint, makeup,' I said airily, waving a hand. I slipped that same hand between us and found his cock, gripping it hard, his scales undulating against my palm. 'It's all the same. As long as it's noticeable.'

'We set Cide up as the Sun King come again,' Callan said, thrusting into my hand. 'Do you know, I think the old king even had red hair.'

I turned him around roughly, unfastening his uniform to the waist and pulling it down, baring his muscular ass, trying to keep my breath steady at the sight. I took his hard cock in one hand and pressed into him with two fingers from the other, finding him slippery and ready for me. It was odd that the Roth were so opposed to male-male couplings when their body was seemingly made for it, but I didn't comment. I dissolved my clothing and guided my cock inside him, feeding it inch by slow inch, until the big pilot was panting and begging beneath me, arching his back as he leaned forward carefully on the control panel.

I purred approvingly at him, pleased and proud at how swiftly he'd thrown aside the shame he'd been raised with to embrace what he wanted. That he was desperately in love with Anna was clear; that he'd *always* been desperately in love with Alcide was even clearer. I had no idea what he felt for me, but I was happy to take his body when he offered it. I thickened my cock, stretching him slightly, and listened with pleasure at the resulting low growl rumbling from his chest and the increase of slick in his hot passage. I hooked one forearm over his chest, encouraging him to rest against me, and licked up the column of his neck before my other hand wrapped around his throbbing cock.

I pumped until hot cum splashed onto the floor to settle in a pool, his ass clenching around me as he came. I gave two hard, punishing thrusts, and emptied myself inside him, my eyes closing as my vision went white. I liked that I could fill him, liked draining myself inside his hard, strong body. There was something primal about it, something instinctual, as if through the act Callan became somehow *mine* in the same way that Anna was.

It didn't help that I could also imagine Alcide under my hands, imagine myself stretching him, opening him up, taking him in the same way. He'd be different; it would be a battle for dominance. Callan was used to being the tallest, the strongest, and his surrender was almost an act of defiance; it would be harder for Alcide, whose entire life was a constant fight for control.

I turned Callan's face to mine and kissed him. He returned it passionately, cupping my cheek with a tenderness I hadn't expected. 'I like this,' he said.

'I'm not Alcide,' I answered.

He stilled, then pulled himself off me, grimacing. 'Fuck, Vesper.'

'I just –'

'I *know* you're not Alcide,' he said fiercely. 'I can tell the fucking difference, starling. Dread gods forbid anyone has *feelings* around you.' He pulled his uniform back over his shoulders and fastened it up.

'Callan –'

'I have work to do,' he said dismissively. 'Thanks for the orgasm, asshole. You can see yourself out.'

'Cal, I'm –'

He held up a hand. 'I don't want to hear it, Vesper. Get out.'

I frowned and dissolved, reforming in Alcide's bedroom.

Anna was on the bed, reading. She started when I dropped down beside her, but managed not to shriek.

She was learning quickly.

She studied me for a moment. 'You look sad.'

I poked at my face. 'Is that what this is?'

She bit her lip. 'What happened?'

My brow creased. 'I think I was an asshole.'

'Vesper, sweetness, you're going to have to be more specific. You're *always* an asshole.'

I cleared my throat and poked her in the ribs, an action that made her squirm. 'I was an asshole to Callan.'

She touched my cheek. 'And now you feel bad.'

'Is that normal?'

She gave a soft chuckle. 'Yes, Vesper. It's normal. You upset someone you care about.'

'How do I make it stop?'

She put the book aside. 'You need to make up. Make him happy again.'

'Anna, I'm not in the business of making beings *happy*. Rather the opposite, in fact.'

'Callan isn't *just* a being. He's part of your family. Part of *our* family.' Anna rubbed her chest, over her heart. 'I know who you are, Vesper. I'd never ask you to change. But I love Callan, and I love you, and I think you like each other, and there's a good chance that with time, that *liking* will turn into something deeper, if it hasn't already. He's not a mark. He's not someone you're playing, not someone you'll leave behind. He's your *future*, Vesper. If I'm your lodestar, then Callan and Alcide are your moons. They're part of your night sky. You need to start treating them like they matter. Like they bring you just as much light.'

I swallowed, then pulled her into my arms. 'Were you always this wise?'

She laughed and kissed me; I felt something swell inside my chest; it might have been joy. 'I'm not wise. I just read a lot of books.'

CALLAN

I STARED DOWN AT Natare, uneasy. I wasn't used to seeing so much water; Scytha was largely a land-locked planet. Our seas and lakes were small and dead, which was part of the reason our species had been so fixed on expansion. If we couldn't get help cleaning our water and nourishing our soil, Scytha would be nothing but dust in two Roth lifetimes.

It was just another reason that this *had* to work.

'Ready?' Alcide murmured.

I turned to take him in, my breath catching. He was magnificent, his shoulders rolled back and his chin set defiantly high. His horns were gilded, his eyes lined with gold, and there was gold shimmer dusted over his high cheekbones and lips. Vesper had stolen more cloth-of-gold from somewhere, and I'd sewn lines of it onto his black jacket, emphasising the breadth of his chest and the graceful lines of his arms, but his unruly red hair made the royal ensemble unmistakably and wholly *Alcide*.

'My King,' I managed.

'Don't start that,' he said, his voice low. His eyes shone as he looked at me. 'You look incredible, Cal. My heart.'

I licked my lips, ruining Anna's careful work. I was dusted in gold, too, and Anna had painted swirls of gilt up my horns. Vesper's cheekbones and lips glimmered, matching ours, and he'd fashioned himself an Earth-style suit of a black darker than the deepest space. He'd stolen Anna a dress, jumping all the way back to Earth to find a gown made entirely of golden sequins. Its neckline fell almost to her navel, though its hem swept the floor and its sleeves stretched to her wrists, the overall cut demure but for that stretch of lovely, smooth skin – a stretch I could barely tear my eyes from. It didn't matter how many times I'd seen her naked now, how many times she'd impaled herself on my cock and ridden me to climax – I still couldn't get enough. Of her, of Alcide – or, if I was honest with myself, of Vesper, who hadn't touched me since the day I'd snapped at him on the bridge. It had been weeks of us being stilted, awkward, and though we'd still worked together to shatter Anna and Alcide to a million pieces more times than I could count, he didn't reach for me, and I'd had to hold myself back from reaching for him. Anna had huffed at me, exasperated, but I wasn't going to make myself vulnerable if the starling wasn't willing to bother.

It hurt more than I cared to admit.

Anna squeezed my bicep. 'You look so handsome, Cal.' She took in her three males with obvious pride. 'You all look so handsome.'

'You look like a star, Anna,' Alcide said thickly. He touched her hair gently; she'd pulled it back into some deceptively simple twist and fixed it with a pin lined with champagne-coloured diamonds, another *find* of Vesper's, one that I suspected was worth rather more than the dress. In place of Alcide's gilded horns, she had a circlet nestled in her fair hair, adjusted so that it was barely visible; *the dress should say enough*, Anna had commented wryly.

'You have your weapons, don't you, Anna?' I said, suddenly anxious, despite the fact I'd strapped them to her lovely thighs myself.

'Yes, Cal,' she said patiently. 'I have a knife on one leg, a stungun on the other, and both my pin and my circlet can be used for stabbing. I will stay close to you or Vesper at all times. I won't go anywhere by myself.' She squeezed me again. 'It will be fine.'

I didn't share her confidence, but I kissed her hair, then smoothed it down. 'I know, my Queen.'

She snorted and poked me in the ribs. 'Nope on that,' she muttered. 'Not from you.'

Vesper's eyes had been closed; he opened them again, the glow so bright it was almost painful. 'There are a lot of beings down there,' he announced. 'Mostly different cephalopod and decabrachia species, but there are a fair few Tirians, too. The Darnagh and the Kjidja have arrived, though I can't see any Levros yet – they are famously always late.' His brow creased. 'There's at least one of my kind, too. There should be more, but they could be resting after the jump.' He closed his eyes again. 'I can see an Illisean ship, and a cruiser from Sector 9 next to it, which I assume would have carried a mixed contingent.'

Anna gaped at him. 'How do you know all that?'

Vesper tugged her into his side without opening his eyes. 'My parents are politicians, lodestar. Criminality runs in the family. Theirs is just ... legalised.'

'Bryn, can you bring the cast up?' Alcide said over his shoulder.

The engineer grunted his assent, and a moment later we could all see what Vesper had observed. A large pavilion had been erected before the grounds of the cephalopod Queen's terra palace, and everything within it was a stream of movement as delegates presented themselves before the Queen's huge golden throne. We could see her, a handsome blonde with storm-blue eyes, wrapped in a short tunic of a regal navy which left her eight thick limbs free to move. I didn't know much about the Enterocti species, but I knew their limbs changed colour; the Queen's were currently a calm sea-green.

Alcide took a deep breath. 'Is everything ready, Bryn?'

'Everything is ready, my King.'

'Tell me again.'

Bryn gave a loud, pointed sigh. We'd been through the plan so many times I could have recited it in my sleep, but that was the point. 'Vesper jumps you down, and we unveil the ship's shields,' he said patiently. 'We play the cast you made. You deactivate your personal sight shields. You and Anna bow to the cephalopod Queen. They are so moved by your speech, so struck by the beauty of our little Queen, that they let you take part in the summit and they promise you an army to take back Scytha. The coup is successful and you reign as King for three thousand years.'

'You added that last part,' Alcide muttered. He straightened his jacket for the seventh time. 'And if things turn nasty?'

Bryn swallowed. 'We shield the ship. Vesper gets Anna back to the orb. We fly away.'

Anna's lips twisted. 'I still think –'

Alcide took her hand. 'I'm not changing my mind, Anna.'

I exchanged a look with Vesper. He'd already agreed to take Alcide, too. I'd stay behind and cause as much disruption as possible as a distraction while the orb escaped. We all had military-grade personal shield activators nestled somewhere in our clothing, but I also had every kind of grenade I could find lining the underside of my jacket hem.

If they tried to hurt Alcide or Anna, I'd use every single one of them.

I'd tried to convince Alcide to stay on the ship, to make a livecast instead, but he'd argued that if they didn't want to listen, they could simply take out the entire orb, which would mean Bryn and the rest of the crew's lives, too. Divided, we gave them an extra target; Alcide suspected they would try to capture him alive if it came to that, which might give the ship – and everyone on it – the chance to escape.

It made sense. I hated it, but it made sense. And it was quintessentially *Alcide*. He wouldn't risk his crew just so he could stay in relative safety.

But it meant the three beings I loved most in the universe would be in danger, and that made me ... twitchy.

Alcide exhaled slowly. 'Right,' he said tersely. 'Let's go.' He took Anna into his arms and held out a hand to me. I threaded my fingers through his, bringing his hand to my lips. Vesper draped his arms around us all and grinned, the space around us beginning to darken.

'This is an intensely unadvisable idea,' he said cheerfully. 'I love it.'

The darkness thickened, and Vesper made the jump.

We'd practised it a few times, so we were all ready for the feeling. It seemed to affect Anna more than us; though I didn't strictly *enjoy* the sensation of being ripped apart and being put back together again, it didn't give me the nausea and vertigo

Anna experienced. When Vesper re-formed us on the ground, Anna staggered; three sets of hands shot out to catch her.

'Thanks,' she said weakly, swallowing determinedly. She took a deep breath in – the air was laced with salt and the scent of kelp – and adjusted her skirt. Vesper smoothed an escaped lock of blonde hair back into place; I gave her waist a tiny squeeze before my hand fell to the antimatter gun at my hip.

'I smell something sweet,' Anna murmured. 'Oh, look at those gorgeous lilies.'

I could hear the ocean from somewhere nearby, and, much louder, the sound of chatter. Vesper's woodsmoke scent swirled around us, making sure Anna would be able to understand the conversations of the summit's guests.

'We're ready, Bryn,' Alcide said into his wrist screen.

The sight shield dropped from the orb ship.

I tensed.

For a long, incredible moment, the chatter continued unabated. In that moment, I could imagine we were here like all the other beings: here to debate the issue of intergalactic peace, and how we might achieve it. That we might be welcomed, our voices heard, our ideas considered. The moment was long enough that – impossibly – my tight muscles began to unwind.

Then a low, savage growl ripped through the chatter.

'Oh, green gods,' someone said.

A shriek came from nearby as the cast of Alcide appeared on the hull of our ship.

'Her majesty Orla, third of her name, most excellent Queen of Natare, we greet you.' Alcide's deep, pleasant voice rippled across the crowd. 'I am Alcide Severson, King of Scytha.'

A burst of uneasy chatter met that announcement; the news of the old King's death seemed to be a surprise to most of the beings in attendance.

'We were not invited to this peace summit, and I acknowledge the reasoning behind this. As Roth, we are part of the problem; perhaps even the largest part. We have been focused on expansion at the cost of other planets and other species, and also at the cost of our own home. We have made the skies unsafe.'

The chatter fell to a low rumble.

'My royal father is dead, and Scytha enters a new chapter. The burden of kingship has fallen on my shoulders, but I will not mimic the King who came before me. I look to Scytha's future, and to learning from her past. Scytha is dying; the Roth diminished. I stand on a precipice. Should the Roth perish, so be it. But I am asking for your help in protecting my people, in protecting mother Scytha, in beginning a new chapter for our world. I know, given the Roth's recent history, this is asking much. I come before you to ask it anyway.'

I saw a slight shudder in the air as Bryn deactivated our personal sight shields and we were revealed to the delegates around us.

A deathly silence fell over the pavilion.

Alcide lifted his chin, then tucked Anna's arm securely through his. 'With the permission of the delegates, I would come before you to plead my case,' he said. His voice was quiet, but it carried regardless. 'My Queen and I seek your ears, and seek your mercy. We wish to seek peace; we wish for Scytha to take its proper place within our universe. We seek to sign the Pact.'

A blonde cephalopod male in his trueform pushed through the crowd, a growl rumbling incessantly from his chest. He was tall, as tall as me, and his chest was just as broad, wrapped in a high-collared military-style jacket that stretched over his massive shoulders. His limbs were a bright red that promised pain, and his fangs were bared over his full lip in a savage snarl.

'Prince Morgan Eventide,' Alcide said calmly.

'Your ship is rather heavily armed for a king come to seek our *mercy*,' the male growled.

Alcide gave a graceful half-shrug. 'We were quite certain you would kill us on sight,' he said. 'The weapons are a precaution.'

'Tell your pilot to stand down, and we might not.'

A Tirian female made her way to stand beside him. Willowy and slender like most of her species, she brushed a strand of dark hair, escaped from a net of sea pearls, from her pupil-less eyes. 'My officers are checking the truth of your claims, Alcide King,' she said. 'It seems the Roth are rather preoccupied at present.'

Alcide bowed his head in agreement. 'My cousin, Fiach, has seized the opportunity of my father's death to consolidate his own power. He has met with some success in the military, but some resistance from the priesthood of the Dread Order.'

She gazed upwards. 'And you have but a single ship?'

Alcide lifted his chin. 'That is correct, Captain.'

The cephalopod prince snorted. 'So you would beg us for support to bolster your claim to the throne,' he said, unimpressed. 'Was what you said about a *new chapter* just pretty words?'

'I meant every one,' Alcide answered softly.

The Tirian Captain's gaze slid to Anna. 'Your consort is human,' she said, her tone tinged with surprise.

I bristled.

'*Queen*, not consort,' Alcide corrected. 'And yes.'

Morgan's eyes went to Vesper for the first time. To my surprise, the cephalopod paled, his mouth parting in shock. 'Fuck,' he said.

I tapped my translator, thinking I must have misheard, but it beeped, telling me it was charged and working properly.

'Ah,' he said, not taking his eyes off the starling. 'I ... Ah. Cy?' he said, his voice strained.

The most beautiful humanoid being I'd ever seen appeared at Morgan's side and touched his shoulder. He was grey-eyed and red-haired, and too perfect to be completely organic; I'd heard of Machina, where flesh was combined with mechanics and systems, but I didn't think cyborgs left their home planet.

'Fuck me,' he breathed, his eyes falling on Vesper.

'Thank you for the offer,' Vesper said politely, 'but my hands are already rather full.'

Morgan let out a sharp bark of laughter. 'This *has* to be the sibling.'

'All available evidence would strongly support your hypothesis,' the cyborg answered tightly.

Morgan crossed his arms. 'And what the everloving *fuck* is Aster's twin doing with the Roth King?'

'You know Aster?' Vesper said warily.

Morgan gave a wide, dangerous grin. 'In *every* sense, starling.'

Vesper stared at them. 'Stars. You're his –'

'Yes,' Morgan interrupted. 'We are. Are you going to come and see him?'

Vesper blinked, looking suddenly unsure.

Anna reached over and tugged his sleeve. 'Of course you have to see him, Vesper!' she hissed.

Vesper took a tentative step forward. I echoed it, my hand still hovering over the weapon at my hip.

Morgan surged towards me. '*Not you,*' he snarled.

Vesper dissolved into his trueform in a heartbeat, wrapping me in darkness and jumping me out of Morgan's way. '*Mine,*' he snarled back at the cephalopod prince as we reformed, his voice echoing across the pavilion. He stepped in front of Alcide, Anna, *and* me, his arms spread at his sides to shield us. 'He's *mine*. They're *all* mine. You don't *touch* them.'

My throat narrowed with some strong emotion before Morgan Eventide threw his head back and roared with laughter. He elbowed the cyborg.

'Did you ever suspect we ended up with the *calm* one?' he chuckled.

Cy cocked his head, studying Vesper. 'It's not something I considered.'

Another Tirian approached. 'Captain –' they began, before trailing off.

'Oh, dread gods,' I murmured.

Because he had fair hair and moss-green eyes, and his pretty face was uncomfortably *familiar*.

Willow cleared his throat. 'Ah,' he said. 'Anna. How are you?'

Anna's face broke into a wide, delighted smile. 'Willow!'

Willow looked nervously backwards. 'Ah,' he said again. 'Ashton, before you –'

A feral snarl rippled through the air, louder even than Morgan's had been. Another Tirian – one with chestnut hair and bristling with weapons – pulled Willow behind him, and I found myself suddenly facing a Tirian gun.

'*You,*' the warrior snarled. '*You're the ones who took him.*'

'Ashton, can you just –'

'No, I can't *just,*' the male snapped at Willow. 'They *took you,* Will.' He pointed his gun at me. 'I demand reparation.'

'What is Ash banging on about?' a voice came from behind them.

Anna went white. 'No,' she whispered.

A human female pushed her way to the front, elbowing the snarling Tirian male in the ribs and giving a convincing, wordless snarl right back. Her canines were sharper than Anna's, and her eyes were glowing a striking blue-green. 'Put your gun down, you –' she broke off suddenly when she saw Anna, her mouth falling open in shock. 'Mother-licking mud cake,' she said, astonished. '*Anna*?'

Anna gave a small, awkward wave, her body tight with tension. 'Hey, Maeve.'

Maeve snapped her mouth shut. 'What in the *fuck*?'

The Tirian Captain frowned. 'Maeve McCarthy? Explain.'

Maeve gestured at Anna. 'Anna is my friend. My friend who should very much be safely on Earth right now.'

There was another growl; it was coming from Alcide.

'Okay, I have had *enough* of people growling today,' Maeve grated out. She strode forward and hugged Anna tightly. 'Anna, I'm loving this whole unexpected reunion thing, but what the *fuck* is going on? Why is half of Australia suddenly on Natare?'

Anna returned Maeve's hug, but her expression was tight. 'It's a long story. This is not going the way we expected.'

'*Anna*?' Another female voice rose in a shriek.

'Oh, fucking save me, she's going to go into labour over this,' Maeve muttered.

A lovely human with a rounded, pregnant belly walked up to the group with difficulty, her cheeks pink with exertion. I stared, but it wasn't at her – on her arm was a humanoid who looked astonishingly similar to someone I knew.

'Tessa?' Anna whispered, her eyes impossibly wide, but she wasn't the only one surprised.

Vesper made a strangled sound.

The pregnant human stared at him, then looked at the man on her arm. 'Um,' she said. 'Aster?'

The male – *Aster* – didn't answer. His black brows lowered. 'I didn't expect to see you here, Vesper.'

'I didn't expect to be here,' Vesper answered tightly.

The human female looked from one starling to the other, then elbowed Aster hard in the ribs. 'You said you hadn't seen him in the fles – in the *starlight* – for *one hundred and seventy years*, Aster. Is that the best you can do?'

'Look at him, Tessa. *He stole my face.*'

The female – Tessa – sniffed. 'No, he didn't. Your eyes are wider, your jaw is squarer, and his curls are tighter. It's not *your* face – it's the face of your *twin*.' She wrinkled her nose. 'Quite frankly, Aster, you're prettier.'

Vesper frowned; Anna patted his arm. *It's not true*, she mouthed.

'Fine.' Aster paused. 'Twin,' he said politely in greeting.

'Twin,' Vesper rejoined.

'Oh, for fuck's sake,' Tessa muttered.

'Aster is right,' Vesper said. 'I did steal the face.' He studied Aster thoughtfully. 'You've made a few changes.'

Anna blinked. 'You can do that?'

Vesper broke off his staring contest with Aster to grin down at her. 'Why, lodestar?' he said playfully. 'Do you have some requests?'

She patted his arm. 'You're perfect as you are.' She pulled away from him and went to Tessa, eyeing Aster warily. Tessa's face broke into a wide smile and she threw her arms around Anna, squeezing tightly.

'Goodness, Tessa,' Anna murmured, her eyes shining with tears. 'I didn't know if I'd ever see you again. And now I can't even hug you properly. There's something in the way.'

Tessa snorted, and adjusted Anna's arms to wrap around her shoulders. 'No one tells you how bloody inconvenient the belly is,' she said. 'Or maybe they do, and no one listens. I can't wear normal clothes, can't see my feet half the time, can't move without bumping into something.' She winced. 'And the larvae seems to like sleeping on my bladder, which is astonishingly inconvenient.'

'Larvae?' Anna's eyes darted to Morgan. 'So ...?'

Tessa nodded. 'It's his,' she said grumpily, though the cephalopod all but puffed up with pride. 'Although Aster is just as responsible.'

Maeve, who had been listening to everything with an increasingly incredulous look on her face, held up her hand. Willow and Ashton stilled immediately, as if she was their commander; the dark-haired Tirian Captain rolled her eyes, though the corners of her lips were tugging up as if she couldn't quite repress a smile. 'There's a lot happening here,' Maeve said, her eyes flicking from Tessa to Anna. 'I think we should understand what's going on, shouldn't we?' She turned to Morgan. 'Is there somewhere we can go to talk?'

ANNA

When someone says *Can we go somewhere to talk*, you'd imagine that to mean a comfy couch in a quiet room, possibly accompanied by a pot of tea and a plate of biscuits, and I was certain that was what Maeve had in mind. But it turned out that our audience – the summit guests – had more curiosity than we'd expected, and when we tried to leave to talk, a sizeable number of them came with us. The Nataran Queen took charge, dismissing all but the other Intergalactic Council members, who I gathered were rather less easy to get rid of, but my dream of tea and biscuits were dashed when we were led under armed guard to a room with tiered seats that vaguely resembled an Earth courtroom, complete with alien microphones, screens, and myriad translation devices. Instead of a casual conversation between some humans far from home, we were carefully watched by a half-humanoid, half-octopus queen; a space-elf with thorns growing along her cheekbones and jaw, and a badge of rank pinned to her shimmering dress; a humanoid being with a two-tufted, prehensile tail; a floating cloud of darkspace with glowing, golden eyes; a bipedal being with claws tipping their fingers and slanted eyes that could only be described as *feline*; and a being that looked remarkably like Callan and Alcide did when they were armoured, only without the horns, their scales a riotous shimmer of green and silver.

Our partners came too, of course, so in the end, the room was rather cosy, even if it was only because it felt so full. It was soon apparent that instead of a *talk*, we humans would be giving some kind of formal *report*, presumably to explain to the Council members what the heck we were doing there.

When a cephalopod in a navy-blue uniform offered me a strong-smelling drink that clearly contained some type of alcohol, I took it.

Morgan had shifted back into his humanoid body, but his mother didn't bother. She occupied a seat at the head of the ringed chairs, her presence quiet and commanding, and every inch the queen. She was beautiful, with sea-blue eyes and strong features, her blonde waves reaching below her waist to where her limbs rested, flickering between sea-green and an anxious burnt orange.

'Tessa, little starfish,' she said without preamble, her voice deep and rich like a singer, 'would you like to begin?'

Tessa was settled next to the Queen, and one of the cephalopod's limbs curled protectively around the back of Tessa's chair, offering anyone watching a clear message: *Tessa belongs with us now*. Morgan and Aster stood behind, shoulder to shoulder, and Cy sat on Tessa's other side, nervously eyeing the screens around the room, which were clearly recording.

Tessa rubbed her hand over the swell of her stomach. Morgan, Aster, and Cy watched the movement, each with a slightly different expression: Morgan's was intense and possessive, Aster's relaxed and indulgent, and Cy's warm and full of love. She reached back blindly; her hand was taken up by Aster, and Morgan bent to press a kiss to her palm, while Cy linked his fingers through her free hand.

It was the kind of adoration that six months ago would have made my heart hurt. As it was, Alcide took up my hand and ran his thumb over my heartline; Callan hooked his boot between my legs and rested his palm on my knee; and Vesper bent to rub his cheek against my hair, his warmth against my back, a silent purr rumbling through his body.

I bit my lip to hide a smile.

'I was at Advena,' Tessa began. 'A club – a bar – in Australia, the country on Earth that I come from. I hadn't been out in a while, and Maeve convinced me that it was time to let loose a little.' She threw Maeve a smile. 'I was having a drink when a man with glowing golden eyes came over to talk to me.'

Aster's lips curled up.

Tessa continued her story, flushing when she talked about taking Aster home, about Morgan and Cy bursting into her apartment. She described how incredulous she'd been, and how the three had worked to convince her to go with them – all in a matter of hours. She talked through how she'd refused at first, and sent them away, but in the few short minutes they'd been gone, she'd realised how empty her apartment felt, and how *wrong* it was to be without them. When Aster came back with a screen Cy had set up so they could keep in contact across galaxies, Tessa had changed her mind and left with him.

Morgan rumbled wordlessly at that.

Tessa described her first few weeks on Morgan's ship, and how they'd been snared by a Roth scuttler. Her voice caught when she detailed Aster jumping out of the ship and flaring supernova to save them; there was a collective shift as Maeve coughed a laugh.

'Ash thought that was you,' she said.

'You almost blinded Maeve,' a silver-haired Tirian female said to Aster, her soft voice reproachful.

'He didn't have much of a choice,' Morgan growled.

The Tirian warrior standing behind Maeve with his hair braided back into a topknot growled wordlessly back.

'Oh, for – *stop that*,' Maeve snapped. 'If I wanted to be in a room full of males comparing dicks then I would have stayed on Earth.'

Tessa smirked, then finished her story quickly, settling back in her chair when she was done.

She'd skipped over one part, though.

'And you got pregnant on the way?' I asked quietly, when a natural silence settled over the room.

'It was an accident,' she said, a blush colouring her cheeks. 'We thought we were being safe, but Aster ...' She chewed her lip and looked up at him.

Aster bent to kiss her brow, then looked across the room at his twin. 'Cy built organic blockers across her fallopian tubes,' he said. 'But starling ... body matter –' he cleared his throat '– heals humans. Well, mine does Tessa, anyway. Even the parts of her that aren't broken. So be careful,' he continued, his eyes falling on me. 'The human body seems to be quite ... receptive ... to other species.'

At this, the being with the fangs and the interesting tail – '*Darnagh*,' Vesper whispered to me – sat up straighter in their seat. 'Cross-species mating?'

Aster gave a half-shrug. 'It's not unheard of, obviously – your own species is the product of it, Rellyn. Cy ran some tests, which seemed to conclude that humans could bear the offspring of most known humanoid life forms. We've sent the results to a specialist lab in Sector 4, and they're running more tests as we speak.'

Rellyn's tail whipped back and forth behind their chair as they brought a projection of Earth up into the air before them, flicking through a stream of shimmering text. 'I suppose that is why the Roth *also* took a human,' they added, their voice coloured with disdain. 'We know your kind is dying.' They paused as they took in some of the information, a frown furrowing their brow; I wondered what they were reading, and what they'd found that made them frown.

'This was not something we were aware of until this moment,' Alcide said calmly. 'And it is not a pressing concern. In fact, we have not discussed it.'

Rellyn's tail gave an agitated jerk. 'As if the Roth *discuss*,' they hissed.

The green scaled being grunted in agreement.

'They do now,' Alcide said, unfazed. 'Vesper took Anna home to Earth. She chose to return to us. She is loved by us, *treasured* by us. And she will continue to be so, whether she chooses to have bairnlings or not.'

The Tirian Captain nodded. 'You are a family,' she said approvingly. She turned to regard Maeve. 'This seems a good place for you to begin, Maeve McCarthy.'

'I fucking hate public speaking,' Maeve grumbled, but began.

Maeve spoke about her worry when Tessa went missing, and of her incredulity at the note Tessa left behind. She spoke of Tessa's cousin, Rian, and how he'd tried to help, but she'd been so desperate that when a stranger – Elswyth – had told her a preposterous story about *beings* and *peace summits*, she'd left Advena with her. She smiled like a cat when she recounted her bond with Elswyth, and meeting the two males, the doctor, Willow, and the warrior, Ashton.

'I don't think we need *that* much detail,' the cephalopod Queen interrupted, when Maeve began straying into her typical overshare.

Maeve grinned over her shoulder as the silver-haired Elswyth blushed bright green. '*Need?* No. Worth it, though.'

The Tirian Captain cleared her throat.

'Right, the very important story I'm telling in the super-formal alien courtroom,' Maeve said, and continued, unruffled, with how Willow was stolen from the peacekeeping ship.

Both Callan and Alcide straightened; I did, too, knowing they'd stolen him because *I* needed help. The tension in the room rose as the big Tirian male began growling without pause for breath.

Maeve smacked him on the thigh with a dull *thunk*. 'For fuck's sake, Ash, give it a rest, would you? We all know you're terrifyingly big and muscly and full of sperm or whatever the fuck it is that males are trying to say through all the bullshit posturing they do. They took Willow to save *Anna*, you pillock, *and* they gave him back. You slayed the dragon, got the magical maiden *and* her wife *and* your boyfriend, and the Captain is considering giving you a nice shiny medal for how stupid you were. Oops,' she went on, sounding completely unrepentant as the Tirian Captain shot her a glare. 'Sorry, ma'am. It just slipped out. I'd make a fucking awful spy.'

The Captain rolled her eyes. 'Then let me finish up,' she said, her voice full of a steely command that made even Maeve blink and pay attention. 'You owe my First Guard a debt, Alcide King. While you were busy shooting at your father's ship, he found a way on board and took out the old King's shields for you.'

'The Pod,' Callan breathed in surprise. 'That's what the Pod was doing during the fight. That was *you*.'

'That was me,' the Tirian warrior growled.

Alcide stood. 'Then we certainly owe you a debt,' he said, and gave Ashton a deep bow. 'You saved me, and my mates. You saved Scytha. You have my deepest thanks. What will you ask of me in return?'

The Tirian's brows creased in confusion. 'I –' he began, staring at Alcide. His pupiless hazel eyes turned to his Captain. 'Roth don't say *thank you*.'

The Captain was staring at Alcide too, her expression calculating. 'They certainly never have before,' she muttered. 'It seems this really is something else entirely.' Her lips pursed. 'What exactly have you come here for, Alcide King?'

I put my hand on the small of his back. He looked down at me, his eyes softening for a moment before they grew determined once more. He took my hand in his.

'We've come to claim our future,' he said.

'I can't believe we're alive,' I said blankly.

Alcide collapsed onto the edge of his bed. We'd come back up to the orb ship to wait on the Council's decision after Alcide said politely that we wouldn't trespass on the cephalopod Queen's hospitality when we hadn't technically been invited to the summit. The Queen had looked surprised – then pleased – by that, but had invited me to return, saying that Tessa would be glad of the extra human company. 'I was sure that Tirian was going to riddle me with holes. He's terrifying. *Your friend* is terrifying,' he added, his eyes on me; I assumed he meant Maeve.

And really, I had no answer to that but *yes*. She'd always been that way, but her time with the Tirians had honed her sharper, as if she'd finally become fully *herself*.

'You weren't in any danger,' Vesper said airily, waving his hand in dismissal. 'I would have gotten you out before anything interesting happened.'

'*Mine*,' Callan said thickly, his eyes darkening as they fell on Vesper. '*He's mine. They're all mine*. That's what you said.' He stepped forward, closer to the starling. 'Did you mean it?'

I held my breath as Vesper's gaze locked on our pilot, his eyes blazing gold. I knew that things hadn't been right between them for a few weeks; Vesper wasn't good at apologies, and it seemed Callan was having trouble overcoming his frustration.

'Of course I meant it,' Vesper answered, his brows drawing together. 'Why would you think –'

Callan strode forward and took Vesper's face in his hands, dragging him up for a fierce kiss.

'Oh,' I sighed, my insides melting as I watched them. Alcide pulled me down into his lap, nuzzling at my neck as Callan and Vesper's kiss softened, then slowed. Vesper cradled Callan's face, stroking his fingers over our pilot's cheekbones, tracing his jaw.

'*Oh*,' Alcide echoed beside me, going still as Callan returned the caresses, his hands tangling in Vesper's dark curls.

'Do you think they need some time alone?' I breathed to Alcide.

His nose brushed my ear as he nodded. 'We can –'

'No,' Callan said, trailing his lips over Vesper's cheek. 'We don't know how long it will take before the Council makes their decision. Neither of you are leaving our sight.'

'I don't think we're in your sight right now, Cal,' Alcide said dryly.

'That can change,' Vesper purred. He surged up to give Callan a final passionate kiss, nipping at his bottom lip. 'I'll make up with you later,' he promised our pilot, his voice low.

'Oh, Vesper,' I said thickly. 'You remembered.'

'I've never forgotten a word you've said, lodestar.' Vesper stalked to the bed, dragging Callan with him by his jacket lapel. I leaned back as my starling loomed over me, intense and dangerous and all kinds of delicious, his eyes flaring gold. 'That was a stressful day, and your skull computers need a break. I've been thinking, and I want to try something,' he said, trailing his fingertips down my throat and over the skin my dress bared, giving me a fair idea of what kind of *something* he meant. 'Do you trust me?'

I swallowed. 'Yes,' I whispered. 'I trust you, Vesper.'

He stepped back, then headed to the doorway. I frowned, wondering what he was doing; he pressed a button on the control panel, and then another.

Callan gave a rumbling laugh; his hair began to fan out around his face in a dark halo. '*Oh*. I've heard about this.'

I squeaked as my limbs began to lift without me telling them to. A moment later, my body wasn't resting on the bed anymore; the skirt of my dress was lifting around my legs as I floated.

A wave of dizziness had me closing my eyes; arms wrapped around my waist, mooring me. 'You'll adjust in a moment,' Alcide murmured. He hooked his knee around the bedpost, keeping himself in place with my back pressed against his chest. It was the oddest sensation, like being suspended, weightless, in water; my stomach churned, settling after a handful of moments as I grew used to the feeling.

Callan reached out, wrapping his fingers around the same bedpost, his legs stretching out mid-air behind him as he took my chin in his free hand and nuzzled gently at my mouth. 'Another thing at the academy I never tried. I had to listen to a lot of jokes about *docking*.' He lifted his face to Alcide, who kissed him with a soft groan. 'This is going to take some set up, starling.'

'Anna's going to be our anchor,' Vesper said, grinning. The low gravity didn't seem to affect his body in the same way it did mine and my Roth's; he walked back to Alcide's bed like nothing had changed. 'If she wants to, of course. We'll put that stick to good use.'

'The bed post?'

Vesper waved his hand again. 'Whatever. And we'll need some of that wet I got on Earth.'

'Wet you got ... Do you mean lubricant?'

'Sure. That. Liquids behave differently in low gravity, so we might need ... extra. But first, clothes.' He fixed his eyes on mine. 'Unless you want to be hit in the face by floating garments, we'll need to put them somewhere contained.'

'Hook your legs around mine, Anna.' Alcide's lips brushed my ear. When I'd done as he said, he let me go, his fingers going to the zipper at the back of my dress. 'I've been wanting to take this off you since the moment you put it on.'

He slid the dress over my shoulders; I wriggled out of the skirt with more difficulty. I hadn't worn a bra, so the instant I was out of the dress, Alcide's hands went to my breasts, cupping and rubbing his thumbs over my nipples until they were hard and aching. I bit my bottom lip, reaching out to help Callan shrug his formal jacket over his huge shoulders, laughing when my dress floated by and I realised Vesper was right.

Callan grabbed it, taking my dress – and an armful of his own clothing – and pushing gently away from the bed, floating towards the built-in shelves that served as Alcide's wardrobe. The door slid open; Callan stuffed our clothes inside and closed the door before anything could float out, the momentum sending him back across the room.

'This might take some practise,' he muttered.

'Learn fast, or I'm going to keep Anna all to myself.' Alcide slipped a hand inside my underwear, tracing over my clit and further down with a featherlight touch.

'Are you,' Vesper drawled. His fingers circled my ankles before sliding up my legs; he took hold of my thighs and gently pulled me from Alcide's hold. 'You're the perfect height, Anna,' he purred. 'Hold on to the stick, brightness.'

I reached back, grabbing the bed post, floating a few feet off the bed. 'Perfect height for wh –'

Vesper sank down on the edge of the bed, then pulled my underwear to the side and buried his face between my legs.

'Oh,' I squeaked, my head tipping back as his tongue swiped a line up the centre of me. He sucked on my clit lightly, holding me still when I squirmed, then turned his attention back to my entrance, pushing his tongue inside.

'*Mmm.*' Callan's rumble sent a shiver down my spine. He hooked a foot around Vesper's calf, reaching to tear my underwear in two, giving Vesper free reign. Our starling immediately took advantage, spreading my thighs further apart, his tongue exploring further than it ever had before.

'*Oh,*' I panted, as his tongue circled my ass.

'Yes or no?' Callan growled, his eyes obsidian as he watched.

'Um,' I said breathlessly. 'I –' Vesper's tongue pressed down gently. 'Oh, *oh*. Yes. That. *Yes.*'

Callan leaned down to kiss me, wrapping his hand around the bedpost, anchoring himself between Vesper and me. His tongue tangled with mine as Vesper's continued its gentle plundering, withdrawing to be replaced a moment later by the tip of a finger slippery with lube.

'Anna?' he said thickly.

I bit back a gasp. 'Yes, but slowly. I haven't ... I haven't done ...'

'I know,' Vesper said. 'I've got you, brightness.'

Callan wrapped his free hand beneath my knee, pulling my leg up to make me open for Vesper. The starling made a wordless purring sound, his lips going back to my clit as his finger pushed inside. My body tightened at the unfamiliar intrusion; Vesper waited until I relaxed, then began to push in and pull out in a gentle rhythm.

'Beautiful,' Alcide said roughly. He'd used the time to undress; he hooked an arm around Callan's waist and pressed himself against the big pilot's back. 'I read that it's harder to get an erection in low grav. You don't seem to have that problem, Cal.'

'And where exactly did you read *that*?' Callan said, tipping his head back to rest on Alcide's shoulder as Alcide palmed his cock. 'Part of your princely studies?'

'Bioscience, obviously,' Alcide answered, straight-faced, working Callan up and down as his scales rippled.

I moaned at the sight, then moaned again as Vesper began to suck. His finger pushed in further, invading and retreating, causing a slight, pleasant sting; my internal walls fluttered, trying to clamp down on nothing as Vesper pushed me further towards the edge.

'*Yes*,' Callan hissed, watching me through slitted eyes. Alcide was sucking a line of shadowed love bites up his neck, one hand on Callan's cock and the other cupping the heavy sac below. I whimpered, closing my eyes, my body arching as my world narrowed to Vesper's mouth and his movements inside me.

'Come, Anna,' Alcide growled.

I cried out as the waves broke; my body tightened around Vesper's finger, throbbing with the mix of new intrusion and emptiness. The sensation was so strong it was almost sharp, and my throat made a series of garbled noises, which Callan swallowed with a kiss until my shuddering breaths calmed.

Vesper withdrew gently; I squirmed, my cheeks hot. He kissed my clit, breathing in deeply.

'An anchor,' I said thickly, realising what he meant. 'You want ... Two at once? Me?'

My core tightened at the thought of *two* of my males inside me.

'Yes, but not there. Not today.' Vesper disappeared, then reformed a moment later, which, he'd told me, *reset his form*, the starling version of taking a shower. 'You have such a pretty mouth, Anna.' Vesper traced my lips, his fingers so light that my toes tingled in response. 'I want to put it to good use.'

My cheeks flared with a mix of pleasure and desire. 'Oh. Okay,' I whispered. I licked my lips without thinking; Callan gave a wordless growl and ran his hand down my side.

'As Cal said, we need some set up.' Vesper glanced at Alcide. 'Cide, back against the post.'

Callan helped Alcide position himself, his back against the bed post, his hands hooked around it, his feet just brushing the blanket. His unruly red hair floated up around the graceful curves of his horns. Despite what he'd said, his cock was swollen and hard, his scales rippling in slow, undulating waves. Vesper had pulled a condom from somewhere, and he slid it down over Alcide with deliberate slowness. They exchanged a passionate, gasping kiss as Vesper squeezed Alcide's sheathed cock.

My mouth watered. As far as I knew, kissing and touching was the limit of what they'd done together so far, but if the heat of their kiss was any indication, it wouldn't stay that way for long.

'Anna.'

I pushed myself to the side, laughing as Callan's hand shot out and caught my ankle when I used too much force. Alcide scooped an arm around my waist and drew me close, nuzzling his lips against mine.

'An anchor,' he whispered. 'That's exactly what you are. An anchor and a guiding light. Not just for this. For us. For everything.'

I wrapped my arms around his neck and buried my face against his chest. 'Then you three are my ship.'

Vesper's hands found my hips and he gently turned me around. He took hold of Alcide's cock and positioned it; I could feel his head pressed against my core, feel the apex of his raised scales vibrating against me. I hooked my feet around the back of Alcide's thighs, pressing down with Vesper's help until Alcide was slipping inside me as his hips moved in a series of small, shallow thrusts. His scales pulsed; my eyes rolled back as the ripples pressed against some sweet spot in a series of rhythmic pulses.

'You feel so good,' Alcide grated out. One hand was on my hip, holding me in place; the other was wrapped around the bedpost to keep us secured.

'Good,' Vesper said, his eyes flaring. He reached out to trace where I was stretched around Alcide; I bit my lip to stop a whimper. His hand fell to his cock, circling his shaft and pump-ing twice before he stepped closer.

'*Oh*,' I managed. I reached out, catching his shoulders, then dropped my hands to his hips, angling down. The action had me stretched out mid-air, pinned in place by Alcide's cock.

'Gods below,' Alcide growled. 'I *like* this.'

'You'll probably like it more in a moment,' Vesper said. 'Anna? Is it comfortable?'

I dropped my head until my mouth was close to Vesper's cock; I let my tongue swipe over his head, tasting his smoky precum. He groaned, his body tensing. I dropped my mouth further, taking him inside, my lips stretching over his head and down his shaft.

'You're right,' Alcide said blankly. 'I do like that more.'

I came off Vesper's cock, licking my lips. I suspected that had I tried this with gravity, my neck would have been aching at the odd angle, and my thighs would have been burning at the stretch. As it was, I could have stayed that way for hours.

'It's comfortable.'

'Good,' Vesper answered. 'Then I'm going to fuck your mouth, and Callan will fuck me. Any questions?'

Alcide's scales pulsed; I mewled in response. 'None from me,' I managed. Callan shook his head and hooked his arm around Vesper's waist, looking as if all his birthdays had come at once.

'Tap my hip, and I'll stop,' Vesper said, looking down at me. His hand cupped my cheek, his thumb stroking over my cheekbone. 'You're so beautiful, lodestar. Your light is so bright when you're with us.'

My eyes stung. 'For a notorious asshole, you're very sweet, Vesper.'

'Only to you,' he said, and reached back to grab Callan's hip. 'Your turn, Callan Sandborn, pilot-who-graduated-in-the-top-section-of-his-class.'

Callan threaded one foot around Vesper's calf to keep himself in place, then did something with his hand that had Vesper panting. My starling's head tipped back to rest on Callan's shoulder; Callan growled, and his hips pushed forward, then Vesper's eyes fell closed.

'Fuck, you're hotter than the seventh hell, starling,' Callan rasped.

'Don't worry, I won't burn your cock off,' Vesper said, his voice strained. 'I think.' He gave a shuddering exhale. 'Stars, those *scales*. I get it now. Anna, please tell me you're ready, because I don't know how long I can last.'

'*Who* needs to work on their stamina?' Callan said, his lips curving up as he trailed kisses down Vesper's throat.

I didn't answer our starling, just dropped my head and took him between my lips again, flattening my tongue against his shaft. He moaned, his hand smoothing up and down my back.

'Vesper, I'm going insane here,' Alcide rasped. 'Now what?'

Vesper shivered. 'I'm hoping those scales of yours do their work, because I didn't think this far ahead, and now I can't think at all.'

Callan barked a laugh. His big hands came to rest over mine, keeping them in place on Vesper's hips and keeping me in place between my males. 'Anna. Anna comes first. Cide, make her come. Vesper and I will work it out.'

Alcide's hips moved in a slow roll, pushing himself deep as his scales rippled in an almost continual wave, sending thrills of pleasure through my body. The movement nudged me towards Vesper, who wasn't affected by it at all; when I pushed back, using Vesper as a brace, I could keep Alcide inside me. My King's fingers trailed over my hip and around to my clit, gently pressing in time to the rippling of his scales.

I moaned around Vesper, trying to concentrate on moving my mouth up and down his cock. He cupped my jaw, holding me in place and thrusting shallowly forward. Behind him, Callan groaned and caught on, and soon it was Callan's thrusts that had Vesper pushing into me, Alcide timing his movements to push deep when Vesper retreated.

I couldn't think of anything but their movements; my world shrank to the feeling of Alcide's cock inside me and Vesper's slipping past my lips. There was nothing but that, and the pleasure; the sensation building deep inside with every undulation of Alcide's scales, with the steadiness of Callan's hands over my own and of hearing Vesper gasp, his silken skin hot against my tongue. I'd never been pinned between them like this, my body a bridge for theirs, moving back and forth between them, my feet hooked around Alcide's hard thighs so I could stay that way. My nerves sparked when Vesper stroked my back, at the way Alcide was working between my legs, when Callan whispered our names. My body began to tighten; I whimpered, then hollowed my cheeks and sucked as Vesper's cock thrust gently deeper.

'Fuck,' he groaned. 'Come, little light. *Come*, Anna.'

I pulled off him as my body tightened and the wave broke, sending pleasure crashing all the way down to my toes. Alcide's scales rippled faster and faster until there was no break, just a continual swell inside me; I cried out wordlessly as I felt his heat through the condom, digging my fingers into Vesper's hips. Vesper swore again, and I lowered my mouth and sucked; a few moments later, my mouth was flooded with his smoky taste, the heat spreading over my tongue and down my throat as I swallowed.

'Dread gods – *Vesper*,' Callan snarled, his hands tightening on mine as he came, and for a few minutes, the only sound was panting as we all caught our breath. Alcide pulled me upright, holding me tight against his chest, his cock still hard inside me, his scales rippling lazily.

I licked the taste of Vesper off my lips. Callan and Vesper watched me do it through hooded eyes; Vesper languidly ran his fingers through Callan's hair.

'What the fuck is that?' Callan said eventually.

'Did you make sure the lid was on the lubricant, starling?' Alcide said; as one, we watched a blob of shining liquid float through the air.

I tipped my head back on Alcide's shoulder and laughed. 'This is the messiest thing I've ever done.'

'Yes,' Vesper said happily. 'Isn't it wonderful?'

Epilogue

'AND THIS IS MY chamber,' Tessa announced, waving her hand in front of some kind of sensor. The veil of flowing water before us ceased, revealing a doorway large enough to accommodate a being as tall and broad as Morgan. 'Not that it's really just *mine*. The others sleep here too, even though Morgan has a literal *quarter* of the palace. They thought I'd share with Morgan, but most of his rooms are underwater, and there's a seal colony that likes popping up unannounced in the parts that aren't. The last time I went in there, a seal cow had pupped *on his bed*. I'm all for nature, but not *that*, and not where I'm sleeping.'

'Is that where you will ... pup?' Maeve said absently, staring around Tessa's massive room with interest.

Tessa moved across the room to perch on the edge of an oversized bed. 'I'm not going to *pup*, Maeve.'

Elswyth eyed Tessa warily; the apricot-coloured flower be-hind her ear budded tight. 'You won't lay an egg, will you?'

'I fucking hope not,' Tessa said cheerfully. 'Cy assured me that the larvae seems to be living in a human amniotic sac. No shell in sight.'

Maeve grimaced. 'Are you *very* sure that's what you want?' she said to Elswyth. 'It sounds … gross.' She waved a hand at Tessa's belly. 'And then there's this business.'

'Fuck off,' Tessa said, grinning as she rubbed her stomach. 'I'm a goddess. Or so Morgan likes to tell me.'

'See?' Elswyth said, arching a silver brow at Maeve. 'It's magical, not gross.'

Maeve lifted Elswyth's knuckles to her mouth and brushed her lips across the Tirian woman's skin. Elswyth blushed a deep green, her hair glowing with a faint light. 'You're already magic,' Maeve purred.

'Now who's gross,' Tessa said, but she was smiling. She patted the bed next to her. 'Anna. I'm *dying* to hear about Vesper.' Her smile widened. 'And the other two, actually.'

I perched next to her. 'How much longer do you think the Council will be?'

'Hours, probably,' Maeve answered. 'The Captain was pretty riled up. She doesn't like diplomacy. Prefers giving orders.'

The corners of Elswyth's lips tugged up; she caught my gaze and gave the slightest shrug, as if to say *that sounds familiar*.

I smiled. 'Vesper was in chains when I met him,' I began.

Tessa blinked.

'What kind of chains?' Maeve said interestedly.

Elswyth swatted her leg.

'The *he-was-in-a-cell* kind. He'd raided Alcide's on-board treasury – twice – but Cide and Cal caught him on the third try and cuffed him with a dark matter chain. He hadn't moved for months when I arrived. I think … I think he was starting to go mad. But he was kind to me. And when the ship's doctor bit me, he –'

'The ship's doctor *bit* you?' Maeve interrupted, her face settling into a familiar *Maeve-on-the-warpath* scowl. 'You were unsafe?'

'That's why I was in the cell with Vesper,' I explained. 'It was the only place on the ship that Cide could fully restrict access to; he and Cal were trying to keep me away from the crew. But my adenomyosis pain flared up, and Vesper panicked, and they sent me to the doctor. The doctor tried to sedate me to send me to the old Roth King, and when I struggled, he …' I trailed off. 'But Alcide killed him, so you don't need to worry.'

'Oh, Anna,' Tessa said, aghast. She rubbed her belly, as if trying to comfort herself. 'Here I was thinking you had an adventure like Maeve and I did, but you were in actual *danger*.' She studied me. 'Do you need to see someone? Another doctor? A counsellor?'

I shook my head and smiled at Maeve and Elswyth. 'Willow helped me. He treated the infected wound and broke my fever. We talked a bit, when I was conscious again. He's an amazing doctor.'

'He is, isn't he?' Maeve said proudly, as Elswyth smiled.

'It wasn't … *great*, the whole getting bitten thing, but Alcide and Callan intervened before anything truly bad could happen. It sounds stupid, but what I need to talk about is something different.' I chewed my lip.

'Nothing you say is stupid,' Tessa said gently. 'What is it?'

'How do you …' I trailed off. 'How do you manage *three*?' I blurted.

Maeve and Tessa looked at each other and burst out laughing.

'Fucked if I know,' Maeve said a minute later, when she'd caught her breath.

'I'm not sure I *manage* them at all,' Tessa said thoughtfully. 'I more just ... exist, and they're there. Morgan prefers to pretend he's managing *me*, Aster is inherently *un*manageable, and Cy is perfect.'

Maeve eyed Elswyth. 'Do I *manage* you?' She paused. 'I mean, Ashton is a given.'

'Ash needs the most management,' Elswyth agreed, then muttered something that sounded like *bark brain* under her breath.

'You just work out your own dynamic,' Tessa said. 'You work out what you need from them, and what they need from you, and what they need from each other.'

I laughed nervously and looked at my hands. 'I haven't dated for years, and now I have three partners. It's ... a lot.'

'It's a lot regardless of *any* dating history,' Tessa said. 'You're doing beautifully, Anna.'

I took a deep breath. 'Would Willow talk to me about a long-term contraceptive? I don't ... I'm not ready for children, and we don't know what's going to happen on Scytha, and ...'

'Of course,' Elswyth said immediately. 'Of course he would.'

'Just make it something the starling super spunk won't affect.' Tessa gave a small smile, rubbing her belly again. 'I didn't really mind, but it still came as a shock.'

I blinked at her. '*Super spunk*?'

'Starlings, they –' Tessa broke off with a soft yelp as darkness flooded the room and Vesper materialised in front of the bed.

She narrowed her eyes at him. 'Just so you know, I house trained Aster *not* to do that, if you need any tips.'

'Vesper?' I said softly, taking in the way his eyes were glowing the way they did when he was excited, but his mouth was twisted. He gathered up both my hands in his warm grasp and knelt before me. 'What's happened?'

'They've decided,' he said hoarsely. 'The Council. They said yes. They'll support Alcide's claim.'

I squeezed his fingers. 'That's wonderful news! But Vesper ... Why aren't you happier?'

He lifted my knuckles to his lips. 'Because we're going to war, lodestar. And you'll be coming with us.'

I took a shuddering breath.

A silence fell over the room; the only sound was that of softly running water. I ran my thumb over Vesper's fingers, trying to sort through what I was feeling. I hadn't expected it to happen so *quickly*, but then, I hadn't expected *any* of this. Not being abducted, not travelling through space, not falling in love.

Now I not only had to work out how to manage a relationship with three partners – I'd have to work out how to be a *queen*.

I exhaled, pleased at how even it sounded. I could pretend to be calm, even if I didn't feel it. 'We're going to war,' I repeated evenly.

Maeve exchanged a long glance with Elswyth, then looked across at Tessa. 'Well,' she said at last. 'Then I guess we're coming with you.'

THE *ADVENA ABDUCTIONS* SERIES will conclude with Claire's story, *Safe Landing*.

Notes on the Text & Acknowledgements

I NEVER MEANT FOR Anna's story to take a dark turn.

I never meant for *any* of the Advena books to be anything other than light, easy reads with plenty of spice. But – fortunately or unfortunately, depending on how much you liked this book – I tend to get carried away by *story*, and my intentions fly unceremoniously out the window.

My beautiful grandmother, Joan, was in an aged care home with dementia when she died of Covid almost two years ago. My husband's grandmother, Robyn, has dementia, and currently resides in an aged care home, where we visit her as often as we can. The references to dementia, those suffering from it, and those who care for them, are informed by my own – and my family's – experiences, which are, of course, deeply personal and shaped by our particular circumstances; any misrepresentations or mistakes are wholly my own, and I hope you can forgive me for them.

I was diagnosed with adenomyosis after five years of frustrating visits to gynaecologists, constant diagnostic scans, invasive procedures, ongoing pain, and unexplained bleeding. Again, the depiction of Anna's adenomyosis is based largely on my own experience, which may differ from that of others; I've also left out some of the more choice symptoms, because this is a romance novel, and literally no one needs that.

As always, I would like to thank my beta readers, wholeheartedly and with immense gratitude. To Kelly, my alpha reader, who still puts up with me, though I often don't understand why: thank you, thank you, a thousand times thank you. Hannah, Erika, Claire, and Charlie – you're absolute stars, and I appreciate your feedback more than I can ever say.

And to those reading this – I am entirely astonished that you are still here with me, though I will never stop being grateful for it. Thank you for reading my weird, smutty little books, and here's to the home stretch.

About the Author

Hollie Hartwright lives on Ngunnawal land in Australia's capital city with her infinitely supportive husband and their two children. She has a degree in Literature from the best university in the country, which she is currently putting to good use writing otherworldly smut. She is currently working on the *Advena Abductions* series, a collection of four high-heat romances featuring human heroines who will not need to choose between their alien suitors.

You can find her on Instagram as @hollie.hartwright, or at holliehartwright.com.